Once,
Twice,
Thrice

Ian Kilgour

1832

— PUBLISHING —

ISBNs:
    978-1-7341563-0-0 (ebook),
    978-1-7341563-1-7 (paperback)

Once,
Twice,
Thrice

In memory of Hunter,
my beloved golden retriever
whose time in my life
was not long enough.

CHAPTER ONE

I t had been a sunny spring weekend, the last weekend in April. Warm, not too humid, not like the hot and humid days soon to come. A nice day for the four friends on their drive home from a girl's weekend away.

They had started with a shopping spree at the outlet mall in Simpsonville. Then dinner in downtown Louisville, followed by the traveling Broadway show *Phantom of the Opera* at the Louisville Theatre. A little celebrating with much after-show chardonnay in the Derby Room of the Hotel Cheval where the women had shared two adjoining rooms. On Sunday morning, they had sunned while brunching outside on the rooftop restaurant, which had a view of the Ohio River, taken pictures in front of the bronze horse statue in the hotel lobby, and then departed for the return trip to Owensboro.

It was midafternoon; all would be home for dinner with their husbands, or in Sue Ellen's case, her husband and two children. Eve was the last of the quartet to be dropped off.

Sue Ellen turned her minivan left from Scherm Road onto Christie Place, slowing at the curve to pull into the single-lane driveway of Eve's house, a red-brick single story with white trim and a large maple tree shading the front lawn. She stopped behind the Mustang in front of the white garage door, placing the gear lever into Park and clicking the button for the sliding door.

"Thanks for driving, Sue Ellen," Eve said as she opened the passenger-side door. "It was a blast to get away like this. We need to do it again sometime."

"It was. Maybe next time there is a good Broadway show our husbands hate!" she said with a chuckle. "Get all your things?"

Eve tugged at her leopard-print overnight case, which had wedged between the second-row captain's chairs, before grabbing the two large shopping bags with her shopping prizes. "I can't wait to show Jeff the shirts I found for him at the outlets. Just hope he likes them."

"He will—if you hide the price tags."

"Maybe," she grinned. "Thanks again." She closed the minivan doors, and watched as her friend backed out into the street, then gave a little wave, which was returned as Sue Ellen retraced her path.

Eve carried the shopping bags in one hand, pulling the suitcase with the other, to the front door. She noticed that the single porch light above the front door was on. *Odd*, she thought. *Jeff must have forgotten to turn it off when he went to bed.*

"Jeff, honey, I'm home," she called as she stepped through the front door. The front room was empty, the television off. No answer. She left the luggage by the door and walked down the hallway to the bedrooms. There were two small bedrooms on the right, for the children they hoped to have someday; the master was last door on the left. She walked into the room. The bed was unmade and empty. She tossed the shopping bags onto the queen-size bed.

"Jeff, are you home?" She slowly walked back down the short hallway, toward the kitchen. "I got some presents for you. I think you're gonna like them."

Eve peered around the doorway to the kitchen. And screamed.

CHAPTER TWO

Robert Hunter grew up in Owensboro, the only son of Betty and Thomas Hunter. His father had been recruited to the English department of Verona College after finishing his PhD, eventually becoming chairman of the department. They lived in an older bungalow near campus—walking distance for Dr. Hunter. Reaching a height of six foot four his junior year, Hunter had been the tallest high school quarterback in the state. He graduated third in his class from St. Andrews, Owensboro's private Catholic high school. After finishing college in Louisville with a degree in criminal justice, he returned to his hometown to join the police force, and turned out to be the youngest officer ever promoted to detective in the department's history.

Hunter's house was situated on a corner lot, the double garage door opening on the side street and the two-story main house facing Citation Ave in an L-shaped footprint. A row of arborvitae had been planted along the edge of the backyard by the previous owners. Over time, the evergreens had grown tall enough to create a somewhat secluded area for the concrete slab patio. A gas grill and a dining set with a center umbrella completed the outdoor setting. He was sitting at the table with his high school pal and fellow football player, Louis Mercier. Mercier was an anesthesiologist who had recently left the University of Chicago, returning to Owensboro to take over his family's farm when his father retired. He had also joined the staff at Daviess County General Hospital.

They were two old friends, enjoying a warm spring afternoon, drinking beer and catching up.

"How do you like being back in Owensboro?" Hunter asked.

"No lie—it's an adjustment. But things seem to be falling into place," Mercier responded before taking a sip from the bottle. "Big change from Chicago, that's for sure."

Hunter tapped a cigarette from the pack of Marlboros, lighting it with a wooden match. He pulled a slow drag before reacting. "Yeah, I can see that. Will there be anything you'll miss?"

He shook his head. "Not really. It's mostly what I won't miss. Chicago winters are horrific, and the traffic is migraine-inducing. It takes me twenty minutes to get to the hospital here. The only thing twenty minutes from my condo on Fifty-Seventy Street was Fifty-Eighth Street."

Hunter laughed. "C'mon, traffic can't have been that interminable."

"Well, maybe fifteen minutes," he grinned. "I will miss the pizza. Chicago has the best pizza on the planet. Period." He rubbed his stomach for emphasis. "Surprised I didn't put on a few pounds."

"Bubba, I did that for you!" Hunter smiled as he pointed to his own stomach. "Living the good life." He drained the bottle before returning to his cigarette. "You want another beer?"

"Not yet," Mercier said, holding up the half-empty bottle. "Getting there."

"Before I forget to ask, how's the farm?"

"Good news there. You remember Paul?"

Hunter nodded. "Yeah, I remember him. Quiet guy, always had a wad of chewing tobacco in his cheek."

"And a little dribble of saliva running off the left side of his lip," he said with a smile as he touched his own chin with his index finger. "Well, he's worked for Dad for a long time. I think he's been running the place the past couple of years. Anyway, I made him an offer: he takes care of the farm; I worry about the hospital and try to stay out of his way."

"Sounds like a plan."

"I think it'll work. He knows the farm a lot better than I do now."

"So, got the farm managed, and you can find your way to the hospital. How's your love life? Keeping any old flames burning back in the Windy City?"

"No long-distance romances. Tried that once, and I can tell you it doesn't work very well." He drank some beer. "I have had a few dates with one of the ER nurses."

"Excellent. Bring her to dinner next Sunday—I'll grill."

Mercier laughed at his friend. "I'll ask. Don't start the charcoal just yet."

Hunter smashed the cigarette butt into the ashtray and stood up. "Ready for that beer?"

"Of course." He gulped what little remained in the bottle in a single mouthful, placing the empty on the table.

As Hunter started across the patio, his wife, Brenda, opened the sliding door with a cordless telephone in her hand. "Bob, you're wanted on the phone." He walked over, took the handset, and slid the glass door closed behind him.

"Hunter," he said as he returned to this chair. After listening for a few moments, he nodded, then said, "Christie

Place. Got it. I'll be right there." He pushed the *end* button on the handset, and set it down on the table.

"Brewski number two is gonna have to wait. Duty calls."

Mercier sat back in the chair, a query on his face. "What's up?"

Hunter reached for his wedding band and twisted it back and forth on his ring finger. "Murder victim." He stared at Mercier. "Lady found her husband in the kitchen, dead, stabbed in the chest."

Mercier's mouth fell open. "Murder? In Owensboro?"

Hunter picked up the cordless handset and arose from the chair. "First murder we've had in at least two years." He looked down at his boat shoes. "I'd better go change."

Mercier stood also. "What? Cargo shorts and a tie-dyed T-shirt are not appropriate crime-scene attire?"

Towering eight inches over his closest friend, Hunter looked down at Mercier with a smirk and roughed his short, dark-brown hair with his left hand. "Glad you're back in town, bubba. See ya Sunday."

CHAPTER THREE

There were three black-and-white patrol cars parked in front of the house on the curve of Christie Place, and the Evidence Collection Unit, or ECU, van was backed into the driveway behind a red Mustang hardtop. Detective Hunter pulled his graphite-grey Cadillac sedan to the curb opposite the house and caught a glimpse of a drape moving in the front window of the house. *Nosy neighbor*, he thought. *May be good.*

He got out of the car and looked around the neighborhood. In the driveway of the next house down, a late-sixties Chevrolet Camaro, Rallye Green, with the passenger door in brown primer, was on jack stands, hood up, a father and son team changing oil. *What I would be doing on a weekend*, he mused, *if I'd had a son instead of two daughters?*

A collection of neighbors had gathered farther down, looking up the street, curious perhaps. Several had their smartphones out, taking pictures of the scene. In the distance, he could hear the hum of a lawnmower. Most of the houses seemed to be the same one-level bricks with a few two-stories here and there; some had carports instead of garages, and all of them had more cars and trucks than space, the vehicles overflowing into the street. That drape moved again in the window. Hunter smoothed the royal-blue pindot tie against his white shirt, buttoned the jacket of his two-piece navy suit, and slowly walked toward the front door of the red-brick house.

As he approached the square concrete slab that functioned as a front porch, the door was opened by a uniform who stepped out to meet him. Even on the sidewalk, Hunter was taller the young patrolman, Officer Michael Wagner—Mike to his friends. When he joined the Owensboro Police Department, Officer Wagner was following in his father's footsteps. He even looked like him: trim, dark eyes, black hair in a crewcut, and an oft-present smile. His father had spent his entire career in uniform, retiring the prior winter after thirty years on patrol, longer than any of his cohorts, who had either moved up into desk jobs or out of the force to the private sector.

"Afternoon, Detective." Mike closed the door. "Let me fill you in while the lab rats finish processing the scene."

"Okay, Mike" he nodded. "What d'you have?"

"Victim is Jeff Miller, thirty-one. Stabbed in the chest. He's a salesman, er, was a salesman at Butler Brothers Ford." He motioned with his right hand to the driveway. "His car. Mustang GT."

Hunter turned to look at the Mustang. "Okay."

Mike continued. "His wife, Eve, she was in Louisville for the weekend with three of her girlfriends. They returned about an hour ago. She found her husband in the kitchen and called 911." He pointed over his shoulder. "She's on the back patio with my partner, Phil. Her sister is on her way over here. We talked Eve into staying with her for a few days."

"Good work. You've got the names of the friends?"

"Yes."

"Confirm the alibi." Mike nodded in agreement. "Kids?"

9

"No kids."

"Has anyone talked to the neighbors yet?"

Mike shook his head. "Next on my list. I was waiting to update you."

Hunter pointed at the house directly across the street, where he had parked his car. "Start there. I think she's Mrs. Kravitz."

Mike looked up at Hunter, his face a question mark. "Mrs. Who?"

"Mrs. Kravitz." Hunter frowned. "Didn't you watch *Bewitched* when you were a kid?"

"What's *Bewitched*?"

"Forget it. Anyway, start there. She probably saw something."

"Will do." He opened the door for Hunter. "Oh, by the way, Dr. Turner is already in there."

Hunter stopped on the porch. "The medical examiner? Already here? Why?"

"I called her after you were called. She was excited and raced over. Said something about it being her first murder."

Hunter ran his left hand through his thinning black hair. "She was excited? That's twisted."

"Yeah, I know, right?"

"Thanks, Mike." He pointed at the house again as he turned into the doorway. "Start there."

∞

The front room was the family room. A flat-screen television was mounted on the inside wall, facing the dark-blue and green-plaid couch under the rectangular picture window. A matching recliner was next to the couch along with end table, upon which was the television remote and an oversized glass half-full of what appeared to be tea, the ice long ago melted. Hunter moved on, stopping at the cased opening to the kitchen.

Dr. Jean Turner was bent over the victim's torso, so that Hunter was unable to see the chest wound. One of the lab technicians was still taking pictures, the other stabbing his finger at a table computer. No one seemed to have noticed Hunter's presence.

Turner suddenly stood up and pulled the teal-framed reading glasses from her curly black hair to her nose, looking intently at the digital readout end of a liver thermometer. In doing so, Hunter was able to look at the corpse. The victim's shirt had been pulled open, exposing his chest; the black handle of a knife was still protruding from the left side. Blood, evidently from the wound, had spread in a pool extending several feet from the left side of the body, almost to the back door. Excepting his shirt, his clothes and hair were untousled.

"Your first crime scene?" he asked.

She looked up at Hunter, eyes wide open with enthusiasm. "Yeah. This is the first time I've used my new thermometer. Cool, huh?"

"You got an idea about time of death, Jean?"

"Twelve to twenty-four hours. The AC was on, but he's at room temperature. Rigor has already set in."

He viewed the kitchen. *Nothing unusual*, he thought. "No signs of a struggle?"

"Not that I can tell. No bruising or cuts on his hands, nothing on his neck," she said as she pointed toward his head. "Doesn't look like he tried to fight his attacker."

"Hard to believe he would just lay down and allow someone to stab him. Could he have been drugged?"

Jean nodded. "I may be able to get a tox screen, but don't get your hopes up."

Hunter knelt next to the body. "Why would he leave the knife?" he whispered to himself. "Any prints on the knife?"

The camera-toting lab technician responded. "None. But there looks like a little of the dust you get from latex gloves. I've got a good close up." He turned the camera for Hunter to see the screen. "Right there."

"Hmm." Hunter stood up. "Any signs of forced entry?"

The techs both shook their heads.

"Any evidence of robbery?"

"No."

"Alright, so we have a victim who likely knew his killer, let him in, and then somehow the killer was able to force him to the kitchen floor for the execution without a skirmish. The killer brought gloves to conceal prints. He was well prepared."

"He? Why not she?" asked the tech with the tablet computer. "You don't know the killer is a man."

Hunter rolled his eyes. "Unless there is some evil Bond villainess roaming the streets of Owensboro, I'm pretty sure this is the work of a man."

Turner added, "Yes, I agree. It would take considerable arm strength to slice a chest like that."

The tech had returned to looking at his computer screen.

"What are you doing?" Hunter asked.

"I'm trying to find out what kind of knife that is."

"It's a Navy SEAL knife."

"How'd you know that?"

Camera lab tech glared at his partner. "Really?"

"Okay, so the killer's a Navy SEAL. So, he's a guy. That should be helpful."

Hunter held up his hand. "Not so fast. That particular knife is available to the general public. Hunting retailers carry them."

"So, why did he, this maybe–Navy SEAL, leave it in Jeff Miller's chest?"

Hunter shook his head. "No ideas yet. I'm working on it." He kneeled again to look more closely at the knife handle. "Did you find any hunting gear in the house?" he asked the techs. "Rifles, shotgun, maybe some camo?"

"No. Several fishing poles and a tackle box in the garage, but no hunting gear," answered camera-tech. "Nothing in the closets."

"The killer brought the knife, then," Hunter surmised as he contemplated the blade.

"I'm ready to move the body, if you're okay with that," Turner said.

"Go ahead." He stood up and moved away from the corpse.

The back door opened. A uniformed officer stepped in, leaving the door open. "Detective, Eve Miller's sister arrived."

Hunter stepped around the body to follow him to the back patio. Two women were seated in rattan chairs. One, whom he assumed was Eve Miller, held tissues in her hands, her eyes bloodshot.

"Mrs. Miller, this is Detective Hunter."

"Thanks, Phil." He offered his hand. "Robert Hunter."

"And her sister."

"I'm very sorry for your loss, Mrs. Miller," he said.

The sister rose from the other chair to shake his hand. "It's Ann O'Neil," she said as she took his hand.

He turned to Ann. "And yours." He paused. "I know this is hard, and you've spoken to the officers already, but can you tell me in your own words what happened when you arrived home?"

Eve recounted the afternoon, hesitating, pausing for tissues, and concluded the saga with the arrival of the officers, Mike and Phil.

Hunter listened quietly, then asked, "Do you know of anyone who would want to kill your husband?"

"No. Most folks seemed to like Jeff. He's pretty easy going, hard to believe for a car salesman, I know."

"Do you know if he planned to be home alone?"

"Yes. Jeff said he was looking forward to some quiet time. He was supposed to work Saturday, and then he was going to watch some movie he said I wouldn't like."

"Who knew that you would be out of town, leaving your husband in Owensboro?" he asked.

Eve gently bit at her lower lip. "My girlfriends, of course. Ann knew," she said, looking to her sister. "Not sure about anyone else. It wasn't a secret–we'd been planning it for a while."

"Is it likely that your husband would have told friends or coworkers?"

"I suppose so." She paused. "Like I said, it wasn't a big secret."

"Did you notice anything unusual in the house–that is, before you found your husband's body?"

Eve turned her head to her sister, then answered as she looked back to Hunter. "The front light was on. Jeff always turned the porch light off when he went to bed. It was still on."

"Thanks, that's helpful." He fidgeted with the cigarette pack in his suit coat pocket. "I know this may seem odd to ask, but were you and Jeff having any marital problems, anything like that?"

"No, well, other than me getting pregnant. We've been having some trouble in that department. Jeff read something about all the chemicals in processed foods being bad for you, so he wanted me to cook only organic food, and we both stopped drinking. He even stopped drinking diet soda, switched to iced tea, said he read something about the antioxidants in tea being good for his sperm count." She looked to her sister and burst into tears. "Guess it doesn't matter now."

Iced tea. The glass next to the chair was iced tea. "Phil, have one of the lab guys collect that iced-tea glass from the front room, it's on the end table."

Ann asked, "His iced-tea glass? Why? Is that important?"

"I think he may have been drugged before he was stabbed. We'll test the tea. It's just a theory. We have to look into any and all possibilities." He gazed at Ann, then returned his attention to Eve. "Can you think of anything else?"

"No, not really."

After a brief silence, Ann stood up, purse in hand. "Can I take my sister away from here now?

"Yes. Do we have your contact number?"

Eve nodded, and Ann answered, "I gave my number to the officer. Eve is going to stay with us for a few days."

"An excellent idea."

Eve joined her sister, and they stepped onto the concrete walk that stretched around the garage side of the house. Ann turned back to look at Hunter once more.

"You're going to catch this bastard, whoever it is that killed Jeff, aren't you, Detective?"

Hunter nodded without answering. After the sisters had disappeared around the corner of the house, he pulled the cigarettes from his pocket and lit one.

CHAPTER FOUR

Hunter arrived at the police station before dawn, having given up on trying to sleep sometime after 4 a.m. He flipped though the pictures, smoked, drank coffee, read everyone's reports, and then started the cycle over again. He didn't find anything new.

He concluded that the attack was personal. The killer left the knife as a statement. He knew that Miller would be alone that night, knew how to get into the house, knew how to evade detection. And was able to easily subdue Jeff Miller. Maybe it was someone with military training, this unknown Navy SEAL. Someone with some very specific knowledge and a vendetta to carry out.

The nosy neighbor who lived directly across the street from the Miller's house had seen something: a woman with dark hair in a blue polka-dot dress had dropped by the house around eight or so Saturday evening. She didn't remember seeing a car. Hunter recalled that there were a lot of cars parked on the street, so that might not be unusual. She did remember seeing her leave not long after arriving and thought that she might be one of Eve's friends. Dark-haired woman— that could be a lot of people.

Hunter reasoned that the murder had to have occurred after 8 p.m. and before Miller would typically have turned out the outside front light and gone to bed, presumably around midnight. That would fit with Turner's time frame for the time of death.

The mystery woman might be the last person to see Jeff Miller alive. Not much of a description to go on—even some hint about her car would be useful, assuming she drove to the Millers. Hunter shrugged his shoulders.

"You ask a guy if he saw a car," he said softly to no one, "he'd give you something like 'A dark-blue Dodge Charger with white racing stripes,' but a woman, you'll get 'It was blue.'"

"Who you talking to in there, Detective?"

Hunter looked up from his desk to find Mike holding a folded newspaper.

"You made the front page of the *Gazette*." He opened the paper so that Hunter could see the headline, "Murder in Owensboro," then dropped it on Hunter's desk.

"Shouldn't you be on patrol somewhere?" He picked up the paper and quickly scanned the article. It was not particularly informative, as Hunter had purposely withheld a number of details when he spoke to the reporter who had been waiting outside the Miller house.

"Heading to the squad room now. Keep the paper."

Hunter reread the short piece. He would start at Butler Brothers Ford. After eating. The breakfast of coffee and cigarettes was not enough.

The Owensboro Police Department was located on Seventh Street, filling a space past Eighth Street, if a street was there, to Ninth Street. Hunter pulled his sedan out of the parking lot onto J R Miller Boulevard, named for the former mayor, and drove south. It was a quick ten-minute ride down the boulevard to the Ford dealer. He turned onto Carlton Drive, then into the customer parking lot. Before he was even out of the car, an eager young salesman trotted in his direction. His zealous smile vanished when Hunter produced his badge and asked to speak to the manager.

He followed the young man through the showroom to the glass-walled offices. They stopped at the last one before the service area, in which sat a thin, gray-haired man, staring intently at a spreadsheet on a large computer screen. His tie hung loose below the collar of his blue-and-white striped shirt, sleeves rolled up to his elbows, and a blazer was draped over the back of his desk chair. The salesman knocked on the open glass door.

"Mr. Butler, this policeman needs to talk to you."

He turned, and seeing Hunter looming in the doorway, stood up from the desk.

"Yes, I was expecting the police. Come in." He nodded to the salesman, who zipped away to find another potential customer.

Hunter held up his badge. "Detective Robert Hunter."

"Yes, of course, Detective. Have a seat." He pointed to the empty chairs in front of the cluttered desk before retaking his own. "You're here about Jeff Miller."

"Yes." Hunter stated, letting the single word hang in the air. He stared silently at Butler, waiting.

"I read the papers, Detective. I know Jeff was murdered. You want to know if there's some connection to my dealership."

"I'm interested in finding out who would want Jeff Miller dead. It may have nothing to do with your dealership."

"Okay." Butler leaned back, letting his shoulders drop. "What can I tell you?"

"What sort of guy was Jeff?"

"Well-liked. He developed this soft-sell approach that really worked. The customers loved him. Many were repeat customers, you know, coming back to find a used car for their teenager, that sort of thing. He got along pretty well with the other salesmen and he liked to hang out with the service guys." He paused to scratch his chin.

Hunter sat quietly, waiting for Butler to continue.

"One time, he arranged for a private tour of the Ford truck plant in Louisville for a group of customers. We sold a boatload of trucks that quarter."

"Any unhappy customers?"

"Detective, this is the car business. I'm not going to tell you that everyone is always happy. Sure, he had some angry ones. We all do. Not angry enough to kill anyone."

Hunter thought about the knife. "Any of your employees have a military background?"

"What's that have to do with Jeff's murder?"

"Do they?"

Butler pursed his lips. "O'Connor. Did a couple of tours in Afghanistan, I think. He's the service manager. Not sure about anyone else."

"I'll need to speak to him. Is he here today?"

"Should be."

Hunter stood. "I may need to ask some of the other employees a few questions. If you think of anything, please give me a call." He handed Butler his card. "Thank you for your time, Mr. Butler."

Butler looked at the card, added it to the chaos of his desk, then returned his attention to the spreadsheet.

Hunter talked to O'Connor, who liked Jeff and had an alibi for Saturday. He then meandered around the showroom and the lot, talking to a few more employees. No one had anything to add to what he already knew. Before leaving, he looked at a new F-150, did a double take on the Monroney sticker, and decided he didn't really need one.

CHAPTER FIVE

Although the bank did not open until 9 a.m., he liked to be at his desk well before eight. An early start to organize his day, to prepare for the bad news he would be delivering to those loan applicants who failed and the good news to those who passed. But mostly to prepare for the unending and mundane tedium of the lending process.

Darryl Thomas had grown up in the shadow of his older brother, the popular one who did nothing wrong, a handsome athlete who lettered in basketball and track, who dated cheerleaders and somehow still brought home a report card chock-full of As. Darryl was none of those things; he was a solid B student, a glasses-wearing awkward kid. Although tall like his older brother, he was lanky and not muscular, never making the cut for basketball despite his best efforts. And he was saddled with the nickname "Skeeter." It started after the popular one thought he sounded like a mosquito buzzing when he was a baby. "Mosquito" soon deteriorated into "Skeeter," and Skeeter stuck. By the time he was in high school, no one actually knew his given name. Darryl Thomas would be forever known as Skeeter Thomas.

Skeeter had a glass-walled office on the first floor of the bank, to the left of the foyer, opposite the lightly stained wood and black-marble teller counter. When there was no traffic on Third Street, he could see the reflection of the gilded double-doored entrance to Bluegrass Bank and Trust in the shop windows across the street and often smiled at the "backwards" stylized name above the doors. His morning had been uneventful, just another Monday. After a trip to the second floor to update the bank manager, he walked down Allen Street to a newly opened coffee shop. Finding the handwritten drink menu options on the oversized chalkboard overwhelming and the pierced and tattooed baristas distasteful, he returned to the bank emptyhanded. Breakroom coffee was just fine.

His head was buried in yet another loan application when a colleague walked into his office, carrying a newspaper.

"Skeeter, did you see this?" as the paper was laid on his desk. "Jeff Miller was murdered. You know Jeff, right?"

Skeeter backed up from his desk, looking down at the paper, then slowly leaned forward and picked it up.

"No. I mean, yes. I mean, well, yeah, I know Jeff. I didn't look at the *Gazette* today."

"Oh. Well, he was stabbed. Not much detail. A murder, right here in Owensboro. Hard to believe."

"You mind if I look at this?"

"Sure. I'm heading out for a client meeting. Later."

Skeeter pushed his too-long blonde hair back, adjusted his steel-rimmed glasses, then turned his chair away from the street view. He slowly and deliberately studied the article. Jeff Miller had been found by his wife, Eve. He thought back to their wedding, a time before he and Jeff had drifted apart. Although not the close friends they once were, the two had been able to collaborate professionally, to mutual benefit. With Jeff's assistance, Skeeter had been able to arrange financing for some of Butler Brothers' customers. Jeff got the and Skeeter got the bank manager's attention, which eventually resulted in him becoming the loan officer in the little glass office with a view.

He contemplated telephoning Eve, hesitating as he reached for the handset. A lot of time had passed since he last spoke to Eve; he no longer remembered the number. May be better to wait, he decided. He would attend the visitation, attend the funeral, see her there.

CHAPTER SIX

The pathology department and the autopsy room were located on the first floor of Daviess County General Hospital, far removed from the main lobby. Hunter strolled through the lobby, reaching the outer office. The receptionist, who was on the telephone, acknowledged his presence and waved her hand toward the double doors, mouthing "Go in."

The chubby Dr. Turner was sitting at a small desk on the far wall of the stark, white room, next to a row of X-ray boxes. Her back was to Hunter and to the steel table on which Jeff Miller's body was lying under a drab-green sheet. She turned around in the chair as he approached.

"Sneaking up on me, Detective?" She rose from the chair.

"Just here to see what you've found, Jean. It's been an unproductive morning."

She walked to the autopsy table, turned on the overhead lamp, and adjusted the focus before pulling back the sheet. Hunter stood opposite. The chest cavity was spread open, the internal organs removed.

"So, as we noted at the scene, there is no bruising to suggest a struggle. No scratches or bruises on his hands to indicate that he tried to hit or claw at his attacker. He has a scar on his lower abdomen. Had an appendectomy as a child." She looked up at Hunter.

"Keep going."

"Okay. Well here's where it gets interesting. The knife entered here." She pointed to the medial end of a wound that extended laterally across the left thorax. "That's the fourth intercostal space, the space between the fourth and fifth ribs. He inserted the knife on the left side, next to the sternum, with the blade positioned so that he could extend the gash. The knife was deep enough to penetrate both the right and left ventricles of the heart. By pushing the knife across the chest, he bisected the heart."

Hunter touched his chest. "Ouch."

"Yeah, big ouch. Death would have been pretty much instant. No one survives having their heart sliced in two."

"Anything else?"

"There was still some urine in his bladder, so I sent it for toxicology a few hours ago. Don't have the results, but should soon."

Hunter pulled on a pair of examining gloves and poked his fingers through the gouge in Jeff Miller's chest. "This guy knew what he was doing."

"What I'm thinking."

"Someone who has medical knowledge, who would know exactly where to insert the knife. Maybe a doctor, nurse?"

Turner pulled the sheet over the body. "Maybe. You are talking someone with a very detailed knowledge of anatomy."

"What about someone who is bright enough to self-educate? Not a healthcare worker? Would that be possible?"

She considered the idea. "Well, perhaps. Most folks seem to know that the heart is on the left side of chest, but don't know exactly where. The placement of that knife was not random. He would need to be able to translate book knowledge into which intercostal space to run the knife through, that is, which rib to run the knife over. That sort of thing is not exactly spelled out anywhere, not even in the forensic books." She paused. "I doubt most medical students would even get that question right."

Hunter tossed the exam gloves into the waste can next to the steel table. "You sent the knife to ECU?"

"Yes. I'm dubious as to whether they'll find anything."

"Thanks. I need to go interface with the chief. Let me know if the tox screen turns up anything."

∞

The office of Owensboro's chief of police was down a long hallway in the far corner of the first floor, with a window through which the squad cars in the parking lot could be seen. Unlike the other workplaces, with half-walls and glass to the ceiling, the chief's office had solid walls and a small reception area for his administrative assistant. It was sufficiently large to house an oversized desk, two chairs facing it, and a six-chaired oblong table. The rumor in the department was that Chief Hartmann had had the desk and matching chestnut leather chair custom-made so that he would be seated higher than any occupant of the "hot seat" in front of him. Hunter wasn't convinced of the tale's legitimacy, but his own height may have negated any elevation provided the chief.

The admin's desk was unoccupied, so Hunter walked to the office door, pressing it open far enough to determine if the chief was there. He was.

"Come in, Detective."

Hunter entered and parked himself in front of the desk.

Hartmann held up the *Owensboro Gazette*, folded so the front-page headline could be seen. "Where are we on this? The mayor has already called me, and I need to get back to him. Soon." He placed his hands on the uncluttered desktop.

"What's not in the paper and will be in my report is that the knife was of the type used by Navy SEALs. The placement of the wound was very precise, so that the heart was sliced into two pieces. Based on my conversation with Dr. Turner this morning, I suspect the killer has either a healthcare background or has a very high level of healthcare knowledge. It's also likely the murderer has military training. There was no evidence of a struggle. The attacker was able to easily overpower the victim before stabbing him."

The police chief leaned back in his leather chair, eyes closed, elbows on the chair arms. He rubbed his temples gently in small circles using his index and middle fingers, taking care so that his heavily sprayed comb-over was not disturbed.

Hunter resumed relaying the details of the case, ending with "and there were no fingerprints or footprints at the scene. No suspects yet, but I'm working on it."

There was a long pause, then Hartmann finally spoke. "This is not good, Detective. What should I tell the mayor? He's gonna want something, and right now you've got much less than something."

"This was a personal attack, Chief, not random. The knife was left in the chest on purpose. It was a statement. The killer knew Jeff, and that's how I'll track him down."

Hartmann tilted his chair forward. "Yeah, okay, I like that. Personal attack, likely knew the victim, we'll be able to use that to find the killer. Yeah, the mayor will go for that. Good."

Hunter smiled and stood up. "I'll get him, Chief."

"Before you leave, Hunter, there's one more thing."

"Yes?"

"I was informed this morning that Detective Maddox will not be returning to the force."

Hunter sat down. "I just talked to him Friday. He thought he would be back in a week or two. Seemed to be recovering well from the operation."

"Change of plan, apparently. He's going to take an early retirement. He meets the department's criteria. You'll be getting a new partner. And Maddox's old office–it'll be packed up today."

∞

After leaving the chief, he took the back stairs to the third floor. He was surprised to learn his partner would retire. Detective Alan Maddox had been more that Hunter's partner, he'd been his mentor. Maddox had joined the Owensboro Police Department after starting his career in Louisville, seeking a change to a smaller, less violent city and a more felicitous life. He brought with him a fund of policework knowledge that Hunter had been eager to tap.

Hunter walked into his now-former partner's office, in the back corner of the third floor, with windows facing Crittenden Street to the east and the parking lot to the south, half filled with an assortment of black-and-white patrol cars and employee vehicles. A row of filing cabinets filled the wall beneath the windows, which Maddox had populated with a hodgepodge of mementos. He turned to the chairs facing the desk in the center of the room. How much time had he spent sitting, listening, and learning from the big-city detective,

Hunter wondered. He had even adopted the Maddox dress code: detectives wear suits, dark suits.

"Guess Chief Hartmann is ready for me to be the sensei," he whispered to no one.

CHAPTER SEVEN

Sunset was approaching as Ann O'Neil turned her British Racing Green Range Rover into the driveway, parking behind Jeff Miller's Mustang. She tapped the power-window switches in the door handle, allowing the warm evening breeze into the cabin while they waited. Eve Miller stared at her house, eyeing the yellow police tape across her front door.

"I never should have gone to Louisville," Eve uttered.

Ann turned in the driver's seat to face her younger sister. "What? Why would you say that?"

Eve shook her head. "Maybe if I hadn't gone, none of this would have happened. Maybe Jeff would still be alive."

"You can't blame yourself, Eve."

"It's all my fault. If I hadn't gone away, Jeff would still be here, our life would go on." She started to tear up.

"Wishing it away won't change the past." Ann ran her hands through her light-brown hair. "You can't wish Jeff back to life."

"If I could, I would." Tears started to flow.

Ann pulled a travel pack of tissues from the center console and handed it to her sister. "The police should be here soon."

"I don't think I can go into the house," Eve sobbed, burying her face into a bouquet of tissues.

"I understand," Ann answered. "I can collect some of your things. Do you know what dresses you want?"

"I can't think about it."

"I'll take care of it, Eve. You should stay with us for a while, anyway. Where do you keep the suitcases?"

"Closet in the front bedroom." Eve stopped dabbing her eyes, pulling the tissues away. "The pink room."

Ann watched in the side mirror as an OPD patrol car pulled to the curb. She opened the driver's door as a uniformed policeman walked up the driveway.

"Dispatch sent me over, Mrs. Miller," he said. "I understand you need to get some personal items from your house?"

"I'm Mrs. O'Neil," Ann replied as she slid from the tan leather seat to the concrete. "My sister, Mrs. Miller, would prefer to wait in the car while I collect a few items for her."

He looked at Eve. "So long as that's okay with you, Mrs. Miller."

Eve nodded. "Yes. I don't want to go into the house, Officer."

He followed Ann to the front porch, stepping in front of her to pull the police tape from the door frame. He opened the screen door, holding it ajar by the handle.

The keys already in her hand, she unlocked the door. The metallic odor of dried blood hit her as she pushed the door open. She remained outside.

"How much longer will my sister's house be considered a crime scene?" she asked the officer.

"I don't know. That's up to Detective Hunter."

"Wonderful." Ann frowned. "This place is in need of a thorough cleaning." She entered the house, flipped the wall switch to light the hallway, then made her way to the bedrooms. The police officer trailed her, then remained in the hallway where he could observe her movements.

She found two large suitcases in the closet, as Eve had stated. She rolled them into the master bedroom and plopped both on the bed. Ruffling through Eve's closet, she chose several dark dresses and matching shoes appropriate for the funeral and viewings at the funeral home. After folding the dresses into the larger of the cases, she pulled an assortment of more-casual clothes from the closet and bureau drawers.

Ann was not sure what cosmetics and toiletries Eve might need or even want. Finding a small floral quilted carry-on bag on the closet shelf, Ann filled it with everything in sight, leaving the items that looked to be used by her now-deceased brother-in-law. She returned to the bedroom, the floral bag's sides bulging.

"May I help you with Mrs. Miller's bags?" the officer asked.

"Yes," Ann responded. She slipped the strap of the carry-on over her right shoulder and walked into the hallway.

He sighed, then closed and secured both suitcases. He heaved them off the bed and rolled them down the short hallway to the front room. Before leaving, he quickly checked the house, confirmed the lights were turned off. After Ann locked the front door, he stopped to place new strips of yellow police tape in an "X" across the door frame.

She pushed the key fob to open the tailgate of the Range Rover and waited for the bags to be placed in the cargo bay by the uniformed officer. With both suitcases in the cargo bay, Ann sat the third one beside them and pushed the button overhead, closing the tailgate.

"Thanks, Ann. I know I couldn't do that," Eve said as Ann returned to the driver's seat.

"That's what sisters are for," she replied. She started the Range Rover and backed out of the driveway. The officer stood by the patrol car, watching the sisters as the SUV headed north on Christie Place.

CHAPTER EIGHT

Hunter's small office was located at the back of the third floor, down the hallway from his now-former partner's office, with a single window overlooking the parking lot. The desk was perpendicular to the left wall, facing the half-glass door, barely enough room for a single visitor's chair.

He stood at his office window, staring out at nothing. Owensboro's first murder in more than two years, and he was stumped. No motive that he could deduce, no obvious killer, and no reliable witness. There was the mysterious "girl in the blue polka-dot dress," who may have been the last person to see Jeff Miller alive, but he had no idea who she was, where she was, or if she had any useful information. A call to Eve Miller had been unhelpful. She was unable to provide any clue to her identity either.

Now it was Tuesday morning, two days had passed, and there was no apparent path to resolving the crime. He crushed the cigarette butt into the blue acrylic ashtray on the window sill and returned to his desk.

The telephone rang. He hit the speaker button, answering, "Hunter."

"Detective, there is a Trevor Reed at the station who wants to speak with you."

Hunter leaned forward in his office chair. "I'm not expecting anyone. Trevor Reed? Not sure I know him."

"Says he has information about the Jeff Miller murder."

He twisted the wedding band on his left hand, tilting back in his chair before answering. *Could this be a break?* "Okay. Can you have someone escort him up to my office?"

"Yes, sir."

∞

After a few minutes passed, Trevor Reed arrived with his uniformed attendant. Hunter stood to greet him, and the uniformed officer left once introductions had been made. He walked Trevor down the hallway to a small reception area next to Maddox's office. The nonconfrontational space was equipped with two chairs, a rather drab brown couch, and a low wooden coffee table.

"Let's have a seat in here," he suggested. "It'll be more comfortable."

Trevor smiled and said, "Thanks." He sat on the couch, crossed his arms on his chest and peering intently at the coffee table.

Hunter notice his jiggling left foot. "Can I offer you something to drink? Coffee, water?"

"No. I'm good." He uncrossed his arms, then started to roll one hand over the other.

Hunter took the arm chair closest to the door, his preferred seat. "Ever been in a police station before, Mr. Reed? Or would you prefer Trevor?"

"Trevor is fine. And no. This is my first, and I hope only, time."

Hunter chuckled. "Okay. Well, you have information about Jeff Miller? What can you tell me?"

Trevor shifted in his seat, clasped his hands, fingers intertwined, and then unclasped them. "This may take a while. It's a bit complicated."

Hunter leaned back in the chair. "Take all the time you need. I'm listening."

He took a deep breath, slowly exhaled, then stopped moving his hands and his left foot. "This goes back to high school." He paused, finally making direct eye contact. "You know, I think I will take some water."

"Be right back." Hunter walked to the break room, taking a cold bottle of water from the refrigerator. He paused at the coffee pot, which had just dripped the last of a fresh brew into the carafe. He pulled his mug from the sink, gave it a quick rinse, and filled it.

"Here you go," he said as he handed the bottle to Trevor. He retook his place in the arm chair. "So, high school."

Trevor swallowed some water and resumed. "Yes, so I was taking my date home. We were on Calhoun Road, I was driving, and we were hit by a drunk driver." He stopped, closed his eyes, head down. Hunter could see a tear in his eyelashes.

"You'd been on Fischer Road, right?"

He nodded without looking up. "Yeah."

"Fischer Road has been Lover's Lane since long before even I was in high school, Trevor, except it was gravel back when I went parking there."

Trevor looked up, a hint of a smile, his posture more relaxed. "Yeah, I guess some things never change. Anyway, I was driving my dad's Cutlass and we were hit head-on. The car crossed the center line. The driver was drunk. Jenny, my girlfriend, she didn't have a seatbelt on. She went through the windshield." He paused, taking some water from the bottle. "Jenny died." He bowed again, shaking his head, eyes closed; a stream of tears began to flow.

Hunter sipped his coffee. And waited.

"The drunk driver was Jeff Miller," he said as he looked up at Hunter. His eyes were bloodshot.

Hunter stooped over the oval table, handing Trevor a box of tissues. He took several, blotted his tears, and after a heavy sigh returned his gaze to the detective. "And he got away with it. Somehow, someway, somebody paid somebody or something, but the whole thing went away."

"Trevor, that story actually makes you a prime suspect. For the record, where were you Saturday night?"

Trevor sat back on the couch. "Me?"

"Yes. You have a good motive. Miller is responsible for the death of your high school girlfriend."

"I was home. With my wife." He took another mouthful from the water bottle. "Number two's on the way, so we've not been going out much. She's the one who talked me into coming here and talking to you."

"Your wife? Why?"

"I keep a picture of Jenny behind our wedding picture. She found it one day, cleaning, you know, and I told her the whole story. I felt responsible for Jenny's death, and then, as I got older, I realized that I was not the one who killed her, Jeff Miller was. I keep the picture as a reminder that she was someone special in my life at one time. My wife thought it might bring some closure to the whole thing, the Miller thing, if I came in to tell you what I know."

"Were you in love with her?

"It was high school. I was in love with someone new every month, detective."

Hunter laughed. "Alright, Trevor. So, how does this help me with Jeff Miller's murder–unless you're going to confess."

Trevor finally smiled; the tears were gone. "When nothing was done, when Miller wasn't charged or anything, Jenny's brother swore that he would make them pay. He swore that he would track Jeff Miller to the ends of the earth and take care of what the police failed to do."

"And?"

"He didn't do nothing. Jenny's brother was in the state pen at Eddyville."

Hunter sat his coffee mug on the table between them. "What's Jenny's last name?"

"Harper."

Hunter closed his eyes and sighed. "And her brother is Billy Ray Harper," he said slowly.

"Yeah. You know him?"

Hunter leaned back, elbows on the arm rests, then drummed the fingers of his right hand on the worn fabric of the chair's arm. "I put him in Eddyville."

"He's out now. On parole. Got out about a month ago."

"Oh?"

"Yeah. He called me, wanted to meet, to talk."

Billy Ray Harper has motive, Hunter thought. "So, did you meet him?"

"I was reluctant at first, but, yeah, I did."

"What did he want?"

"He mostly wanted to tell me that he held me responsible for his sister's death for a long time. But, over time, he realized that we were just doing things normal teenagers did, and that I was not the one at fault, that Jeff Miller was, and that he was thankful that I had been Jenny's friend."

Hunter returned to his coffee. *Harper out on parole, need to check on that. And the connection to a DUI death?* "Trevor, did he say anything about revenge, anything about making Jeff Miller pay for what he'd done?"

"No, that's the interesting bit. He quoted some Bible verse about the Lord avenging for you, as if he thought he didn't need to go after Miller."

"Something like 'Say not thou, I will recompense evil; but wait on the Lord, and he shall save thee'?"

Trevor shook his head. "No, that's not it."

"How about, 'Do not say, "I'll pay you back for this wrong!" Wait for the Lord, and he will avenge you'?"

"That's exactly what he said. How'd you know that?"

"Proverbs twenty, verse twenty-two. I was educated in Catholic schools." Hunter drained the remaining coffee from his mug. "Many prisons, Eddyville included, allow inmates to keep only the Bible. They have plenty of time to read it. Did you believe him?"

Trevor looked up at the ceiling, took a deep breath, then looked Hunter straight in the eye. "No."

CHAPTER NINE

Back in his office, Hunter adjusted the computer monitor and opened the program in which the closed cases were cataloged. Realizing that Jeff would have been a minor when the DUI occurred, he toggled to the tab marked Juvenile and entered his security code. Once verified, he typed "Jeff Miller"; there were no cases. Then he tried "Jeffrey Miller"; same result. *There should be a case file*, he thought. At least he was not getting a Restricted Access screen.

Next, he typed in "Jenny Harper." No cases. "Jennifer" didn't produce any results either. Remembering that "Ginny" is a diminutive of both Virginia and Ginger, he tried "Ginny Harper," "Virginia Harper," and "Ginger Harper" without success.

Frustrated, he decided to abandon the search for the moment and left his office to find Lieutenant Keith Embry, who was in charge of parolees. He had a plausible suspect. It was time to question Billy Ray Harper.

Lt. Embry was in his windowless ground floor office, seated behind his desk, upon which were haphazardly stacked files in dark-brown folders. There were more files stacked on the two four-drawer grey metal filing cabinets against the wall; several drawers were open with more files peeking out. The files were joined by a collection of used paper cups from the coffee shop across the street. He didn't notice Hunter's presence.

"Keith, you got a minute?" Hunter asked, getting Embry's attention before leaning against the jamb, his six four figure filling the doorway.

Embry looked up from the file in his hands. "Yeah, Bob. What's up?"

"Billy Ray Harper. I need to talk to him."

He grabbed at a lock of uncombed brown hair at his temple. "Harper ..." he repeated. He pulled a few files from one of the stacks on his desk, flipping through until he found Harper's. "Yeah, Harper. He got out last month. Got a job with that janitor company, uh ... It's here somewhere."

"Craig's Custodians?" Owned by a rehabilitated former ex-con, Craig had discovered a market for, and found success in, cleaning business offices after-hours. He purposely hired parolees to aid in their return to society, hoping others would turn from their parlous ways as he had. To Hunter's knowledge, Craig had achieved some wins in the battle against recidivism. And the former felons learned a skill from someone who had walked in their shoes.

"Yeah, that's the one." Embry turned in his chair and looked around his office for a place to set the file.

"Before you put that away, can you tell me where's he living?" Hunter asked.

"Oh, yeah." He opened the file again and flipped past several sheets, before stopping and running his finger down the page. "He's staying in the halfway house on Manor Court." He looked up at Hunter.

Hunter glanced around the office. "Harper been checking in with you?"

After turning a few more pages in the files, he answered. "Yep. Every week, like he's supposed to. I have a note from Craig also. Says that Harper's been a good worker, for what it's worth."

Hunter nodded, "Okay."

"Anything else, Bob?"

He stood up from the doorframe. "Yes, actually. You know anything about a sister? Harper had a sister, Jenny, who was killed in a DUI."

Embry scratched at the stumble on his chin. "No, don't think so." He stood up to hand Hunter the file. "You're welcome to look. Just return it when you're done."

He took the thick file. "I'll look, but I'm dubious about the possibility of finding anything. The accident happened over ten years ago, but it was after Harper was put away. I checked the database, couldn't find a case."

"Hang on. You said over ten years ago?"

"Yes."

"Wouldn't be in the database, Bob. That's too old." He returned to his chair, leaning back, hands clasped behind his head. "That would be an old paper file."

"Hmmm. Didn't think about that."

Embry smiled. "Really? You didn't think about it?"

"No."

"You're slipping, Detective."

He chuckled. "Yeah, guess so. Thanks, Keith." He tapped the file. "Get this back to you today."

∞

Back in his office, Hunter dropped Harper's file on his desk, then cranked open the casement window. He pulled the pack of Marlboros from this suit pocket, tapped one out and lit it with a wooden match. He looked out onto the half-empty parking lot and contemplated his strategy. Harper was his only suspect so far. He had motive and a not-so-pristine history. He could bring him in for questioning, try to pry out a confession. Or, drop by the halfway house for a more casual, "good-cop" approach.

He finished his cigarette before taking his seat. No, "good-cop" would not work with Billy Ray Harper. He would go with the beige walls of an interrogation room.

Hunter punched the speaker-phone button and called the dispatcher.

"This is Hunter. Is Officer Wagner on patrol?"

"Yes, Detective. You need him?" the female voice answered.

"Is he busy?"

"Not that I'm aware. Just finished a domestic-violence call."

"Okay. Put me through to the patrol car. I need Wagner to pick up a suspect."

CHAPTER TEN

L unch was at noon. The residents of the halfway house were responsible for making their own meals. They alternated the kitchen chores, preparing, cooking and cleaning in a routine that was followed for breakfast, lunch, and dinner. That Tuesday, Billy Ray Harper was washing the pans and rinsing the lunch dishes. After loading the dishwasher and drying the cookware, he joined the others to watch whatever sporting event could be found on the television.

The transitional home had been converted from a wooden two-story house on which the city had foreclosed after a decade of unpaid property taxes. A large room in the front of the house served as the social area, with a television and a little-used foosball table. The kitchen was in the back of the house, along with a small office and living space for Amos Weller, the manager. The residents had their own single-man rooms on the second floor and shared a lone bathroom. Harper's room had a window overlooking the small back yard.

Officer Wagner pulled the patrol car in front of the Manor Court halfway house, leaving the engine running. As Phil joined his partner on the covered front porch, Amos opened the front door and stepped out, closing the door behind him.

"What's going on, boys?" he asked.

"We're here to pick up Billy Ray Harper," Mike answered. "Hunter wants to question him about—"

Amos interrupted. "About the Jeff Miller murder, right?

"Yes. Did he call you?"

"No. But somehow, I was expecting it." Amos sighed. "Let me get him for you. I don't want uniforms in the house. You okay with that?"

Mike looked to Phil, who nodded approval. "Yeah, we'll wait out here."

∞

Amos Weller retired from the Owensboro Police Department not long after losing most of his left leg. He had been engaged in a high-speed training exercise for the newly formed motor unit when his custom police motorcycle was pinned against the squad car by the chased vehicle, crushing his left leg below his knee. The unit was never put into service and quietly disbanded.

Returning to the force had been a formidable, and finally overwhelming, challenge. Managing the halfway house for the city became the most viable option for the confirmed bachelor to keep a hand in law enforcement. He soon reappeared at the door. Billy Ray was close behind.

Mike spoke first. "Mr. Harper?"

Billy Ray glowered at the uniformed officer. "Yep. What do you want from me?" he stated flatly.

"Detective Hunter needs to question you. Downtown."

Amos interjected, "It's about the Jeff Miller murder, Billy Ray"

"Let us handle this, Amos," Phil scowled.

"You can ask me right here, Officer. I ain't going nowhere. And I gotta go to work at five thirty." Billy Ray responded.

Mike groaned. "Well, Mr. Harper, we could question you here, but we don't intend to. Do I need to remind you that you're on parole? How about a little cooperation here? You want to do this the hard way?" He stared at Billy Ray as he hovered his left hand over the handcuff case on his duty belt.

Amos looked to Billy Ray. "Go to the station, get this over with."

Billy Ray grumbled an unintelligible response.

"Good choice," Mike said. "Let's go."

∞

There was no soundtrack on hold, so Hunter left the call on speakerphone and untwisted a paper clip while he waited. The old paper case files were kept off-site in a small warehouse, along with case evidence that overflowed from the evidence room at the station. He'd provided the case information to Frenchy, the warehouse manager whose real name no one knew, who went on the search.

"Bob, you still there?"

"Yeah, Frenchy, I'm here. You find it?"

"There's no file for a Jenny Harper, or Jennifer, or any of the other names. There's a Janice Harper from the same month, busted for soliciting. Wasn't her first time, either. That's it. You sure you got the right info?"

Hunter picked up the handset. "Doesn't make sense." He set the paper clip in the desk. "How about Jeff Miller, or Jeffrey Miller?

"Hang on, Bob, and I'll look. Let me put you back on hold." The phone went back to silence.

He switched back to the speaker and pulled another clip apart. He thought back to his conversation with Trevor Reed. No arrest, no prosecution, as if it had never occurred. His thoughts were interrupted by Frenchy.

"Well, Bob, something's amiss. There should be a file, there's a Jeffrey Miller in the database, had a few run-ins as a juvie, but there's no file. Nothing else on anyone named Miller for that time period."

Hunter curled the paperclip around his left index finger. "Okay, that's good news. Who checked Jeff Miller's file out of storage?"

"No one. By the records, it should be there."

"Frenchy, you're killing me. Could it be misfiled?"

"Doubt it. But for you, Bob, and only you, I'll take a look around. Call you if I find anything."

"Thanks." Hunter hit the speaker button to end the call. "Jenny Lynn, your case is an enigma," he whispered softly.

∞

The interrogation room was a familiar one to Billy Ray, the same bolted-down table with a ring in the center, the same two-way mirror, and the same stagnant air. Hunter observed him through the mirror. The Billy Ray Harper he knew had aged, and not well. His still prison-short dark hair was greying, and there were prominent crow's feet framing his black eyes. Clad in the tan Craig's Custodians uniform, he could have easily been mistaken for a much older man. After Hunter decided Billy Ray had baked long enough, he left the viewing chamber to start the grill session.

Hunter opened the door and placed a bottle of water on the table in front of Billy Ray before taking the chair on the opposite side, his back to the mirror.

"This gonna take long, Hunter?" Billy Ray looked at the bottle before turning his glare to meet the detective's eyes. "I got a job and I aim to keep it."

"I've missed you too, Harper. How did you like your extended state-funded vacation?"

He picked up the bottle, uncapped it, and took a slow draw. "You didn't drag me down here to talk about that hellhole you put me in. Whadda you want?"

"Did you kill Jeff Miller?" Hunter leaned back in the chair.

Billy Ray sighed. "No."

After a quiet pause, Hunter leaned forward, elbows on the light-gray table. "You expect me to believe that?"

"Am I glad he's dead? Yeah, damn right I'm glad. My baby sister ain't around here no more 'cuz of Jeff Miller," he said, emphasizing the name. "But I didn't do it."

"Where were you Saturday night?"

Billy Ray shook his head. "My alibi?"

"Yes"

"Craig's van picks me up at six on Saturdays. We worked until almost midnight. Then they take me back."

"You always work that late on Saturday?"

"No. Saturdays are usually easy. But we waxed the floors. They do that about once a month, I'm told."

"And if I call Craig, he'll confirm?"

He nodded.

Hunter ran his right hand down his dark purple pindot tie, pressing it against the white shirt. "Well, somebody executed Jeff Miller. Ever think about doing it? About murdering the man who took Jenny's life?"

"Yep. Every day. Until one day when I didn't." He took another drink of water. "And it ain't my problem now."

"Just one day? Poof? And how did that happen, Harper?"

Billy Ray inhaled deeply, eyes closed. When they reopened, he looked up into Hunter's eyes. "The Bible was about the only book I had to read in Eddyville. Yeah, I read it. The whole Bible. More than once. And it helped me to look beyond my criminal past and hope for a better future." He paused. "I didn't kill Jeff Miller, but I'm glad he got what he deserved."

"So, it's just a coincidence that you get out on parole, and Jeff Miller, the man who's responsible for Jenny's death, turns up dead?"

"Guess so."

"Policemen aren't supposed to believe in coincidences, Harper." Hunter stood up and walked out of the room, closing the door behind him.

CHAPTER ELEVEN

C raig returned Hunter's call and corroborated the time frame. Billy Ray was back at the house on Manor Court just after midnight on Saturday. What if he had somehow slipped out of the halfway house unnoticed and made his way to Miller's house? Would time of death fit? Dr. Turner did not have a very exact time to work with. Hunter had assumed between eight and midnight, however it could have been after midnight.

He walked into Maddox's office to find an Owensboro street map. The space was almost barren, a cardboard box of the last of former detective's personal effects on the desk, the remainder of the pictures and keepsakes gone. After pulling a few drawers of the filing cabinets, Hunter found a folded, yellowed map.

"Does anyone even use these anymore?" he murmured as returned to his office. Once it was unfolded, he tacked the map to the corkboard on the office wall. He marked the halfway house on Manor Court, and the Millers' on Christie Place. He traced a route connecting the two, then using a plain three by five index card, estimated the distance. Between 2.2 and 2.4 miles.

"Hmmm. No access to a car." Hunter walked to the window. "At a normal walking pace, he could have covered the span in about forty-five minutes. He would need about fifteen minutes to subdue Miller, maybe less."

He went back to the map. "It's possible. Two hours, out and back. Residential streets, might not even be noticed."

Hunter sat at his desk, still gazing at the map, when his thoughts were interrupted by Mike Wagner knocking on the open door.

"What are you up to, Detective?"

"You get Harper home?"

"It was a quiet ride back."

"Thanks." He turned in his chair. "I appreciate it."

Mike nodded. "You like him for it?"

"Yeah, I do. He's not a nice guy, and what I got today was mostly deplorable mendacities."

"Huh?"

Hunter stood up, and using his hands he pointed out the two houses on the map. "Harper could have made it from Manor Court to the Miller's house and back in less than two hours, on foot. Fits with time of death. He's got motive and certainly has the knowledge."

"You know, you could have done this on the internet with one of those map programs." Mike moved closer to study the map. "Okay, but how did he get past Amos?"

"I'll need to talk to Amos to determine that, Mike. When does Harper go to work?"

He pulled a black notebook from his left breast pocket and flipped a few pages. "Craig's van picks him up at five thirty on weekdays, six on Saturdays."

"Got it." Hunter smiled. "Nice work. Anything else on your mind?"

"Yes, actually. Word is that Alan Maddox isn't coming back. Is that true? His office is packed up."

Hunter nodded. "You didn't hear it from me—Chief Hartmann has yet to make an announcement. Maddox is taking early retirement."

"Who's moving into his office?"

"Me."

Mike put out his hand. "Congrats, Bob."

Hunter shook his hand. "Thanks. And that's not public knowledge yet, either."

He smiled. "Of course. I guess the next question is, well, who replaces you?"

"Don't know. You took the exam, right?"

"Yes."

Hunter winked at him. "Good."

∞

After Mike left his office, Hunter returned to his chair and focused on his computer monitor. Since he had been unable to find a police file for Jenny Harper or Jeff Miller, the newspaper might be useful. Trevor Reed had given him the date of the accident, so he planned to look in the paper for the week following, expecting a report in the Crime Brief section.

He opened the website for the *Owensboro Gazette*, looking for the archives. The paper had been one of the first in Kentucky to have an online version. Prior editions were easily searchable on the website, but, unfortunately for Hunter, only available for the past three years. He found the circulation desk number and called.

After two transfers, he was connected to a raspy-voiced man named Cooper who was in charge of the archives. Hunter explained why he wanted to look though the old papers, to which Cooper responded, "Well, Detective, we have old copies of the *Gazette* back to 1936, but they're in storage. We only keep the prior thirty-six months on the website."

"Can I access the stored papers?"

"Well, not easily. It's a climate-controlled building in Philpot. Take me a few days to get what you're wanting."

Hunter leaned back in the office chair. "I was hoping for something a little quicker."

After a long pause, Cooper replied. "Well, you could try the library."

Hunter sat up. "The public library?"

"Yep. Or the college libraries. They should have copies going back at least as far as you need."

"Like the microfiche I had to look through in high school?"

Cooper laughed, which then turned into coughing. "Well, no, they'll be digital. We ain't had no microfiche for about twenty years now. But that's how the library has the archives before we switched to digital. You won't be needing to plug in the old microfiche reader, Detective."

"Thanks. Appreciate your time, Mr. Cooper."

"You're welcome."

Hunter placed the handset on the base and looked at his watch. He had time to drop by the library before going to the halfway house to question Amos Weller.

CHAPTER TWELVE

When he arrived at the funeral home, the few parking spaces in front were taken. Skeeter Thomas drove his silver Toyota Camry into the side lot. He rolled down the driver's window before turning off the engine. He wasn't ready yet. He checked the dash clock, almost six. Visitation was from four until eight; he had plenty of time. He still wasn't sure if he wanted to go inside. He checked his hair in the mirror, straightened his tie, and popped another breath mint.

His teenage friendship with Jeff Miller had grown into a business relationship but had not grown into an adult friendship. They were business associates who had once been buddies. And Eve, a woman he barely knew. Eve disliked Jeff's high school chums and discouraged the boys' nights out. Jeff Miller had been one of his closest friends at one time. He needed to say goodbye. Yet he sat outside of Fulkerson Funeral Home, hesitating, unsure, indecisive. He wasn't ready. He closed his eyes, pondering what exactly to say.

Then a rap on the rear window startled him.

"Skeeter, you taking a snooze?"

He opened his eyes and turned to look out of the car window. He immediately recognized Wayne Peterson, who had kneeled next to the driver's door to face Skeeter through the open window.

"OMG, Wayne, haven't seen you in a while!" Skeeter unlatched his seat belt as Wayne pulled on the door handle. "Never thought we'd be here." He snatched his suit jacket from the passenger seat before closing the door.

"Yeah, who'd want to kill Jeff?" asked Wayne.

Skeeter slipped the jacket over his thin frame, then righted his glasses, as Wayne watched. He noticed Wayne then look over his own clothing—work pants and a light brown Carhartt jacket, both speckled with concrete dust.

"No idea. You talked to Eve at all?" Skeeter asked.

"Nope. I haven't seen or talked to either of them in a long time." Wayne leaned against Skeeter's Camry and pulled a pack of cigarettes from his jacket. "Never thought that Eve liked me very much, thought I was a bad influence on Jeff."

"You were a bad influence on both of us, Wayne."

Wayne lit a cigarette, took a long drag then slowly exhaled, blowing a smoke ring. "Maybe. We had fun, no doubt about that."

"Fun, yeah, and a lot of trouble." Skeeter shook his head, then smiled. "I haven't seen the inside of a police station since I stopped hanging with you."

"Me neither." They stood quietly while Wayne finished his cigarette, crushing the butt into the asphalt with his work boot. "Anyway, makes no sense, Jeff being killed. I can't figure it out."

"Yeah, no sense." Skeeter shivered. He nervously adjusted his glasses again.

Wayne looked over the Camry. "Nice car. You get it new?"

"No. It was a trade-in. Jeff got me a good deal on it." He sighed. "Actually, got it for Tracy."

"Yeah, I heard she left you. Sorry to hear about that, Skeeter. I know what that's like."

"I know you do." Skeeter motioned with his head. "Let's go." The pair walked silently to the front entrance.

∞

After his stemmery burned down, Zacharias Fulkerson, like many entrepreneurs in 1900s Owensboro, tried his hand at distilling bourbon. He adopted a wheated-bourbon recipe of corn, wheat, and barley for its smooth characteristics. He had hoped to distinguish his bourbon from the more common varieties, and for the effort, he expected to command a premium price. His dream was crushed when the small warehouse with his first and only run was struck by lightning during a summer thunderstorm. Due to the combination of dry wood and highly combustible bourbon, it burned to the ground. Not a single barrel survived.

Following the failure of his distillery, Zacharias decided he would enter a somber, more stable and less flammable business. He built Fulkerson Funeral Home during a period of the city's rapid growth, opening in 1907 at what eventually became the corner of East Parrish Avenue and Moseley Street, a few blocks from the then-new Union Station.

Passenger trains to Union Station ceased in the 1950s, but Fulkerson's parlor remained the family business Zacharias had intended. The success of his third venture allowed for diversification into other concerns, more of which thrived than not. The Fulkersons grew to become one of the wealthiest families in Owensboro, with a large home on

Griffith Avenue and the first Cadillac in town, a 1915 Type 51 Phaeton in maroon and black. The Cadillac continues to be driven in the annual Christmas Parade.

Zacharias's great-granddaughter, Jill Fulkerson Miller, attired in a simple black dress, was standing nearby the open casket next to her daughter-in-law, Eve Miller, and Eve's sister, Ann, in an abbreviated receiving line. They welcomed guests. They shook hands and hugged friends and extended family members between episodes of tears. Everyone avoided talking about the cause of Jeff's demise, to Eve's relief, politely tiptoeing around the subject. She was glad to not have to discuss it.

Skeeter and Wayne warily approached the trio. Skeeter spoke first, offering his hand to Eve. "I'm very sorry for your loss, Eve."

She hesitated, then shook his hand, responding softly with "Thank you."

Wayne silently offered his hand, which Eve accepted. He remained quiet.

Skeeter then rotated to face Jill Miller. "Mrs. Miller, you may not remember me, I'm Darryl Thomas, but everyone—"

Jill interrupted him. "Everyone calls you Skeeter. Yes, of course I remember you. And Wayne."

Wayne finally spoke. "Been a long time, Mrs. Miller."

"Yes, it has." She turned to Ann. "Jeff went to high school with Wayne and Skeeter. They were quite the cadre."

"Very nice of you to come. I'm Eve's sister, Ann O'Neil."

Skeeter nodded, then tugged at Wayne's sleeve to move closer to the casket. Jill shifted with them, maneuvering so that she could stand between the men. They stood over the open head panel, gazing at Jeff Miller's body, his hands folded across his chest so that the wedding band on his left ring finger was easily visible.

"I can't believe he's gone," Skeeter said.

"I never thought the day would come that my only son would be laid out in my family's funeral home," Jill stated flatly. "Thanks for coming, boys. Jeff really loved the two of you."

Wayne nodded, gave a hard swallow, then a tear ran down his right cheek.

∞

After sitting in the visitation room for an appropriate duration, Wayne suggested to Skeeter that they leave. They walked past Eve, who, with her sister, was looking over an assortment of flowers, to say goodbye.

It was dark when they emerged from the funeral home, the now-full parking lot lit with a soft glow by a series of overhead lamps. Wayne stopped as they approached Skeeter's car.

"You wanna get some dinner, or grab a beer?" he asked Skeeter.

Skeeter clicked the key fob to unlock the doors. "Thanks for the offer, but I'll pass." He opened the driver's side door and slipped behind the wheel.

"Later," Wayne said. He turned to walk to his truck. On the way home, he pulled through the drive-thru lane of a fast food restaurant for the overworked, single, construction-worker dinner.

CHAPTER THIRTEEN

The public library was quiet, as he expected it to be. It was always quiet—patrons whispering to one another, the library staff answering questions in hushed tones. Hunter was unfamiliar with the new library, albeit the library was not that new anymore. The Owensboro Public Library had relocated to the new facility on Ford Avenue long after he finished high school. He walked to what appeared to be the front desk, a circular wooden affair with two librarians, each one at the extremes of the arc. He walked to the closest, where a young woman was seated, her auburn hair pulled back into a low ponytail, half-glasses perched on her nose. She looked up to him once he gently tapped the dark countertop.

"May I help you?" she asked softly as she removed her glasses.

He produced his badge. "I'm Detective Hunter with the Owensboro Police Department. I'm looking for the newspaper archives."

"They're housed on the second floor." She pointed over his right shoulder. "Take the stairs just past the bank of computers. We keep the old newspaper and magazines in an area on the left. How far back are you looking to go?"

"Fourteen years. There's a particular date range in which I'm interested."

She stood up and pushed the chair under the counter. "That's going to be digital. I'll need to show you. I assume you've not used our systems before."

Hunter smiled. "Correct. My first time in this library." He looked around. "A big change from the old place."

"I wouldn't know, I've only been here two years." She made her way to her counterpart. "I'm going upstairs to show this policeman how to access the digital archives. Be right back."

The other librarian barely acknowledged her and returned to her book.

"I'm Cheryl, by the way," she said as she joined Hunter at the counter. "Please follow me." She started toward the stairs. "May I ask what this is about? Or is it one of those 'I can't comment on an ongoing investigation' sort of things?"

"It may impact a current investigation. This is more about background research."

"We don't often have police detectives looking for old newspapers. Does this have anything to do with that murder? Everyone is talking about it." She stopped at the bottom of the staircase, turning to face Hunter. "What's your name again, Detective?"

"Hunter."

"You're the detective who was in yesterday's *Gazette*. This is about that murder, isn't it?"

"Yes, I'm the detective who was quoted in the paper."

Cheryl swiftly moved up the stairs, Hunter trailing a few steps behind. She led him to a glass-enclosed room in the far corner of the second floor. There were rows of shelves with metal containers of what Hunter assumed to be old microfiche. There was an ancient microfiche viewer, protected by a yellowed plastic cover, bolted to a rectangular wooden table, and on the other end a flat-screen computer monitor. *The juxtaposing of old and new*, Hunter thought. Cheryl pulled the chair in front of the monitor and turned it on.

"Don't even ask me how that thing works," she said as she pointed to the microfiche reader.

Hunter stood over her, watching the monitor. "That old thing? I actually do know how to use it. Spent many an evening in my teenage years looking through microfiche to write those high school research papers. But that was in the old library."

"You want the *Owensboro Gazette*, right?"

"Yes."

"Okay. Here you go. It's organized by year, then month." She pointed to the left of the screen. "Then, from there you can get the date. Unfortunately, you will have to scroll through each day's paper, page by page. There's no Search function. The scroll arrows are here, on the right."

"Got it."

"If you want to print anything, let me know. I'll do it for you. There is a charge for printing, but of course, we wouldn't charge for official police business, Detective." She rose from the chair and smiled. "So, this Miller murder, the vox populi is that his wife did it. Caught him fooling around, you ask me."

"You've been very helpful, Cheryl. I think I can handle it from here."

"Okay. I'll be at the front desk if you need anything else."

∞

Cheryl closed the door as she left. Hunter sat on the chair and worked the mouse to find the correct date. He decided that he should start from the day of the accident, November 2, and work forward. He scrolled through the first day's newspaper to get a feel for the time. Fall, football season, anticipation of Thanksgiving. November 3, a Sunday, the crime brief section had two charges for first-degree possession of a controlled substance, a third-degree burglary, and a firearm discharge with no injuries. No DUIs. The next day was much the same. Tuesday's paper, November 5, included the obituary for Jenny Lynn Harper, age sixteen. No mention of the cause of death.

Hunter scrolled back through the prior two days of newspapers. Nothing. No DUI, not a single indication there had been an automobile accident on Calhoun Road on November 2 that had taken the life of Jenny Harper. He looked forward for two weeks, no reports. Miller was a minor at the time of the accident, could that be the reason there was no report of the event in the newspaper?

"I'm missing something," he murmured, as he stood up from the computer.

∞

The sun had set, leaving the moon in a cloudless sky to light Manor Court. Amos Weller was sitting in a lawn chair under the front-porch light, reading a magazine, when a familiar graphite Cadillac sedan pulled to the curb.

"Is that Detective Robert Hunter?" Amos Weller asked as Hunter walked to the covered porch of the halfway house. He curled the magazine into his left hand and got up from the chair.

"All two hundred fifty pounds of me, Amos." They shook hands.

"Had a feeling I'd be seeing you." Amos returned to his seat as Hunter leaned on the porch's wooden rail and lit a cigarette.

"You keeping this pugnacious group under control?" Hunter asked.

"On the straight and narrow, Bob. I just threaten to take off my prosthesis and start swinging. None of these guys want anyone to find out they've been taken down by a one-legged man."

Hunter smiled at the mental image. "Yeah, I can see that. What about Billy Ray Harper? He behaving?"

"So far, he's been a good boy. Does his chores, doesn't socialize much with the others, always ready when Craig's van picks him up for work. Not much to report."

"I like him for the Jeff Miller murder, but you already know that. You think he could have done it?"

The lawn chair creaked as Amos leaned back in it. "Could he? Yeah, he could. Would he? Not so sure about that. And from what I understand, the logistics just don't work."

"How so?"

"Billy Ray was here Saturday night after he finished work with Craig."

"Are you absolutely certain, Amos?"

"As certain as I can be."

"Let me limn it for you. Billy Ray could slip out of this house, walk to Christie Place, and be back in what I determine to be two hours." Hunter finished his cigarette, leaning forward to crush the end into an ashtray on a small glass-top patio table. "You'd never know he was gone."

"You have any evidence to support that theory?"

"I'm working on it."

"Here's another question for you, Bob. What's his motive? From what I can determine, Billy Ray didn't know Miller." Amos pursed his lips. "I guess that should have been my first question."

"He had a younger sister who was killed by a drunk driver when she was in high school. Billy Ray was in Eddyville at the time. Jeff Miller was the driver of the other car. There's your motive, Amos."

After a heavy sigh, Amos looked up at Hunter. "What was her name?"

"Jenny Lynn Harper."

Amos closed his eyes. "Oh."

"Odd thing, Amos. There's nothing in the database about it. Frenchy found Jeff Miller in the old-case database for some juvenile offenses, but there's no file. There should be one, but there just isn't. There's nothing about Jenny Harper. I checked the newspaper archives before I came here, and the only thing I can find is her obituary. Miller's DUI was not in the *Gazette*, although he was a juvenile at the time."

"I seriously doubt that there's a file for that incident, Bob."

Hunter stood up from the railing. "What?"

"That case was hushed up PDQ. Way above my pay grade."

"Would explain why I don't remember it. How?"

"Not sure who pulled the strings. It got quiet, real fast. No investigation, no arrests. And no one talked about it."

Hunter tugged at his wedding band. "Amos, do you know if there ever was a file?"

"Not sure, Bob. Can't believe that I just put it together. Miller, drunk driver, Jenny Harper. I hadn't made the connection until now."

"Change your mind about Billy Ray?" Hunter leaned back on the railing.

"Maybe. I agree, he's got motive. Just not sure he would act on it, not now when he seems to be trying hard to return to society." Amos exhaled through pursed lips, making a soft whistle sound. "Look, Billy Ray's not the brightest bulb, but he's not an idiot either. More like idiot-adjacent. I'm not convinced he would go after Miller."

CHAPTER FOURTEEN

The plastic, yellow moving totes were finally packed and stacked against the wall. Hunter decided to take one last break in his soon-to-be former office before he moved his gear to his new one. He leaned his large frame against the window sill, holding the cigarette in his right hand near the opening. Friday—move day. He could start the next week fresh in his new space.

He had reached an impasse in solving the murder of Jeff Miller. Dr. Turner's final report, issued earlier in the day, added nothing new. No substances had been found in Miller's system by the toxicologic analysis of his blood and urine. The iced tea in the glass from which Miller had been drinking was not drugged. No unusual marks on his body consistent with a struggle. As if he had been lying prone on the kitchen floor Saturday night, waiting for a knife. There was no evidence to connect Billy Ray Harper to the murder, just a potential motive and a hypothesis. No witnesses, unless he could determine the identity of the "girl in the blue polka-dot dress." Maybe she was a witness, maybe not. Or maybe she could add something to the paucity of clues.

Hunter finished his cigarette, adding it to the collection in his ashtray, and looked around the space he'd occupied for the past several years. Time to move on.

Mike Wagner appeared in the hallway with a pushcart, accompanied by Irwin Betts, the department's one-man computer unit. Irwin fit the expected stereotype of a geek, with an ever-present three-day scruff joined by an untamed goatee and man-bun, black-rimmed glasses and skin pale from the glow of monitor screens and lack of sunshine.

"Could you use a hand, Detective?" Mike asked.

"A cart? Really? I'm only going down the hallway."

"Make it one trip then. Ready?"

"Yep. All packed," he answered. "Except the computer, of course. Right, Irwin?"

"Yeah," Irwin responded. "Leave that to me."

While the cart was being loaded, Irwin disconnected the desktop computer and components, placing the items on top of the tote stack. Mike pushed the cart down the hallway, into the corner office. The office, except for the furniture, was bare. They stacked the boxes while Irwin started with the computer. He had it connected and powered up before Hunter had the first tote emptied.

"The telephone should be active shortly. I'll take care of that remotely," Irwin said. "Oh, and I set you up with a new keyboard. Do try not to spill coffee on this one." He pointed to the setup. "Any questions?"

"Not yet. I know how to find you, Irwin."

The office was beginning to take shape. Hunter found suitable spots for pictures of his wife, Brenda, their two young daughters, the football from the last game of his senior year. He placed his blue ashtray on the cabinets under the window, which were mostly void of files. He was sorting the books stacked on his desk when the telephone rang.

"Hunter," he answered on speakerphone.

"Can you take a call from Chief Hartmann?"

"Yes." He sat down and picked up the handset.

After a moment and a series of beeps, Chief Hartmann spoke. "Hunter, can you hear me?" His voice echoed in the receiver.

"Yes, Chief. I can hear you. Connection's not too good, though."

"I just got a call from the mayor. He's getting pressure about this Miller case. And he's looking to me for answers. Shit rolls downhill, Detective. You have anything?"

"Nothing new, Chief."

Hunter could hear some mumbling, as if Hartmann had his hand over his cell phone while he was relaying a message. "Not good, Detective. We need to have some movement on this case. Soon."

"Yes, Chief. I'm working on it."

"Short leash on this one, Hunter. Stay on top of it and keep me in the loop." The line went silent.

Hunter glared at the handset.

"I need a cigarette," he murmured softly as he placed the handset into the cradle.

CHAPTER FIFTEEN

Another Saturday evening. Much like the Saturday evening before, and the one before that. Although, now that baseball season had started, there would be a game to watch. The parking lot was half full, with several empty spaces in front of Fat Tony's Pizzeria. Skeeter Thomas pulled his sedan into a vacant spot and made for the restaurant. He wanted to be early to secure his usual seat in the bar before the game started.

The bar side of the pizzeria was getting crowded, most of the high-top tables filled by twenty-somethings clad in Cincinnati Reds gear, and few unoccupied stools at the bar. Skeeter walked through the bar to his favorite spot, a still-empty, small two-seater next to the side wall that separated the bar from the dining room. He could see the big screen televisions over the bar, which were already tuned to the pre-game show. Skeeter sat down at the high-top and pulled the menu from the holder, although he didn't need to look at it. He would order the same pizza as every other Saturday, drink a few beers and watch the Reds game.

The waitress, petite with rose acrylic framed glasses, eventually made her way to his table and opened with a friendly smile. "Back again, Skeeter?"

He returned the smile. "Yes. Big game tonight. Wouldn't want to miss it. I even have my lucky shirt on," he added, pointing to the Reds logo on the left breast of his golf shirt.

"We're expecting a crowd. At least, that's what Tony said." She clicked the ballpoint pen. "How're you doing?"

"I'm good, Carrie. You?"

"Still waiting for Mr. Right," she giggled. "What'll it be?"

"The usual. A Hudy and the Sicilian with extra pepperoni. Small."

"You got it." She winked before she turned away.

∞

Fat Tony's prediction was correct. By the time the game started, all the tables were filled, and people were standing three deep in front of the bar. After a feckless first inning, the top of the second started with a triple. Skeeter was so focused on the game that he didn't hear her at first.

"Excuse me, is this seat taken?" she asked a second time.

Skeeter looked at the empty stool, realizing that it was the only unfilled seat in the room, and then to the inquirer. She was wearing a white Cincinnati Reds jersey, the placket pulled taut across her chest, and jeans. Her dark-brown hair was pulled through the back of her Reds baseball hat.

"Uh, no. You can have it."

He assumed that she would be taking the chair to another table, but instead she slipped up into the elevated seat.

"Do you mind if I join you?"

"I think you already have," he answered.

"I suppose so," she smiled. "Does a waitress come around for drink orders?"

"Yes, she'll be back soon. I'm almost ready for another." He held up the near empty mug in demonstration.

She moved the menu holder to set her purse on the edge of the round table. "So, what'd I miss?"

"Not much. The first inning was a no-hitter. They're just getting warmed up." He returned his focus to the televisions.

"I'm Andrea, by the way. What's your name?"

"Darryl. But everyone calls me Skeeter," he answered without turning his head.

Third out, a runner left on second base, and the Reds came off the field. Skeeter pulled his blond hair back over his ears and shifted in his chair to face Andrea.

"You look familiar. Have we met?"

"I don't think so. I'm told I have one of those faces, you know. That I look like somebody."

Skeeter scratched at this chin. "Yeah, maybe. I work at Bluegrass Bank and Trust. Maybe I've seen you in the lobby?"

"Oh, no, I don't think so."

The waitress arrived, eyeballed Andrea, then turned to Skeeter. "You want another Hudy, Skeeter?"

"Yeah, Carrie, thanks," he answered.

"And your friend?"

Andrea asked, "Do you have Corona Light?"

"In the bottle."

"That's fine. And can I have a glass?"

"Sure thing." She clicked her pen. "You want anything to eat?"

"Maybe later, thanks."

Andrea watched the waitress return to the bar before touching Skeeter's left arm to get his attention.

"So, is she an old girlfriend?"

"Huh?"

"The waitress. An old girlfriend?"

"Uh, no. Why?"

"Just curious."

It was the top of the third inning when Carrie came back, placing Skeeter's mug on the table first, then the bottle and empty glass for Andrea.

"There ya go. Anything else?"

"I'm good," he answered. She winked at Skeeter before resuming her beer deliveries.

Andrea squeezed the lime wedge into the glass, then tilted it to pour the beer. "I don't think she likes me very much. Not very friendly."

Skeeter crooked his head. "Why are you here?"

"To watch the Reds game. Why are you here?"

"That's not what I mean. I mean, why are you here at my table? Why are you talking to me?" He took a large gulp of beer.

"Well, I came to watch the game, and I was told that Fat Tony's is the local Reds bar. As far as this seat, well, when I came in, it was the only vacant place. I don't like to stand in a bar. Not very ladylike."

Skeeter nodded. "Okay."

"And as far as talking to you, well, you're a nice-looking guy, and it seems you're here alone. So am I." She sipped at the glass. "You do like girls, right?"

"Yeah. I like girls. It just that, well, I, uh ..." He ran his hands through his hair, pulling at the ends with his left hand at the back of his head, then corrected his glasses. "It's been a while since a woman has, uh, talked to me. Other than at the bank, I mean."

Andrea smiled. "Okay. Let's watch the game, Skeeter. We don't have to talk a lot. I kinda like just sitting here with you. Watching the Reds."

Skeeter turned away so that Andrea would not see his grin.

∞

The Reds finally scored in the bottom of the fifth inning, a home run with two men on base, to put a nice number *3* on the scoreboard. The enthusiasm of the room was palpable. And Skeeter, feeling the vibe, gained confidence in talking to this woman who had wandered into Fat Tony's Pizzeria and sat at his table, this Andrea.

"Let me ask you something," he said.

"Go ahead."

"What kind of work do you do?"

Andrea chuckled. "You're not very good at this, are you?"

"No, not really," he admitted.

"I'm between jobs, so I thought I'd visit my sister and take a break."

"You don't live in Owensboro?"

"No, but who knows. My sister is here, I might find something."

"I've lived here my whole life, except for college." He picked up his mug, only to realize that it was empty. "Ready for another round?"

"Sure, if you can get your girlfriend to come over here." She grinned at him.

Skeeter laughed. "Ouch."

∞

A few more hitless innings later, it was the top of the ninth, the Reds still winning, the game soon coming to an end. Andrea emptied her glass and reached for Skeeter's left arm, moving her right hand down his forearm to turn his hand over, gently pinning his thumb against the tabletop.

"So, Darryl who everyone calls Skeeter, what's the story?"

"What do you mean?"

"I can see where you wore a wedding band." She pointed to his left ring finger. "But not now. So, what gives?"

Skeeter gazed at his hand. "My wife left me a few months ago."

She released his thumb and looked into his eyes. "Bad for her. Good for me."

"You want to watch the post-game at my place?"

Andrea put her hand on his forearm, softly rubbing her thumb against his flesh. "Whatcha think, Skeeter?"

CHAPTER SIXTEEN

Sunday, his day off. Wayne Peterson was up early, before sunrise, like every other day of the week. The job was in Lewisport, and the construction company was behind schedule. They were converting what had been a small grocery store in a strip mall into an office for a chiropractor. Behind schedule meant overtime. Working construction since high school, Wayne welcomed overtime. It was better than "no time." They had been working Saturdays to catch up, but never on Sunday. Hancock County was quiet, sparsely populated, and religious. No construction on Sundays, and no sales of alcohol, ever. And having Sunday off was good with Wayne.

His muscles aching from the prior six days, he stumbled to the bathroom for a warm shower. The stream of hot water eased his sore back, shoulders, arms, legs. He remained in the stall until the water turned cool.

Wayne lived alone in a two-story townhouse, in the middle of a row of almost-identical townhouses, on the south side of Owensboro. He had worked on the development and the builder liked him. When initial sales were tepid, Wayne acquired his two-bedroom unit below market. With a single garage large enough to accommodate his pickup truck and a paver-brick patio in back, the space fit his needs.

Showered and relaxed, Wayne pulled on a pair of worn jeans and a long-sleeve T-shirt. He walked barefoot down the straight flight of hardwood stairs to the kitchen. He set up the automatic-drip coffee pot, then pressed the Start button. He returned to the second floor while the coffee brewed.

In the closet of the second bedroom, he pulled out the plastic bins storing his old life. After rummaging through several, he found what he was looking for, his high school yearbook. He also found the wedding album that Karla had assembled.

"Wonder how I ended up with that," he whispered. He took the yearbook and album downstairs to the kitchen, to his waiting coffee.

He filled a large mug, added a spoonful of sugar, then took a seat at the kitchen island. Flipping through the yearbook, he stopped at the Senior Class Halloween party. There it was, the picture of Wayne centered between Jeff Miller and Skeeter Thomas, all dressed in pin-striped suits they had found at a thrift store, with black shirts and ties. A trio of hitmen, like extras in a mafia movie. A few pages on, the last football game of senior year. He could still find his face in the stands, next to Karla, wearing a plush bulldog hat on his head, a leftover from Halloween. A few more pages and there was Karla in her cream-colored, frilly prom dress dancing with Wayne, clad in a regrettable burgundy tuxedo. Wayne shuddered, closed the book and pulled the coffee mug to his lips.

"A lifetime ago," he uttered. "Wish I could take back that tux."

Wayne walked to the front room, the living room, to retrieve cigarettes from his jacket. Pulling one from the pack, he lit it on his way back to the kitchen. He leaned against the back of the counter stool and blew a few smoke rings. After finishing the cigarette, he resumed the memory lane trip.

They had met sophomore year in English class. Karla was a transfer student, and Wayne had fallen in love at first sight. He was taken with her shoulder-length blonde curls and how her lower left eyelid moved up when she grinned, giving her face a certain asymmetry he found adorable. By Thanksgiving, he had mustered enough courage to ask her out on a date. The first date, a Saturday-night movie to which Wayne's mom had provided the transportation, led to a second, and a third. They were "going steady" through sophomore, junior, and senior year, until Wayne proposed. Down on his knee in that horrid burgundy tuxedo, in the middle of the dance floor during a rare slow number, he pulled out the black velvet cube, opened the box, and asked Karla to be his wife.

The first pages of Karla's wedding album were filled with pictures of a young Karla and a young Wayne, school dances, and both Junior and Senior proms. Photos of Karla being primped by her mother and younger sister before the ceremony, after several pages from their graduation day.

Karla had wanted an outdoor wedding. The service took place on the grass amidst the shady oak trees of Moreland Park, with a tea-and-cake reception following in the screened picnic shelter. On a sunny June day, mere weeks from high school graduation, they became Mr. and Mrs. Wayne Peterson.

The last picture in the album was a group shot—the wedding party and friends, including Jeff Miller and Skeeter Thomas. The remaining pages were empty. An unfinished project, like their unfinished marriage.

"Time passes quickly," he said with a sigh.

Wayne slowly closed the wedding album and carefully placed it on the counter next to his high school yearbook.

CHAPTER SEVENTEEN

Brenda Hunter stood in front of the full-length mirror in their second-floor master bedroom, looking at her pink, violet, and turquoise sundress. She had changed three times, not sure what was appropriate to wear for a Sunday afternoon barbeque, even though it was in her own backyard. She leaned closer to the mirror. A few gray stands in her wavy dark brown hair. And crow's feet. *I'm too young to have crow's feet*, she thought. She tugged at the skin under her right eye. Wrinkles. Wrinkles around her hazel eyes.

She went downstairs to the kitchen, checked on the dessert in the refrigerator, and poured herself a glass of chilled white wine. Walking onto the concrete patio, she found her husband hovering over the grill, tending to a pile of glowing charcoal briquettes.

"Bob, you did you tell Louis five, right?"

He looked at his watch. "Yeah. He'll be here. Coals should be ready soon." He looked up from the grill. "Did you change your dress again?"

"Do you like it?" she asked.

"Yes, dear. I liked the last one too. And the one before that. Why are you so anxious about how you look? It's just Louis, and you've known him most of your life."

"It's not just Louis, Bob, it's Louis and this girl he's bringing." She sat down at the table and took a sip of wine.

"I'm sure it'll be fine. And I doubt she's going to be critical of your clothing." He joined her at the table and picked up the bottle of beer he had already started.

"It's a girl thing. You guys can wear cargo shorts and it's no big deal."

Hunter laughed. "But, Brenda, these are my best cargo shorts."

She shook her head. "I know."

After a little more wine, she asked, "Bob, do you think I'm looking old?"

He slowly placed the beer bottle on the table and reached for her hand. "Honey, what's this about?"

"Well, am I?"

"You're serious, aren't you?"

"Yes."

He smiled at her. "No, Brenda, I don't think you're looking old. I think you look great. Just like the day I married you."

"You are sooo full of it, bubba," she said with a laugh.

Mercier appeared around the corner of the garage, wearing chinos and a white tennis shirt. He was holding hands with his date, who was olive skinned, with raven hair pulled back into a low pony-tail, which ended past her shoulders. The blue-and-white seersucker dress hung loosely on her tall, slender frame, which, even in her flat sandals, put her three inches taller than him.

"There you are. We rang the doorbell, and when no one answered, I guessed you'd be here," he said.

Bob stood up from the table. "Didn't hear it. We've been back here."

Brenda joined him as the pair moved from the grass onto the patio.

Mercier started the introductions. "Brenda, Bob, this is Carmen."

"Nice to meet you, Carmen," Brenda said, offering her hand.

"Thank you. Louis has told me all about you," she answered.

"I hope not," Hunter said with a smile as he winked at Mercier.

"Well, maybe not everything," Mercier added. He handed a gift-wrapped bottle of wine to Brenda. "Thanks for having us over."

She peeked at the label. "Thanks. I'll put it in the fridge."

"What can I offer you to drink?" Hunter asked.

Carmen pointed to Brenda's wine glass. "What are you having?"

"Pinot grigio."

"I'd love a glass."

"And you, bubba?" Hunter asked.

"Beer's fine." He looked at the patio table, which had been set with four places. "The girls aren't joining us?"

"They're at Bob's parents. A little Grandma-and-Grandpa time," Brenda answered.

∞

Once he was satisfied with the coals, Hunter put the corn and chicken kebabs on the cooking grate and closely monitored their progress. Mercier soon joined him at the grill, along with the women.

"Smells great," Mercier observed.

"Don't start with that. His ego's big enough already," Brenda said.

"Bob is the maestro of the charcoal, Carmen. A true serial griller."

"And you, Louis? Do you grill?" Carmen asked.

"Cook, yes. Grill, no. Those Neanderthal skills have been lost to the more advanced and sophisticated Mercier clan," he said with a wink.

Hunter shook his head. "Carmen, he grew up on a farm. He moves to the big city of Chicago for a few years and somehow is magically transformed into a bon vivant."

"The two of you still behave like Neanderthals when you get together—just like in high school," Brenda added.

"We were just preparing to be backup singers for Blue Swede," Mercier chuckled.

"Ooga-chaka Ooga-Ooga," Hunter and Mercier chanted together. "Ooga-chaka Ooga-Ooga."

Brenda shook her head, then looked at Carmen. "See what I have to put up with?"

Carmen grinned. "You're a saint."

Once the chanting died down, Hunter glanced at Carmen. "Speaking of Neanderthals, how did this nice young lady meet a caveman like you?" Hunter elbowed Mercier.

Carmen answered. "Louis stumbled into the ER, setting off one of the alarms. Claimed he was lost trying to get to the operating rooms."

"In all fairness, it was my first day," Mercier said.

"Interesting way to meet women," Hunter uttered. "Dinner time. Brenda, can you hand that platter to me?"

∞

Midway through the kebab fest, Carmen could wait no longer to satisfy her curiosity. Taking a sip of liquid courage, she looked directly at Hunter.

"Bob, what's the real story with that Miller murder?"

"I wondered when that question would be asked," Hunter answered. He put down his fork and glugged some beer. "I assume you've read the papers."

Carmen nodded, as Mercier answered, "Yes."

"I can add a few things. We're working with the theory that the killer knew Jeff Miller and knew he would be home alone. The murder was clearly planned. The killer left no fingerprints, nor was he seen by any of the neighbors."

"So, a career criminal? That sort of killer?" Mercier asked.

"Possibly. At least an intelligent criminal. He was able to subdue Miller without a struggle and stab him in the chest very effectively. We also suspect there may be an element of revenge." He reached for his beer bottle.

"Buzz in the ER is that the wife did it," Carmen said.

"Sounds like it to me, too," Mercier added. "Stabbed in the chest? A crime of passion, you ask me."

Brenda joined in. "Yeah, like a love spat that went terribly wrong."

"Don't disagree. However, Jeff Miller's wife, Eve, was in Louisville at the time of the murder. I think she can be ruled out as a suspect." Hunter swallowed more beer. "And there's been no reason to speculate on her involvement. And it wasn't a robbery. Nothing was missing from the house."

"Do you have a suspect?" Carmen asked.

"Yes. But I can't talk about it yet."

"Pretty gruesome way to go," Mercier shivered as he put his hand to his chest. "Knife in the heart."

"Eek. Louis, mind if we change the subject?" Brenda said.

"Of course," Mercier answered.

"Well, Louis, now that you are back in town, and, being a doctor and all, who's the best plastic surgeon?"

"Brenda ..." Hunter rolled his eyes.

"Hmmm. I assume you mean for you, right?" Mercier asked.

"Yes."

"Most of the plastic surgeons specialize. Some limit themselves to cosmetic procedures, like face lifts. Others may only do reconstruction, like after breast cancer or trauma. What exactly are you looking for?"

Brenda eye-checked Hunter before proceeding. "I was thinking more along the lines of, well, these lines on my face, my crow's feet. I'm getting those 'old-lady' eyes."

"I think you look great the way you are, honey," Hunter said.

"A plastic surgeon can certainly do something about the wrinkles, and in general change your appearance, make you appear more youthful." Mercier stated. "Sometimes, it's an improvement, but not always."

Carmen turned to him. "How so?"

Mercier emptied the bottle of beer. "A lot can be done to alter one's appearance, from a simple face lift to look younger, to facial reconstruction. And more, like body sculpting, if you consider it that way. Much like the way a woman can increase breast size with implants, or decrease with a reduction, other parts of the body can be transformed. Those stories about criminals having their face modified to avoid recognition and capture are not urban legends."

"Wow. Anything that can't be improved?" Brenda questioned.

"Hands. I saw it a lot in Chicago. The socialites would come in for a nip and tuck. They'd go home looking great, yet still have their same old hands. Wearing flawless diamonds, of course."

"I'll have to remember that, bubba," Hunter said with a chuckle. "Who's ready for another drink?"

Carmen gazed over the table. "Looks like we all are."

CHAPTER EIGHTEEN

Skeeter Thomas was not at his desk on Monday. Or Tuesday. When he failed to appear at the bank Wednesday morning, Carol became worried. She unlocked his office and checked his desk. The drawers were locked, nothing of note on his desk-pad calendar, just the typical scribbles of names and telephone numbers. None of the tellers had seen Skeeter since Friday.

She returned to her desk on the second floor in the anteroom of the bank manager's office. After viewing the bank's vacation scheduler, she confirmed that Skeeter Thomas was not slated for time off. She called the telephone number listed in the internal bank directory, which she assumed was a cell phone. Straight to voicemail. Becoming more anxious, she knocked on the door and then walked into the manager's office.

William Hayden, Bill to his friends, had been the manager of Bluegrass Bank and Trust for almost five years. A small man, he kept his red hair in the tight, close style of his high school days at a military academy and wore suits to the office as an update of his former uniform. He looked up at Carol from the thick document on his desk, removing his half-lens reading glasses.

"Mr. Hayden, Skeeter Thomas hasn't been in the bank since last week. He's not supposed to be off."

"I thought he was on vacation." He twirled his reading glasses by the temple. "Did you call him?"

"Yes, sir, and there was no answer. He never misses work."

Hayden set his glasses down on the leather-topped, antique walnut-burl desk and leaned back from it in his brown leather chair. "Hmmm. He's married, right? Did you try her? What's her name?"

"Tracy." Carol hesitated. "Uh, Mr. Hayden, Tracy left Skeeter several months ago."

"Yes, Tracy, that's it. Went to the wedding." He rubbed his lips. "Left him, huh? Well, I'm sure there's a perfectly good explanation. Call Tracy Thomas, even if they are separated."

"Yes, sir."

"His dad's retired, but his parents still live in town, as far as I can recall. Give them a call also."

"I'll check." She started for the door.

"Let me know. No need to get nervous about it, Carol. Skeeter will turn up." Hayden put his glasses on and returned to the papers.

Back at her desk, Carol pushed her dark-brown hair over her left ear and removed the gold hoop earring before putting on the telephone headset. Looking though Skeeter's personnel file, she found his alternative contact information, which included numbers for Tracy Thomas and his parents. She decided to try Tracy first, as Hayden had suggested.

"Tracy Thomas, this is Carol from Bluegrass Bank and Trust," Carol stated.

"Is this about Skeeter?"

"Yes. He didn't show up to the bank today, and I'm trying to track him down. Have you seen or spoken to him?"

There as a pause before Tracy answered. "You know we're separated, right?"

"Yes, I do."

"Well, why would I know?"

Carol shook her head. "If you hear from him, please ask him to call me."

"Sure," she said shortly, and terminated the call.

"Lovely. He should have left you, not the other way around," she said with a sigh. She scrolled down the page to Skeeter's parents, and punched in the number.

Mrs. Thomas answered on the second ring.

"Mrs. Thomas, this is Carol from Bluegrass Bank and Trust."

"Carol, yes, I remember you. You're Mr. Hayden's secretary."

"Yes, I am, Mrs. Thomas."

"Oh, call me Dorothy, dear."

"Yes, well, Dorothy, Skeeter didn't show up for work today at the bank, and I'm trying to locate him. Have you spoken to him today?"

"No. He's always got that cell phone in his hand. Did you try calling him?"

"Yes, ma'am. There was no answer."

"Oh my," she said. "Well, since that wife of his up and left him, Skeeter's just not been himself."

"When was the last time you spoke to Skeeter?"

Dorothy Thomas hesitated. "Let's see, he came to dinner on Friday. I made meatloaf, that's his favorite. I put a hard-boiled egg in the middle. Skeeter likes to get a slice with the egg."

"Sounds yummy. Well, if you hear from him, will you have him give me a call at the bank?"

"Yes, I will."

After putting the headset on the charger, and replacing her earring, Carol walked around the first floor again. She confirmed that Skeeter's office remained vacant. There were a few employees in the breakroom, none of whom had seen or heard from Skeeter since Friday. Convinced that something was awry, Carol returned to Hayden's office to report.

Bill Hayden was seated at his antique desk, glasses off, rubbing his eyes, when Carol entered his office. He appeared mildly startled by the intrusion and uttered a simple "Yes?"

"I'm worried, Mr. Hayden. Nobody's seen hide nor hair of Skeeter since Friday, not even his parents."

"His ex-wife? Or, rather, soon-to-be-ex?"

"Unpleasant. I'm not surprised they're breaking up."

"Okay. Well, I'm not sure he's exactly a missing person yet, at least legally." Hayden leaned back in the leather chair. "Carol, get his address for me. I'll make a call."

"Yes, sir. Thanks." She backtracked to her desk and jotted the address on her notepad, before returning and handing it to Hayden.

CHAPTER NINETEEN

It was Wednesday afternoon, and Hunter knew no more about Jeff Miller's murder than he had the prior Wednesday. No new information, no quiet revelation from the umpteenth time he had scrutinized the crime-scene photographs, no "ah-ha" from Jean Turner's or the ECU reports. A young man taken down without a struggle, his heart expertly fileted.

Chief Hartmann would return to the office tomorrow. Hunter had no update to provide. It would not be a pleasant encounter. He pushed back from his desk and walked to the window of his new office in the back corner of the second floor, with a view of Crittenden Street and the patrol cars in the back lot. He pulled his blue ashtray to the corner and lit a cigarette.

"My first case as lead detective," he whispered, "and I'm stuck." He took a long, slow drag, gently exhaling. "Maddox, you couldn't wait a few more weeks before retiring?"

His mobile telephone rang, vibrating off the desk. He answered as he retrieved it from the carpeted floor.

"Hunter."

"Bob, Bill Hayden here. Hope I'm not disturbing you."

Hunter crushed the cigarette in the ashtray. "No, actually, I'm in my office. What's up?"

"I'm sure it's nothing, but one of my employees has not shown up at the bank this week, and no one's seen or heard from him since Friday. Carol, my secretary, is worried."

"Do you want to file a missing person report?"

"Well, I'm not sure, as his boss, that would be the correct thing to do. But he does seem to be missing. Carol called his parents and his ex-wife. Uh, she's not his ex-wife yet. Nothing. And none of the other employees have seen him."

"Did you check the hospital? Does he have any medical issues that you know about?" Hunter asked.

"Can you hang on a sec and let me check with Carol?"

"Of course." The bank's hold music started promptly, then a soft female voice reminded Hunter that his call was important before the music resumed. After a few moments, Hayden returned.

"She's calling now. I didn't think of that," Hayden said.

"Okay. If he's not been hospitalized, I can have a black and white check his house. What's his name?"

"Darryl Thomas. He uses a nickname, Skeeter."

"Skeeter?" Hunter questioned. "Sounds like a moniker one outgrows."

"I agree. He seems to like it though—everyone calls him that," he answered. "Carol just walked into my office."

Hunter could hear a muffled exchange, then "Thanks, Carol. Bob, he's not at the hospital."

"Alright. What's his address?"

After Hunter ended the call, he opened the closed-case file program and typed in "Darryl Thomas." Nothing. He toggled to the regular database. He found two files for a Darryl Thomas. The first was a sixty-one-year-old man who presently was in the United States Penitentiary Big Sandy in eastern Kentucky for credit card fraud; the second was a forty-two-year-old with a series of speeding and reckless-driving tickets and two DUIs that had resulted in the temporary loss of his license. Neither was the missing Darryl "Skeeter" Thomas, who did not seem to have any criminal record.

"Maybe he was arrested over the weekend," Hunter whispered softly. He called the Owensboro Detention Center. No one by the name of Darryl Thomas was incarcerated there.

Then he called the dispatcher to find Mike Wagner.

"Mike, I need a favor. Are you busy?" he asked.

"Phil and I were just about to head back to the station." Mike answered. "What's the favor?"

"The manager at Bluegrass Bank and Trust called me. One of his employees has been missing since Friday. Can you drive by the house on your way and check on him?"

"Did he file a missing person's report?" Phil asked.

"No. He called me directly. The bank manager is a friend of mine. He doesn't think it's a serious matter."

"Okay, we can drop by," Mike responded. "You have a name and address?"

∞

As they turned onto Lisbon Drive, a group of teenagers playing basketball stopped their game, observing the police presence. Another teen was pushing a lawn mower a few houses down, but seemed to not notice. The street was otherwise quiet.

Once the patrol car passed, the basketball game resumed. Mike parked on the street in front of Skeeter's house, a single-story ranch, with pale-yellow aluminum siding and white trim, the lawn and landscaping neat, with a row of purple flowers framing both sides of the concrete walk from the sidewalk to the front step. A silver Camry was parked in the carport. And it looked as if no one was home.

Mike and Phil slowly walked to the front door and rang the doorbell. Mike leaned toward the door to listen to the barely audible tones, and then, the lack of a response. He opened the screen door, ready to knock on the white wooden door, when Phil grabbed his forearm.

"Mike," he said, pointing to the small gap at the frame; the door was slightly ajar. "It's open."

"'Do me a favor,' Hunter says. 'Just drop by,' Hunter says. 'It's nothing serious,' Hunter says," Mike muttered.

"Yeah."

Phil pulled the handgun out of his holster.

"You really think that's necessary?" Mike asked.

Phil nodded, his handgun held forward. "Don't touch the doorknob. Push the door open with your elbow."

Mike leaned his shoulder and elbow on the door, easing it open a few inches.

"What's that smell?" Phil asked.

"Oh, no. This ain't good." Mike retrieved his handgun before pushing the door open while yelling "Police!" No response.

The duo walked through the door into the front room of the house. The intensity of the putrid odor increased, the stench of the dead pervading the entire house. Mike pointed to the adjoining room in front of them. "That looks like the kitchen." They moved slowly, Phil turning to look down the hallway.

"I'll check the bedrooms," he said before splitting off from Mike.

Mike halted as he stepped into the kitchen. Skeeter Thomas was lying supine in a pool of blood on the tan linoleum floor.

He swallowed hard, holstered his weapon, and backed into the front room.

"All clear," Phil said as he returned from a bedroom. "God, that odor is about to make me puke."

Mike pointed to the kitchen. "That's the smell of a decomposing body."

Phil grabbed his mouth and ran through the front door. He kneeled in the front yard, emptying the contents of his stomach into a flower bed.

Back on the front step, Mike called Detective Hunter.

"Hunter, we found Mr. Thomas."

"Good," Hunter replied.

"No, not good. He's got a knife sticking out of his chest."

CHAPTER TWENTY

The basketball game was over, replaced by adult neighbors of Lisbon Drive, clustered twos and threes in the front yards, all fixated on the collection of police vehicles in front of Skeeter Thomas's house. Some of the onlookers were snapping pictures with their phones, perhaps taking videos. The ECU van was backed into the driveway, tail doors open. Mike Wagner placed yellow police line barrier tape in the front and along the side yards before walking toward the nearest neighbor gathering.

He approached the group, pulling a black notebook from his chest pocket. The trio of men stood in the adjoining front yard. The older one, wearing bib overalls and a plaid shirt, was leaning on a shovel wedged into the mulch under a hedgerow.

"I'm Officer Mike Wagner. Just want to ask a few questions, if that's okay," he started.

"We were expecting that," answered the tall one, a dark-haired young man still wearing his office clothes, blue shirt with sleeves rolled up and paisley tie loosened. "What's going on with Skeeter?"

Mike visually inspected the assembly before responding. "Mr. Thomas has been murdered."

"Murdered? Really? How?"

"Yes, he was murdered. Have any of you seen anything unusual going on at his house in the past few days?"

Tall guy looked at overalls. "Mr. Myles here knows better than us."

"Yep," he said. "I'm retired."

"Well, Mr. Myles, have you noticed anything unusual?" Mike asked.

Myles chopped the wad of chewing tobacco in his left cheek and spit under the hedge. "Not directly. Skeeter mowed his lawn Saturday, like always. Keeps it real good, that lawn. Never a weed. Anyways, he don't talk much since that no-good wife of his up and left."

Mike started writing notes. "Have you seen him since he was mowing the lawn?"

He looked at the other men. "Can't say that I have. Boys, you seen Skeeter?"

The third man, not quite as tall as the tall man, spoke. "I saw him leave Saturday evening in his car."

"Do you recall what time?"

"Hmmm. It was before the Reds game, so maybe around six?"

"Anyone see what time he came back?"

"I didn't." He looked at tall guy. "You see anything?"

"Me? No, me and Connie were in Evansville having dinner with her sister's family Saturday. I haven't seen Skeeter in weeks."

"What about you, Mr. Myles?" Mike asked.

"No. I fell asleep watching the game."

"So, no one has seen Mr. Thomas since Saturday." Mike looked at each of the men.

Myles peered at Mike. "Yeah, but I know he's been home since then."

"Can you explain?"

"Sure. I saw lights coming on and going off in the house," Myles answered.

"But you didn't actually see him."

"Nope."

Mike turned back to look at the house, spotting the Camry in the carport. "Did you notice if his car was gone during the day? Like he was at work?"

Myles stood up from the wooden handle of the shovel and spit again under the hedge. "Come to think, no. Don't think that I have."

"Just to clarify, you don't think the car has been used recently?"

"Yep. That's right."

"Thanks. Let me get each of your names before I'm done here." After collecting the names, Mike closed his notebook, replaced it in his pocket, and handed each of the men his card. "You've been very helpful. If you think of anything, anything at all that might be useful, please give me a call."

"I've got a question," tall guy said.

"Yes, go ahead."

"Any idea who would kill Skeeter?"

"We're just starting our investigation."

∞

Hunter was standing on the front walk, watching Mike and waiting for his interview to conclude. Mike joined him, shaking his head.

"Just drop by and check on Darryl Thomas, isn't that what you said?"

"Good thing you did, bubba. Wonder how long it would have been before someone else discovered his body," Hunter responded.

"Yeah, well, everyone's here except Dr. Turner. ECU is just getting started. Oh, and the smell is horrible. Phil even puked in the yard."

Hunter laughed. "That happens. He probably didn't want you to tell me."

Mike smiled. "True. He's staying outside, talking to some of the other neighbors."

"You get anything from that bunch?"

"They haven't seen Mr. Thomas since Saturday. And it sounds like he's been keeping to himself lately. Mr. Myles, the older gent in the bib overalls, said he doesn't talk much since his wife left him." Mike frowned. "Didn't think to ask how long ago that was."

"Don't worry about it. We can get that later. Her name is Tracy Thomas. They're separated, in the process of divorce. I've got her number. She'll need to be contacted."

"I'll take care of that," Mike offered.

"Thanks. I'll call his parents. They still live in town, apparently know Bill Hayden well. He's the manager at Bluegrass Bank and Trust."

Mike pointed to the front door. "Ready to go inside?"

Hunter ducked under the yellow tape across the open door and stepped on the tan linoleum of the entryway, which extended into the kitchen. A half-wall with a series of unused candles on top divided the entrance from the carpet of the front room. A chocolate-brown couch was centered under the large picture window, with a leather recliner beyond, angled toward the flat-screen television hanging on the opposite wall. A few magazines were carefully stacked on a side table next to a cork coaster. A shelf below the television held a DVD player and a row of DVD keep cases, which appeared to be arranged in alphabetical order, and another row with a complete set of *Star Wars* movies organized chronologically. On the wall behind the chair hung a framed movie poster, *Revenge of the Jedi*, a small glass-doored curio cabinet with *Star Wars* collectibles underneath. The room was neat, tidy.

Mike pointed to the movie poster. "Hunter, that's odd. I thought the movie was *Return of the Jedi.*"

Hunter eyed the poster. "It is. Look in the cabinet—he's a *Star Wars* fan. The movie's original title was *Revenge of the Jedi*. A batch of promotional posters was distributed before the name change to *Return*. If it's an original poster, it's valuable."

"Hmmm, okay," he responded.

A floor lamp next to the couch suddenly turned on, startling Mike. "That explains that," he said.

"Explains what?" Hunter asked.

"Mr. Myles said he knew Mr. Thomas was home because he saw the lights going on and off. They're on a timer."

"Which supports the theory that he's been dead since Saturday. The smell certainly does."

In the kitchen, the lab techs were still at work. They had propped the back door open in an attempt to mitigate the odor. Skeeter Thomas was lying next to a round oak kitchen table, a knife sticking out of his right chest, with blood pooled beneath him, extending under the table on the linoleum floor. His shirt was pulled up to his neck like a red bandana.

Hunter knelt next to the body. The knife was the same type used in Jeff Miller's murder. There was a tear across the right chest with the handle almost resting on the floor.

He leaned closer to the knife, then stood up. "Something doesn't fit," he whispered.

"So, let me guess. You didn't find any prints on the knife," he said to the lab techs.

"Correct. In fact, we're finding only one set of prints, which I'm guessing are the victim's," the camera-toting tech answered. "I was waiting on Dr. Turner before getting a set off the victim, if I still can. He doesn't seem to have bloated at all."

"Have you uncovered anything useful yet?"

"Yes," replied the other tech. "He keeps his car keys and wallet in a basket on the counter. His cellphone is there also, but the battery's dead. His driver's license confirms his ID. And there were receipts from Saturday." He handed Hunter a plastic bag with three small slips of paper.

Hunter examined the contents, holding the bag up to the light so that Mike could also see.

"Okay, he filled his car," he said as he pointed to the smaller of the three receipts. "But this is much more interesting. Two receipts from Fat Tony's Pizzeria."

Mike looked at the slips. "Why two?"

He handed the evidence back to the tech. "When you dine out, the waitress or waiter will bring you an itemized bill. Assuming you pay with a credit card, when the bill holder is returned, it will have three receipts: the itemized bill, the credit slip for the restaurant that is to be signed, and the copy for the dinner guest. Most people keep the credit card copy, not both the itemized bill and the card copy."

"So, why keep it?" Mike asked.

Hunter shrugged. "This place is well-ordered. He's got OCD. And now we know where he was on Saturday night." He surveyed the kitchen. "Mike, let's see where Phil is with the neighbors while we wait for Dr. Turner. And get some fresh air."

They were met by Phil on the front walkway. There was little more to be learned. No one had seen Skeeter Thomas since Saturday, he had not been very social since separating from his wife, and in general he was a quiet neighbor. One of the older teenagers added that he was "a real nerd who knew way too much about *Star Wars*," and was a lousy basketball player.

Phil was finishing his report as Dr. Turner pulled into the driveway in front of the ECU van. She made straight for Hunter. "Another stabbing?" she asked.

"Yes. Killer even used the same knife." Hunter motioned with his right hand to the open front door. "After you."

Turner stopped as she neared the front door. "I know that smell. Don't think I'll be needing my liver thermometer."

"Best we can determine, the victim was last seen on Saturday."

"Smells about right."

Once in the kitchen, Turner stopped again. "Right chest?"

"I was wondering about that. Miller was stabbed in the heart, his left chest."

"I'll know more after the autopsy." She looked at the lab techs. "You got all the pictures you need?"

Camera guy nodded.

She crouched next to Skeeter's right side. "No marks on his neck, his chest." She lifted his right arm, looking at both sides of his forearm, then his hand. "I think he may have scratched his killer. There's something under his fingernails." She pulled plastic bags from her kit and wrapped both hands for protection.

"Let's roll him." With the assistance of Hunter and both techs, Turner was able to look at Skeeter's back. "No. nothing here except a little livor mortis."

"We'll like to fingerprint him, Dr. Turner," the lab tech said.

"It'll have to wait until after I get a look at his fingernails. Drop by the morgue tomorrow, and we'll take care of it."

"Yes, ma'am," answered camera guy. "Ready to move the body?"

"Yes. Make the call." She turned to Hunter. "See you tomorrow. I'll know more then."

"It's a date."

CHAPTER TWENTY-ONE

The sun had long ago set when Hunter parked his Cadillac on the street in front of the Thomas house, a red brick two-story with a detached garage at the end of a long driveway on the left. Two grand oak trees were bathed with landscape spotlights, the front walk illuminated by the glow of a series of low path lights, casting a collection of overlapping shadows on the neatly cut lawn. He could see the faint flickering of a television set on the curtains of one of the first-floor windows.

Hunter took a deep breath, then pushed the doorbell. The door was opened by a thin man with sparse grey hair and rimless glasses, who was almost as tall as Hunter.

"Mr. Rodney Thomas?" he asked.

"Yes?"

"I'm Detective Hunter with the Owensboro Police Department," he said as he showed his badge. "Is your wife also at home?"

"Yes, she is. What's this about?"

"I'd prefer to speak with both of you, Mr. Thomas."

"Okay. Let me get her." He hesitated. "Uh, would you like to come in, Detective?"

"Yes, thank you." Hunter followed Rodney Thomas into the entry hall and was directed to a formal living room on the right. Two matching floral-patterned love seats faced each other in front of a stone, open-hearth fireplace with a low cocktail table in between. A silver tray with a blue-and-white patterned vase holding an arrangement of dried flowers sat on the table. "Please have a seat. I'll get my wife."

Mr. Thomas disappeared deeper into the house. Hunter heard the faint sound of the television stop, then he returned with a stout older woman whose grey hair matched his own.

"Mrs. Dorothy Thomas?"

"Yes," she answered. "What's this about, Officer?" They sat together on one of the love seats. Hunter remained standing next to the opposite one.

"I'm afraid I have some bad news. Your son, Darryl Thomas, has been found dead this evening."

Rodney Thomas looked up at Hunter with a blank face. "Oh, my. Skeeter's dead? How? What happened?"

Before he could answer, Dorothy Thomas started crying.

"We just had dinner with him Friday," he said. "How did this happen?"

"He's been murdered." He let the sentence linger, waiting to see their reactions. Rodney remained blank, Dorothy ran a tissue under her eyes, then looked up at Hunter.

"Murdered? How?" Rodney asked.

Hunter did not want to add to the stress of what he just told the elderly couple. He decided to keep the details to a minimum. "He was stabbed."

Dorothy turned to Rodney. "The paper said that Jeff Miller was stabbed." She then addressed Hunter. "You think it's the same person who killed Jeff?"

"You knew Jeff Miller?" Hunter asked as he took a seat on the opposing couch.

"Jeff and Skeeter were friends in high school," she replied. "They were in the same class at Owensboro South. Jeff, he'd eaten a lot of dinners here back in those days. They were big buddies."

"But then Jeff married that Eve girl, and well, they kinda had a falling out," Rodney added.

"No, that's not right, Rodney. They just took different paths," she clarified.

Hunter leaned back on the couch. "Do you know if they had been in contact with each other recently?"

"Skeeter told me that he had been arranging car loans for Jeff. Seemed to think that the bank could do a lot more business with Butler Brothers Ford if they just put a little effort into it," Rodney said. "But I think that was mostly over the phone."

"Do you know of anyone who would wish your son harm?"

Rodney shook his head, then looked at Dorothy.

"No," she answered. "I'm sure he made a few folks unhappy about turning them down for a loan, but I can't think of anyone who would want to kill Skeeter."

"I understand," Hunter said. "We've had difficulty in reaching his wife, Tracy. Are you in contact with her?"

"Good luck with that," Rodney said. "She's been a problem since the day they got married."

"That girl is nothing but trouble," Dorothy agreed.

Lacking any further inquiries, Hunter stood up. "I'm very sorry for your loss, Mr. and Mrs. Thomas. If you think of anything, please contact me." He pulled a card from his jacket and handed it to Rodney. "I'll see myself out." Hunter made his way to the front door.

Dorothy began weeping again as the reality of her son's death sunk in.

CHAPTER TWENTY-TWO

The sun was just rising Thursday morning. Wayne Peterson was sitting on the front step of his townhouse, right elbow on his thermos of coffee, cigarette in his hand, waiting for Earl Cravens, his coworker. The job site was upriver in Lewisport, twenty miles away, so Earl and Wayne had decided to take turns driving.

Wayne stubbed his cigarette into the concrete of the small porch as Earl's truck half-pulled into the short driveway. Collecting his white hard hat, thermos, and lunch-box cooler, he made his way around the front of the lifted Ford F-250 pickup truck to the passenger door and climbed inside.

"How ya doin', bro?" Earl asked as he backed into the seat.

"Friday eve, Earl. Almost there."

"You got any big weekend plans?" He backed the truck into the street.

Wayne smiled. "Got another date with Arlene."

"The paralegal with the big tits?" he asked as he winked at Wayne.

"Oh, yeah," he nodded slowly. "You? Anything going on?"

Earl shook his head. "I was supposed to go fishing with my brother, but sounds like we're going to be working again this Saturday. So, fishing's out."

"The fish will still be there, Earl." Wayne reached for the radio controls in the center of the dashboard. "Mind if I switch stations? Want to find out who won last night."

"Have at it," he responded as he turned the truck onto the Wendell Ford Expressway. "I went to bed after the sixth inning."

Wayne found the news just as the weather report was starting, followed by a series of commercials. The news headlines were first.

"Our top story this morning: another murder in Owensboro. Details and sports right after this message."

Wayne looked at Earl. "Did I hear that right? Murder?"

"I think so. Turn it up." He accelerated around a slow-moving hatchback. "Another murder? Here in Owensboro? Can't be right."

He twisted the dial to increase the volume sufficiently to overcome the modified exhaust system of the diesel engine. The news resumed.

"Back to our top story. According to the Owensboro Police Department, a second murder has taken place in our town this month. The victim has been identified as Darryl Thomas. Mr. Thomas was found at his home last evening by an Owensboro policeman who had been alerted to his disappearance. Details of the murder are being withheld at this time. This incident follows less than two weeks after the brutal murder of another Owensboro resident, Jeff Miller. There had not been a murder in Owensboro for three years prior to these events. It's not clear that the two murders are related. We will provide more details as they become available."

Wayne turned the radio off. "Earl, something bad is going on."

"What's up?" Earl asked.

"I know Darryl Thomas—we were buddies in high school. Just saw him last week, at Jeff Miller's funeral. Jeff was also one of my high school buddies." He looked down. "This is just too weird. Something's going on. People I know are being killed."

"Wayne, this doesn't have anything to do with you does it?"

"I don't think so. It's just odd. Two guys I know, well, used to know, are dead. Murdered." He scratched at the stubble on his chin.

"You good to work today?"

He looked through the windscreen at the sunrise. "Yeah, hanging drywall should take my mind off this."

Earl pushed the accelerator, charging on to Lewisport. No radio, just the drone of the big diesel engine.

CHAPTER TWENTY-THREE

Brenda started coffee while her husband was in the shower, like she did most mornings. After breakfast, Hunter would head to the police station, or wherever, and she would start her day. While the coffee was brewing, she stepped through the front door to retrieve the morning paper, still wearing her black-and-red plaid cotton long robe and fleece-lined moccasin slippers.

Although she knew firsthand about murder of Darryl Thomas, Brenda was still surprised to see it as the front-page headline. She folded the newspaper so that the headline was hidden, placing it on the kitchen table.

"Good morning, dear," Hunter said as he kissed Brenda on the cheek, his faint scent of lavender making her smile. He slung the navy suit jacket across the back of an empty chair and sat down to his coffee and toast. "Have you looked at the paper yet?"

"Took a peek, Bob," she answered. "You're not going to like it."

He reached for the newspaper, flipping it open to the front page. "That's an understatement."

In bold print under the *Owensboro Gazette* flag, the headline read, "River City Ripper Claims Another Victim." A black-and-white head shot of Darryl Thomas, complete with his nickname, was centered beneath the headline, surrounded by the article. Hunter skimmed the page as he sipped coffee.

"Well, Brenda, they've already connected the murders." He laid the newspaper on the table, picking up a piece of toast and spooning strawberry preserves on it. "When I informed Mr. and Mrs. Thomas last night that their son had died, I found out that Jeff Miller and Darryl Thomas were friends. They both went to Owensboro South High School. I believe that the murders must be connected. But I haven't told anyone yet."

"How do you like the name 'River City Ripper'?"

Hunter smiled. "Clever. It certainly has flare. The allegorical reference and the cadence of Jack the Ripper. Let's hope I'm more successful than Scotland Yard was."

"So, what do you think?"

"Likely someone who knew both of them, knew their habits. The killer struck when both Miller and Thomas were isolated, home alone. Miller's wife was out of town. Thomas lived by himself, estranged from his wife. These murders were planned, thought out." He sipped from the coffee cup. "There also seems to be an element of revenge."

Brenda got up from the table, reaching for the carafe of coffee. "Revenge? How's that?" She refilled his cup, then her own, before sitting down.

"Not in the paper, and not to be repeated. The killer left the knife in each of the victim's chests." Hunter drank from his mug. "One of the details we withheld."

Brenda shuddered. "That definitely sends a message."

"They got the point, no doubt." He winked.

"Oh, Bob," she laughed. "That's terrible."

∞

Bill Hayden unlocked the door to what had been Skeeter Thomas's office, then held it open for Hunter. Once inside, he allowed it to drift slowly and silently until closed.

"I confirmed that his office was locked after you called me last night. No one has been in here, as far as I know, since Skeeter left work last Friday," Hayden said.

"Did he usually lock the office, or leave it unlocked?" Hunter asked.

"Locked when he left. There's a lot of personal information in loan documents."

Hunter scanned the desktop. The desk-pad calendar was centered in front of the slim computer monitor, notes on many of the weekdays printed in small, neat left-slanted letters and numbers. There was a two-tone grey multi-line business telephone on the right, next to a *Star Wars* logoed desktop clock, and a pen holder on the left, storing red and black pens, all of the same brand. He pulled the chair back to open the top drawer. The front flipped down for the wireless computer keyboard and mouse. There were two left-side drawers. The top one was filled by a steel-mesh organizer, holding more of the same pens, mechanical pencils, a stack of small yellow sticky-note pads and loose change, the bottom a basket of business cards which seemed to be alphabetized, and several charger cords. On the right, a tall drawer file was locked.

"Don't happen to have a key, do you Bill?"

He spun through the keys on the large ring. "Should be loan documents. Try this one." He handed Hunter the ring.

"Works," he said. The tab on the first file in the drawer had a black-and-white plastic label, "Divorce." The remaining files were organized alphabetically by family name, with similar labels. He pulled out the divorce file and laid it open on Skeeter's desk. Taped to the inside of the file were business cards for two law offices, with corresponding names "Tracy" and "Skeeter" neatly printed underneath.

"There's nothing here out of the ordinary, Bill. I may need to contact their attorneys. We've been unable to reach Tracy Thomas to notify her."

"Carol may have another contact number for her. I'll check." He eyed the computer monitor. "Do you need access to his computer?"

"I can't see why. And, frankly, I'd need a warrant for that, Bill. I don't think the loan business is germane to his murder." He surveyed the desk again. "The only personal things I see are his divorce file, and the *Star Wars* clock."

"I'll keep it locked up for now, of course."

"Okay." Hunter adjusted his dark-navy pindot tie. "What do you know about Skeeter's interactions with Jeff Miller?"

"Professionally speaking?" he asked.

"Yes, and personally, if you know."

"I don't know that much about his personal life, Bob. I didn't even know he was separated from his wife Tracy until Carol told me yesterday. Anyway, professionally speaking, Skeeter was convinced we could get more business from Butler Brothers Ford. He bent over backwards to make loans work for their customers. I was for it, of course. They're the highest volume Ford dealership in western Kentucky. We forwent some level of profit to build volume. It was working, too. Skeeter had a good head for that sort of thing. His strategy development skills were impressive. Of course, his relationship with Jeff Miller made it all the easier to work with Butler Brothers."

Hunter nodded. "Makes sense to me. I think the murders may be related. The relationship may not have anything to do with the bank or the car dealer."

Carol knocked on the glass door, then opened it. "Mr. Hayden, the employees are in the conference room, ready for you and Detective Hunter."

"Good. Oh, Carol, do you have another number for Tracy Thomas? The police have been unable to reach her."

She shook her head. "No. I only had the one." She paused, looking away, then turned her gaze to Hunter. "You'll not be too fond of Tracy when you do speak to her, Detective. I'm not surprised they're getting divorced." She hesitated. "Uh, were getting a divorce."

They walked upstairs to the conference room, Hunter trailing behind. All the seats were taken, with several of the bank employees standing along the sides and in the back of the room. The low rumble of chit-chat died down as Hayden walked to an open space in the front, with Carol at his side. Hunter remained at the open double doors.

"As many of you are aware," Hayden began, "our friend and colleague Darryl Skeeter Thomas was found dead last evening in his home." A soft murmur began, then faded quickly. "Most of us at the bank interacted with Skeeter on a regular basis. He was a valued asset to our team. He will be missed, both as a friend to many, and as a dependable coworker to all. At this time, we do not know what arrangements have been, or will be, made for Mr. Thomas. Once we are aware, Carol will communicate that information to everyone." He turned to Carol. "Would you like to add anything?"

Carol cleared her throat. "We will, of course, be sending a flower arrangement on behalf Bluegrass Bank and Trust.

I'll circulate a card later today for anyone who would like to sign it."

Hayden nodded. "Thanks, Carol." He motioned to Hunter. "I've asked Detective Robert Hunter of the Owensboro Police Department to join us this morning. I know this seems a bit unusual. Detective Hunter and I have been friends for a long time. He's leading the investigation into Skeeter's death." He turned to face Hunter. "Thanks for coming in this morning, Bob.

"Thanks, Bill," Hunter said as he walked to the front of the room, joining Carol and Hayden. "If you've seen this morning's *Owensboro Gazette*, you are aware that Mr. Thomas was murdered. There is speculation that his murder may be related to the murder of Mr. Jeff Miller, which occurred last week. I cannot comment any further as to the connection at this time, only to say that it is a possibility that is being examined. If any of you have any information that you think may be of aid in our investigation, please let me know." He nodded to Hayden. "Are there any questions?"

One of the employees standing in the back raised his hand.

"Yes?"

"Is it true that Skeeter was stabbed in the chest?"

"Yes. Both Jeff Miller and Skeeter Thomas were stabbed." He looked around the room for another question. A young woman in the second row shot up her hand. He pointed to her.

"Skeeter hasn't been at work since last week," she said. "When you think he was murdered?"

"As Mr. Thomas lived alone, we are unable to confirm at time of death," Hunter answered.

After answering a few more questions, Hunter turned to Hayden. "I'll remain in the room after your meeting."

"Just one announcement," Hayden stated. "Skeeter's office will be locked until the police have completed their investigation. If you need any documents from his office, please check with Carol."

Hushed conversations started as the employees filed out of the conference room. A petite woman in a striped, pale-yellow-and-white dress with light-brown hair in a pageboy lingered in her seat. When the room was almost empty, she walked up to Hunter. She looked up at him through the bangs which extended just past her eyebrows.

"Detective, I worked closely with Skeeter," she disclosed. "He was quiet and kinda nerdy, sure, but I can't believe someone would want to kill him." She looked down at her matching yellow heels, then back up to Hunter, a few tears in her eyes. "Ever since Tracy left him, well, he wasn't the same. Sad, melancholy. We were wondering, uh, well, it is possible that Skeeter committed suicide?"

"We don't think so at this time," he replied. "Thank you for asking."

After she vacated the conference room, Carol tapped Hunter's arm to get his attention. "I've thought for a while that she had a crush on Skeeter."

"Interoffice romance is frowned upon," Hayden quickly added.

"Of course." Hunter smiled, then checked his watch. "I'd better get going."

"Thanks for speaking to the team," Hayden said. "I'll walk you out."

CHAPTER TWENTY-FOUR

Sergio Perez was the assistant manager at the Southside Health Club, where he also taught fitness classes and provided personal training. After a brief career as a body builder, collecting a few trophies, he dropped the bulk on his five foot nine frame to a slimmer, trim physique. With his dark complexion, longish black hair, and lightly accented English, it was not surprising that his fitness classes were often crowded with women.

This morning's indoor spinning class was no different. He had opened the club at 5 a.m. and had a packed studio for the 5:30 a.m. class. And the seven o'clock session. It was well after 9 a.m. before he could take a break to down a protein shake and turn on his computer. His desk was contiguous with the bar-height front counter, an accessible appendage where he could meet with prospective clients yet still supervise the club. As he clicked through the weekly schedule, readying to upload to their website, he overheard two walkers on nearby treadmills talking about a "second murder." Thinking about the recent murder in Owensboro, he decided to walk over to discover if the "second murder" was Owensboro news, or the latest airport novel being read in some book club.

"Julie, did you say something about a 'second murder'?" he asked one of the walkers.

"Did you hear the news?" she responded.

"Yeah," the pudgy woman on the second treadmill added. "There was another murder. I saw the paper this morning. They're calling the killer the River City Ripper on account of he cuts his victims with a knife."

Sergio shook his head. "I don't know what to say. I thought Owensboro was a peaceful town."

Julie hit the pause on her treadmill. "I didn't see the *Gazette*. Bet we can find it online."

"C'mon," he said. Julie joined him as he returned to his desk, with Pudgy close behind.

On opening the *Owensboro Gazette* website, the first article was headlined "A Second Kill for the River City Ripper." With the ladies looking over his shoulders, Sergio scrolled down the page until he saw the black-and-white photograph of Darryl Skeeter Thomas. He leaned back in his chair, his head bumping into Pudgy's breasts.

"Are you okay, Sergio?" Julie asked.

"I, uh," he hesitated. "I need to go home. Excuse me, *chicas*." He closed the website, and looked to the receptionist. "Something's come up. I gotta get out of here. Cancel my classes."

∞

The duplex was quiet when Sergio walked through the front door. He dropped his keys on the kitchen counter, picked up Tracy's cellphone and entered her code. There were an uninterrupted series of missed calls with similar numbers and three unopened voicemails from the same number. He placed the phone back on the counter and walked to the bedroom at the back of the duplex. Tracy Thomas was asleep on her left side facing away from the doorway, her dark-brown hair a halo on the white pillowcase. Sergio gently shook her shoulder.

"Tracy, wake up."

Without turning, she answered, "I don't have to work today. Leave me alone. I'm sleeping."

Leveraging her right shoulder, he spun Tracy onto her back. "Wake up. We need to talk."

She stared at him. "Shouldn't you be at the health club?"

"Get up, Tracy." He turned on the bedside table lamp. "Your husband's dead."

"Skeeter?" She rubbed her eyes, adjusting to the light. "What's that have to do with me?"

"A lot. You're still married."

"Hang on." She sat up in bed, pulling strands of wavy hair away from her face. "How did he die?"

"Murdered."

"I didn't do it."

He stood up from the bed. "Tracy, you had a bunch of calls last night. I'm guessing the police have been trying to reach you. Get cleaned up. There are things you need to do."

"Like what? I filed for divorce. Not my problem."

Sergio sighed. "Yes, your problem. You're still legally married. You need to call your divorce attorney." He pulled the sheets and blankets from her, baring her naked body. "And we need to go to the police station before you become suspect *número uno*."

"You can be a real ass sometimes, Sergio," she said as she reached for the covers.

Chapter Twenty-Five

F at Tony's had started as a small pizzeria, a few tables covered by red-and-white checkered vinyl tablecloths with candles in fiasco basket Chianti bottles, a limited menu, and a mostly delivery business. Over time, Tony DeLuca was able to expand into the adjoining space on Eighteenth Street, adding a large seating area and turning the original space into a sports bar. He added big-screen televisions and sports memorabilia from the Cincinnati Reds, his favorite team. His uncle, Marco DeLuca, had played for the Reds in his brief professional career and had even provided Tony with the pizzeria's slogan: "I'll make you a pizza you can't refuse."

During baseball season, it was pizza, beer, and all the Reds games you can watch. Fat Tony's Pizzeria was the go-to Reds bar.

There was a tall, thin man cleaning the wooden bar, spray bottle in one hand and a white rag in the other, when Hunter approached the full-frame glass front door. Before he could reach the handle, the bar cleaner pointed to a Hudepohl-branded analog clock above the bar, and mouthed what looked like, "We're not open yet."

Hunter checked his watch. Just after 10:30 a.m. He pulled his badge from his suit jacket and held it up to the glass. The barman nodded, walked around the bar and unlocked the door, standing in the doorway, blocking the detective with his height.

"We don't open until eleven."

He put his badge away. "I need to see Tony. Is he in yet?"

The door was fully opened. "Yeah. I'll go get him," and disappeared down the narrow hallway beyond the Restroom sign.

Hunter looked around the bar, and seeing several Red's jersey in frames, walked between the high-top tables to the side wall. When Brenda and he had eaten at Fat Tony's with the girls, they always sat in the dining room. He'd not been on the bar side in years. There were framed jerseys, most signed by the players, faded hats, two well-worn gloves. In one box, some ticket stubs and a program from a 1976 World Series game against the Yankees, signed by several players, including Marco DeLuca.

"Well, Detective, what'd my son Mario do this time?" Tony asked.

"How did you get all these memorabilia?"

"Uncle Marco. Most of it was his, from when he played shortstop with the Reds."

"Great collection." Hunter turned to face Tony. "I didn't drop by to talk about baseball. You know Darryl Thomas?"

"Yeah, I know him. But everyone calls him Skeeter."

"He was murdered. His body was found yesterday. We found a credit-card receipt for Fat Tony's in his wallet, dated Saturday. This was likely the last place he was seen alive."

"How'd it happen? How was he killed?"

"Stabbed in the chest."

"Oooh," Tony shuddered as he grabbed at his chest. "Have a seat. You want some coffee? Espresso? Cappuccino, maybe?" He pointed to the high-top table next to them.

"Regular coffee is fine," he said as he unbuttoned the jacket of his navy suit and sat on the stool.

"One of these days, Bob, I'll make you an espresso you can't refuse," Tony said with a grin. Then he turned to the bartender, who had resumed cleaning. "Vinnie, can you get us a coupla regular coffees?"

"Sure, boss. Comin' right up."

Tony turned back to Hunter. "So, Skeeter, well, he's been here every Saturday night since his wife left him for some personal trainer. Sits in the same place—where you are right now—has a few beers, orders a small pie. He's always alone. Watches the game, now that the season has started. I try to take a few minutes to talk to him, not just as a restaurant owner, you know, but he's not like a close friend or anything." He paused, looked up at one of the framed jerseys, then continued. "Seems like an okay guy, I guess. And he was murdered?"

"Yes. Do you know if he was alone last Saturday?"

Tony tugged at his black goatee. "Don't know. Reds played the Cardinals Saturday. Had a big crowd. We were down to our last keg of Hudy."

"Hudy?"

"Hudepohl beer. We're the only place in town that serves it."

Vinnie placed two mugs of coffee on the table. "You need any cream or sugar?" he asked, looking at Hunter.

"No, thanks, I take it black." He picked up the mug for a sip.

Tony leaned back in in the chair, his left index finger up. "Vinnie, you remember seeing Skeeter Thomas Saturday?"

"Yeah, he was here, like always, in his usual seat, right there." He indicated Hunter's side of the table with his head.

Hunter asked, "Was he alone or with someone?"

"You know, he's usually by himself, but Saturday, this place was packed. We do good business when we play the Cards. There was this girl who sat at the high-top with him, but I don't think they were together. I remember her coming in around the second inning or so, and it was like she just needed a seat."

"You remember what she looked like? Get a name?"

"No name. Dark hair in a ponytail pulled through her Reds cap. She had on a Reds jersey. Her face was like a five, six maybe, but her rack was a nine, ya know?" He held his cupped hands in front of his chest to demonstrate. "Pretty sure they were fake."

Tony glowered at Vinnie, then added, "I don't remember her."

Hunter considered the receipt. Three beers, small pizza. That was for one, for Skeeter, not for two of them. "How did she pay her bill?"

Vinnie thought for a moment. "Skeeter paid with a card. She had two Corona Lights, paid cash."

"Do you know if they left together?"

He shook his head. "No idea."

Tony held up his right hand. "I think I can help with that. We've got two surveillance cameras on the parking lot. You may be able to see something." He stood up. "Grab your mug. Let's go in the back."

∞

Tony sat at the desk in front of the two large computer monitors, Hunter standing over his shoulder, coffee in his right hand. He keyed in a few sequences, bringing the monitors to life.

"Let's see. Saturday. The game ended around ten, as I recall," Tony said.

"Run it back a little before then."

"Sure." Tony moved the computer mouse, and a few clicks later, the front of the restaurant from two angles was on the monitors, a timer in the right lower corner reading 9:48. "Here ya go."

"Can you speed it up?" Hunter asked.

"Yeah, hang on."

The black-and-white video stream showed a couple having a cigarette just beyond the front door, then returning to the restaurant. Nothing until ten fifteen, when Skeeter emerged with a woman.

"Stop it there, Tony." Hunter moved closer to the monitors. "That's Skeeter Thomas, all right."

"I'll get Vincenzo, see if that's the girl."

With a white dishtowel in his hands, Vinnie entered the small back office with Tony. Looking at the monitor, he confirmed, "Yeah, that's her."

"Thanks. Tony, can you resume the playback, going slowly?"

He tugged at his goatee. "I gotta remember how to do that." He returned to the desk chair, typed a series of letters, and the screens started again. The slowed speed exaggerated their actions into a flounced progression of jerky movements.

The couple walked to Skeeter's Camry, which was parked within the camera range. Standing next to the sedan, they appeared to have a discussion. Skeeter's left hand went to the driver's door handle, but he did not open the door, then removed his hand and turned back to his companion.

"Audio would be nice," Hunter observed.

Tony looked up at Hunter. "I'll look into it."

The woman pointed across the parking lot. They walked behind the Camry, out of range.

"That doesn't help much," Tony said.

"Wait, bubba. They're returning."

"How do you know that?"

Hunter smiled. "Trust me."

A light-colored Volkswagen Beetle appeared at the top of both screens, slowly approaching Skeeter's car. The Beetle stopped at the Camry. The passenger door opened, and Skeeter emerged. The Beetle backed up slightly as Skeeter got into his sedan. He backed out of the space, pulling in front of the Beetle, and cruised past the front door. The Beetle followed close behind.

"Stop." Hunter said. "Can you zoom in on the Beetle?"

"I think so, but I don't know how to do that," Tony answered.

"Who does?"

"Mario. He'll be here after school."

"What about sending that file to me? I'll have the tech guys look at it."

Tony shook his head. "Same thing. Mario knows, I don't."

"Okay. Let me know if Mario can or can't. I get a number off of the license plate, I find Skeeter Thomas's last date."

"Sure thing, Bob. I'll call you later."

He sat the empty mug on the desk. "I owe you one."

Tony grinned. "I'll put it on your tab."

CHAPTER TWENTY-SIX

When he arrived at office, the chief's administrative assistant, Laura, was seated at her desk. Single and in her early forties, she was preoccupied with projecting a more youthful appearance. Her straight, auburn-dyed hair was worn in a stylish, windblown updo, her makeup was always fresh, her dresses colorful and fashionable. On Hunter's arrival, she looked up from a magazine and pointed to the closed door of Chief Hartmann's office with an emery board.

"He'll be off the phone in a minute, Detective."

Hunter sat in one of the reception-area chairs to wait. "How's his mood today?" he asked.

"Surprisingly calm."

"Two murders, back to back. I didn't expect the chief to handle it well. Not something for which anyone is really prepared."

"I can see that. Anyway, he's kept that door shut except when he wanted coffee. Some reporters have called, one from some Louisville TV station, wanting to know if we're going to have a press conference. The mayor called twice this morning. He's on the phone with him again right now." She checked her nails, setting the emery board aside. "You planning to hold a press conference?"

"Not my call, Laura. That's up to the chief."

"Yeah, uh, okay. How's the new office?"

"View's better."

Laura glanced across the room at Hunter and smiled. "I bet." She looked down to the charcoal office telephone as the glow from one of the line buttons ended. "He's off the phone. Hang on."

She picked up the handset, and punched the chief's line. "Detective Hunter's here." There was a brief pause, then she answered, "Yes," and replaced the handset.

"Go ahead. He's free."

Chief Hartmann was curled over his large desk, focused on the file he was holding open. The collar button of his white shirt was undone, his sleeves rolled up to his elbows, his striped tie loosened. Not wearing a suit jacket, his bright-red suspenders were revealed.

Hunter closed the door, then slipped into the "hot seat" before Hartmann diverted his attention to the detective. He closed the file and sat it on the smooth wooden desktop.

"Have you seen today's paper?" Hartmann asked.

"Yes. The *Gazette* linked the two murders and christened the killer the 'River City Ripper.'" He turned in his seat. "There was a fair bit of detail in the piece. Someone's leaking."

Hartmann nodded. "There's always a leak. No department is immune." He returned his attention to the file he had been reviewing when Hunter entered the office. He slid it across the desk.

"Here's the file you're looking for."

Hunter looked at Chief Hartmann, trying to read his face. Nothing. He slowly leaned forward in the chair to retrieve the thin file and turned it so that he could read the name on the tab label: *Jenny Lynn Harper.*

"Go ahead. I'll wait," Hartmann said.

He opened the folder. The first page was a hand-drawn diagram of the accident on Calhoun Road. It was as Trevor Reed had described it to Hunter. A head-on collision in the northbound lane, Car A, the Oldsmobile Cutlass coupe that Trevor had been driving, and Car B, a Mercedes-Benz S-Class sedan, the oncoming car travelling southbound, which had crossed over into the northbound lane and caused the accident. Four distinct skid marks were depicted behind Car A, with a slight curve to the outbound side of the lane; none were on the drawing for Car B.

A summary followed. Jenny Harper was found on the crinkled hood of the Cutlass, covered in blood and broken glass. She was taken directly to Daviess County General Hospital by ambulance, where she was pronounced dead less than an hour later. The driver, Trevor Reed, agreed to a preliminary breath test by a handheld breathalyzer, which showed a blood alcohol concentration of zero. He was treated and released from the emergency room. The Cutlass was an older model, lacking airbags. Reed had been wearing his seatbelt.

The front airbags of Mercedes-Benz had deployed. Several empty beer cans and a broken whiskey bottle were found on the floorboard of the vehicle. The driver, Jeff Miller, and front-seat passenger, Darryl Thomas, had been wearing seatbelts and were unharmed. The rear-seat passengers, Elroy Beggs and Wayne Peterson, were unrestrained. Both rear-seat passengers had been injured; Beggs dislocated his right shoulder and fractured two ribs, and Peterson fractured both bones of his left forearm and his left zygomatic arch. He also had a concussion. All four were transported by ambulance to the hospital. Miller and Thomas were treated and released,

Beggs and Peterson admitted. All refused to be tested with the breathalyzer.

Both vehicles were undriveable and appeared to be totaled. They were towed to the police impound lot.

Hunter closed the file, placing it on the desk. He leaned back, smoothed his tie against his pale-blue dress shirt with his right hand, and sighed.

"It's not even a proper report, Chief."

Hartmann nodded. "I know."

"Where's the rest of it? There're no crime scene photographs, no arrest reports, not even the officers' names."

"Photos were deleted, no arrests were made." Hartmann looked down, rubbing his forehead without disturbing his comb-over. "I knew this would come back and bite us in the ass."

"What happened?" Hunter asked.

"Jeff Miller's mother is what happened. Jill Miller. Or rather, Jill *Fulkerson* Miller."

"As in 'the Fulkersons?'"

"Yes," Hartmann answered. "She's the granddaughter of Bruce Fulkerson. She knew the right strings to pull with the administration. Elkins was chief then. He went along with the mayor, and we made it all go away."

Hunter shook his head. "So, three-time former mayor Bruce Fulkerson was still a potentate from the grave."

Hartmann pulled the folder from the desktop, and, rotating his chair to the credenza behind him, dropped it into a file drawer. He closed and locked the drawer.

"The murders are related," Hunter stated. "Why didn't you tell me any of this after the Jeff Miller murder?"

"The mayor believed that Miller's murder was an isolated event. I was hoping that to be the case."

"And now?"

"Now, we should assume the two are related."

"If someone has a dead list, there are two more to go. Elroy Beggs and Wayne Peterson. My prime suspect, Billy Ray Harper, is looking even more guilty." Hunter ran his fingers through his hair.

"Unless Wayne Peterson is the culprit," Hartmann observed. "Or Trevor Reed."

"What about Beggs?"

Hartmann turned his chair back to the credenza, pulled several blue plastic folders from the metal file sorter, and opened one as he spun back to face Hunter; the others he placed on the desktop.

"Private First Class Elroy Beggs was killed in action in Iraq. The Department of Defense was light with details." He closed the file and pushed it across the desk to Hunter.

Hunter didn't touch the file. "You've kept tabs on them?"

"Yes. Like I said, I knew this would come back to haunt us someday."

"I've met Reed. I don't think he's involved. Peterson's on the suspect list now."

Pointing to the one of the other blue folders, the chief continued. "Peterson's information. Raised by a single mother. Divorced, no kids. Works construction. Lives alone in a townhouse on Goetz Road."

Hunter left Peterson's file untouched.

"You need help, Hunter. I've let you run solo only because Alan Maddox was supposed to have returned to duty by now, instead of retiring." Hartmann leaned back in his chair. "The promotional exam results are back. Phil will be joining you as the junior detective, effective tomorrow."

"Phil? I have a good working relationship with Mike Wagner. What about Mike?"

"Won't consider it." Hartmann sighed. "Phil passed the test. Mike didn't. Phil will do well under your tutelage."

Hunter picked up the blue folder with Peterson's information. "Dr. Turner should be done with the autopsy of Darryl Thomas soon. I'll track down Wayne Peterson next."

"And Billy Ray Harper?"

"I'll have him picked up again for questioning. Amos Weller knows he's a suspect."

"What about Trevor Reed?" Hartmann picked up one of the blue files.

"Like I said, I don't think he's involved."

Hartmann nodded. "That file, and the information about Jill Miller's involvement, the whole Fulkerson thing, remains in this office." He pushed a notepad toward Hunter. "I don't think I need to add, but I will: Jill Miller is off limits."

"Got it, Chief."

Hunter opened the file, made a few notes, and placed the closed file back on the desk. He stood up, buttoning his navy suit jacket. "If that's all, I'll get back to work."

The desk phone blinked. Hartmann punched the speakerphone button, answering "Yes, Laura."

"Sorry to interrupt, Chief. Tracy Thomas has shown up. She's in reception."

Hunter looked at Hartmann. "We've been unable to reach her. I'll take care of it."

Speaking into the phone, he said "Have her escorted to Detective Hunter's office."

"Yes, sir." The line went silent.

CHAPTER TWENTY-SEVEN

Taking the back staircase to his third-floor office, Hunter exited the stairwell as the elevator doors opened down the hallway. Tracy Thomas and Sergio Perez walked out of the elevator car accompanied by Teri, a petite uniformed policewoman. He walked toward the group, stopping at the small reception area next to his office. Tracy, wearing jeans and an oversize and untucked white shirt, her brown hair pulled back, stood close to Sergio, still clad in his gym gear.

"Mrs. Thomas, this is Detective Hunter," Teri stated, motioning to Hunter with her open hand. "He's leading the investigation into your husband's case." She turned to Hunter. "Tracy Thomas and Sergio ... uhh—"

"Perez. Sergio Perez."

Hunter offered his hand, which Sergio shook and Tracy avoided. "I'm very sorry for your loss, Mrs. Thomas."

"Don't be," she responded.

Sergio glowered at Tracy, then turned to face Hunter. "I had to drag her down here."

"Please have a seat," Hunter said, pointing to the brown couch. "Can we get you something to drink? Coffee? A bottle of water?"

"Nothing, thanks," Sergio answered. After Tracy was seated on the couch, he joined her, taking the side nearest the door.

"Do you need me for anything else, Detective?" the policewoman asked.

"No. Thanks, Teri," he answered. She turned and walked back down the hallway to the elevator.

"We've been trying to reach you, Mrs. Thomas. Thanks for coming to the station," Hunter began as he took the chair opposite the small table, facing Tracy and Sergio. "There are a few questions I need to ask you."

Tracy stared at Hunter without responding. He continued.

"How long have you and Mr. Thomas been separated?"

"Why does that matter? We're getting divorced," she answered.

"I understand that. Please, just answer the question."

"About six months," Sergio answered. "Tracy moved in with me about six months ago."

"When did you last see or talk to Mr. Thomas?"

Tracy looked at Sergio. "We had to meet with the lawyers a coupla weeks ago. Haven't seen or talked to him since then."

"Does your husband have any enemies? Any who would want to murder him?"

"He's not my husband," Tracy said with a sneer.

Sergio shook his head. "Tracy, Skeeter is still your husband. You're still married." He looked at Hunter. "Actually, she's not married now, right? She's a … What's the word? Widow? Is that right? Widow?"

"That's correct," Hunter answered. "Widow." He considered Sergio for a moment. "Your accent—I can't seem to place it. Portuguese? Spanish?"

"I'm Cuban," he replied. "I'm legal, Detective," he added defensively.

"Your immigration status is not in question, Mr. Perez," Hunter stated. "Let's get back on track. Anyone you can think of who would want Mr. Thomas dead?"

Tracy glared at Hunter. After a pause, she simply said, "No."

"What do you know about the relationship between Mr. Thomas and Jeff Miller?"

"Do you think the murders are connected?" Sergio asked. "I read the article in today's *Gazette*. They seem to think so."

"It has not been determined that the murders are linked at this time." Hunter studied Tracy, who was looking down at the empty flower vase on the low table between them. "Mrs. Thomas, do you know anything about Jeff Miller and your deceased husband?"

"Him and Jeff was buddies in high school. We never did anything with 'em, the Millers." Tracy reached for Sergio's hand. "If Skeeter was involved in something with Jeff, I don't know nothing 'bout it."

"One more question. Where were you, both of you, on Saturday night?" Hunter watched for a change in facial expressions. Sergio returned his gaze with a quizzical look.

"Are we suspects, Detective?" he asked.

"Anyone may be a suspect, Mr. Perez. I'm assuming that Mrs. Thomas and you have nothing to hide." He sat upright in the chair, straightening his tie and smoothing the jacket of his suit. "Can you account for your whereabouts Saturday?"

The couple exchanged glances. "We were in Cincinnati. At the Reds game," Sergio answered.

"Stay the weekend?" Hunter asked.

"We drove up Saturday afternoon, after Tracy got off work. After the game, we stayed in a downtown hotel. Came home Sunday morning," he replied.

"And you'll have receipts to verify, if needed?"

"Yes." Sergio nodded his head slowly.

"Okay. Do either of you have any questions?"

"What happens now?" Tracy asked.

"Did Mr. Thomas have a will?"

"Yeah," she said. "But it's old. Before I filed."

"It's valid, Mrs. Thomas, unless there's been an updated version of which you are not aware," Hunter explained. "I suggest you contact your attorney. He can help you sort out the details."

Sergio held up his hand. "I've got a question. What about this body?"

"There will be an autopsy today. The body of Mr. Thomas should be released tomorrow to the funeral home."

"Wait," Tracy uttered. "There's an autopsy?"

"Standard in these cases, Mrs. Thomas."

Sergio stood up. "Detective, can I speak with you privately, for a moment?" He looked down at Tracy, who remained seated on the couch. "Just be a minute, Trace."

"Of course, Mr. Perez." Hunter pointed to the adjoining room. "Let's step into my office." He led Sergio into his corner office and closed the door.

"Would you like to have a seat?" Hunter stood next to his desk.

"No, that's okay." Sergio said. "Look, Detective, Tracy didn't do this. We were at the game, and I can give you my Visa bill to prove so if you need it. I know she's not crying or anything, like she's upset or sorry. When I started seeing her,

I didn't know she was married. Their marriage was broken a long time ago. I didn't break it up."

"I'm not passing judgement, Mr. Perez."

"I understand. She just wants to move on with her life, her life without being married to Skeeter."

Hunter leaned against his desk. "Did you know him?"

"No. I met him once. He came into the club with Tracy. I'm the assistant manager at the Southside Health Club." Sergio hesitated. "Not much of an athlete, really. I didn't see what they saw in each other."

"If you think of anything that will aid the investigation, please contact me." Hunter pulled a card from the gun-metal grey holder on his desk, handing it to Sergio.

∞

After escorting the pair downstairs to the reception area of the station, Hunter was met by Teri as he waited for the lone elevator to return to the ground floor.

"She's a piece of work," Teri said.

The elevator doors slid open. Hunter held the door as Teri entered and waited until the door closed before speaking.

"The general feeling from talking to everyone who knows Skeeter Thomas and also knows her, is that no one seems to be very fond of Tracy Thomas." He punched the button for the third floor. "No obvious sign that she was grief-stricken." He paused. "Not a tear, her eyes weren't even red."

"Think she did it?"

"No. She lacks motive. There's no grand estate to inherit, the Thomas's lived a modest life. Tracy Thomas would gain little from killing her husband." The doors opened on the third floor. "Although it's crystal clear she doesn't care that her husband is dead."

"What about the boyfriend?"

"Same thing. He seems to be more concerned about running into an immigration agent than anything as mundane as the murder of his girlfriend's husband."

Teri followed Hunter to his office. "Devil's advocate, Detective. She didn't want to be married to him anymore, filed for divorce. The relationship's over, almost like some long-ago school age fling. Would you be grieving if your high school sweetie suddenly died? I think I would."

"I get your point. And for the record, yes, I would be absolutely devastated." Hunter looked down at Teri and smiled. "I married my high school sweetheart."

CHAPTER TWENTY-EIGHT

The reception desk of the pathology lab was unoccupied. Hunter pushed through the metal double doors into the sour aroma of the autopsy room. Dr. Turner tilted her head to look at Hunter over her half-frame reading glasses.

"I was about to call you," she said. "The knife's been sent to ECU. Doubt they'll find anything. It was the same brand." She pointed to a box on the steel autopsy table. "Put on some gloves. Lots to show."

He walked up to the right side of the autopsy table, slipping on a pair of blue latex gloves. The chest cavity was splayed open in the same manner he had seen at Jeff Miller's autopsy, heart and lungs removed.

Turner poked her left index finger through the knife wound in the right chest. "Same as Miller. The knife sliced through the fourth intercostal space, except on the right side, not the left." She removed her hand, then pointed to the corresponding area on the left chest. "See these three small wounds on the left chest?"

Hunter leaned closer to examine three parallel skin wounds, superficial, each less than an inch in length. "The same space, right? The fourth intercostal space?"

"Correct. I missed those at the house when I first examined the body. Those are called *hesitation marks*. Usually seen with suicide attempts. When a person commits suicide using a knife, they will often hesitate before actually stabbing themselves. They may feel the sharp pain of the instrument and have to build up a bit of courage with a few dry runs before actually executing the final cut that causes death. The self-inflicted wounds tend to be superficial."

"You think he committed suicide?" Hunter asked incredulously.

"Not very likely," she answered. "But the hesitation marks have led me to another idea."

"Okay, that idea is?"

"Hang on, Bob. This takes a minute to explain. The heart is situated in the left chest. But his heart was on the right side."

Hunter peered across Skeeter Thomas's body into Turner's hazel eyes. "Dextrocardia," he whispered.

"Very good. Yes, dextrocardia. A rare congenital abnormality. The usual position is levocardia."

"Left-sided heart."

Turner pulled the green sheet over Skeeter's body, then tossed her gloves into the waste bucket.

"Not just dextrocardia. He had a condition known as *situs inversus totalis.*"

"Latin. Sites inverted in total," Hunter murmured slowly. "All his organs were reversed, like a mirror image?"

"That's right. Situs inversus totalis is a rare condition, occurs about one in ten thousand people. I've only seen it once, in medical school."

"I'm guessing that he would have known he had it?" he asked.

"Yes. Although they usually have no medical symptoms. The organs all still function properly."

Hunter pulled off his gloves, then leaned against the empty autopsy table behind him. "That explains why he was stabbed in the right chest."

"And the killer knew it. My theory is that the killer started to stab him in the left chest, the normal heart position, then stopped and switched to the right chest. There's no hesitation marks on the right chest." Turner reached up to switch off the ceiling-mounted LED lamp. "I checked the photographs of Miller's chest. No hesitation marks there either."

"Who do you suppose would know he had dextrocardia?" He twisted his wedding band around his left ring finger.

"His physician, of course. His family, perhaps some of his friends. Situs inversus is not exactly what I would expect for dinner party chitchat." Turner smiled at Hunter. "Unless the host was a pathologist."

"Last night I informed his parents about his death. They didn't say anything about a heart condition."

Turner shrugged her shoulders. "Probably not the first thing they would think to tell you. They'd have known about it since infancy. It would be their normal."

"Makes sense. Assuming the killer didn't know Skeeter Thomas had dextrocardia, would he be able to determine that quickly in the midst of the murder?"

Turner walked around the table to stand in front of Hunter. "In medical school, we were taught to palpate the heart. This is done by gently laying your right hand on the left chest over the area when the heart is located. That region is called the *precordium*." She pointed to Hunter's left chest. "In thinner patients, you can feel the pulse related to the contraction of the heart's apex. It's called the point of maximum impulse, or PMI."

Hunter peered at the green sheet covering the body. "He was fairly lean."

"Yes. But remember, you're talking about a physical exam technique that has to be taught, and it's done in controlled circumstances."

"So, possible, but not very likely," Hunter summarized.

"That would be my professional opinion."

Turner walked to the desk, taking a seat in front of the computer monitor. "Let me see if the tox screens are back."

Hunter followed.

"What about his fingernails? Did that turn out to be human tissue?"

"Oh, yeah. Almost forgot. I got a good amount of tissue. I asked for a rush on the DNA. I may have something tomorrow, certainly by Monday."

He acknowledged with a nod.

"Here it is," Turner said. "Nothing in his blood or urine except alcohol. And that level wasn't very high."

"Not drugged," Hunter stated deliberately.

"Definitely not, Bob. And not drunk." She spun around in the desk chair. "Subject change. You see the front page of the *Gazette*?"

"The River City Ripper headline? Yes," he smirked. "What'd you think?"

"Exciting, in a ghoulish way." She shook her head. "But, then, death is my business."

"Evil sells papers," he observed. "Rare is the top news story about a good Samaritan."

Hunter's phone vibrated in his suit jacket. He pulled out the phone, looking at the number on the screen. "Mind if I take this, Jean?"

"Of course not."

He punched Answer. "Hey, Tony."

"Bob, I got good news and bad news," Tony DeLuca said. "Good news, Mario already emailed you the video file."

"And the bad news?"

"He doesn't know how to zoom in on the license plate."

"I'm confident we can take care of that. Thanks." He ended the call.

"What was that about?" Jean asked.

"The recently deceased Skeeter Thomas had a date Saturday before his untimely demise. The pair can be seen on surveillance video from Fat Tony's. I'm after the license plate number of her car."

"You think she's the killer?" Jean looked at him skeptically.

"I doubt it, but you never know. She may be the last person to have seen him alive." He slipped the phone into his pocket.

CHAPTER TWENTY-NINE

Finished with drywall in Lewisport for the day, Earl Cravens climbed into the driver's seat of his truck, Wayne Peterson joining him on the passenger side. A few miles into the trip back to Owensboro on Highway 60, Earl pulled into the parking lot of a convenience store.

"How about a home beer, Wayne?" Earl asked. "I'm buyin'." He pulled a twenty from his pocket.

"I got it," Wayne answered as he popped the door handle, waving off the cash. "I sure could use one today."

He walked down the snack aisle to the glass-doored coolers at the back of the store, pulling two cold cans from the front of a middle shelf. As he joined the three-person line for the lone cashier, he spotted the newsstand next to the counter, and the boldly printed headline of the *Owensboro Gazette*, "River City Ripper Claims Another Victim." Two copies remained in the slots. He pulled one as he neared the cashier, placing the newspaper on the counter with the beer cans.

"Will that be all?" she asked.

"Pack of Camels," he said.

"It's three for two this week." She turned to the wall of tobacco products behind the counter. "Sure you don't want three packs?"

"Okay, three then." He drew his wallet from the back pocket of his jeans, removed a credit card, and slipped it into the reader.

Returning to the truck, Wayne handed a can to Earl before climbing back into the passenger seat. He put the newspaper on the center console armrest, then opened his own beer and took a long swig.

"Since when do you read the newspaper?" Earl asked as he pulled onto the two-lane highway.

"The front page is about Skeeter." He reached for the paper. "Uh, Darryl. Darryl Thomas. We always called him Skeeter growing up."

"Your friend who was killed, right?"

"Yeah. We were tight in high school. Things change." He folded the paper to look at the front-page article.

"Sorry to hear that, bro." Earl opened his beer, downing half in a single gulp. "You need me to do anything?"

"Nope," he answered, reaching over to increase the volume of the radio.

∞

Wayne read the newspaper's lead story twice. *Senseless*, he thought. Who would want to kill Skeeter? Sure, he was a bit nerdy, but he wasn't a bad guy. He was one of the good guys. He regretted losing touch with his high school pals, and now it was too late.

"Jeff and Skeeter," he said to no one. "Why?"

He carried his beer out to the patio, taking a seat in one of the chairs. Karla had not wanted the three-piece white cast-iron set, a small round table with two chairs, so Wayne had ended up with it. He lit a cigarette, staring blankly at the tendril of smoke rising from the smoldering end. His mind returned to his deceased high school friends. And the lost opportunities.

His thoughts were interrupted by the doorbell. He pushed the butt into the empty beer can, leaving it on the table, walked through the townhouse, and opened the front door.

"Detective Hunter with the OPD," Hunter stated, showing his badge. "I'd like to ask you a few questions."

Wayne eyed him warily, holding the door partially open. Even though he was standing on the step above, Wayne had to look up to the six foot four detective.

"May I come it?" Hunter asked.

Releasing his grip on the knob, he silently stepped back and let the door swing fully open. The front room of his townhouse was a ragout of mismatched essentials: an oversized bachelor's television on the inside wall opposite two recliners, remote controls and an ashtray on a small single-drawered table between the chairs, the hardwood floors lacking a rug. Wayne's work boots were on the floor next to a wooden bench that looked better suited for outdoor use.

"I'm investigating the murders of Jeff Miller and Darryl Thomas," Hunter said. He remained standing just inside the front door. "I understand you were acquainted with them."

Wayne sat in a recliner. "High school friends."

"When was the last time you saw Jeff Miller or Darryl Thomas?" Hunter moved to the bench.

"Skeeter. We always called Darryl Skeeter."

"Mind if I sit down?" he asked.

"Yeah, go ahead, Detective."

Hunter took space on the bench. "Back to the question. Last time you saw either of them?"

He looked up at the ceiling, then responded. "I haven't seen Jeff for years."

"Why?"

"His wife, Eve, well, Eve didn't like me so much." He looked at Hunter. "Almost like I wasn't good enough for the likes of her. I was invited to wedding, but that was about the last invite I got."

"And Skeeter Thomas?"

"I saw Skeeter at the Fulkerson Funeral Home when I went to pay my respects to Jeff. Before that, must have been a while. Coupla years at least. I heard Tracy left him a few months ago, was gonna call but never did. Never could figure out why he married that good-for-nothin' trailer trash."

"I take it you didn't like Tracy Thomas."

"Not one bit. Skeeter, well, he done real good for himself. Went to college, got a good job at the bank. Tracy was a bad idea."

Hunter twisted his wedding band, considered Wayne. He seemed remorseful for the loss of former friends, not ready for vengeance of any sort. There was nothing to avenge.

Wayne continued. "And Jeff, he did good too. Eve didn't like me, but that don't mean she wasn't good for Jeff." He pursed his lips. "You know, the last time I saw Jeff was at the Ford dealer. About two, maybe three years ago. I was looking for a new truck, but it didn't work out."

"Any particular reason why?"

"Financing. I've been working construction since I got outta high school and was in a hurry to get hitched. Karla, my ex, she used to say that with construction, sometimes it was chicken and sometimes it was feathers, and that time when I was looking to get a new truck, it was mostly feathers."

Hunter recalled from the file Chief Hartmann kept that Wayne was divorced. "Karla, she was your wife?"

"Yes. Was. We had one of them long feather times, and we started to fight about money. Like that Billy Joel song."

"'Scenes From an Italian Restaurant,'" Hunter said softly.

"Huh?"

"The Billy Joel song is 'Scenes From an Italian Restaurant.'"

"Yeah, whatever," Wayne said. He suddenly stood up from the recliner. "You want a beer, Detective?"

Hunter shook his head. "No, I'll pass."

Wayne walked past him to the kitchen, returning with two cans of beer. He handed one to Hunter. "If you change your mind," he said as he returned to the recliner. Wayne opened the can, guzzling a long swig.

"You have any reason to want Jeff or Skeeter dead?" He put the beer on the bench.

He stared at Hunter. "You gotta be kidding me. They was my friends. Yeah, life turned out better for them than me, 'cepting they got killed by this River City Ripper, but I have no reason to want them dead."

"Can you account for your whereabouts last Saturday night?"

"Am I a suspect?"

"Just answer the question."

"I had a date. We had dinner, then came back here and watched the Reds game."

"And after the game?"

Wayne took another drink. "Whadda you think, Detective?"

"She stayed the night?"

"Most of it, anyway."

"And the prior Saturday? The night Jeff Miller was murdered?"

"Don't remember," he answered. "I did something with Arlene, not sure what. I remember what we did later, though," he said and smiled.

"Arlene will collaborate the dates?" Hunter asked.

"Sure. You want her number, Detective? You might like her. She got a nice rack." That smile again.

Second time I've heard that today, Hunter thought. "Yes, we may need her to confirm."

Wayne finished the beer in a single quaff, setting the can on the end table, and glared at Hunter.

Hunter shifted on the uncomfortable wooden bench. "Are you familiar with a Trevor Reed?"

Wayne closed his eyes, slowly shaking his head. "Yeah," he finally uttered.

"You want to tell me about that night?" Hunter asked. "About the accident?"

"You think that's why Jeff and Skeeter are dead? Because of a car accident a long time ago? How does that matter?"

"An accident that resulted in the death of a young girl, Mr. Peterson. I'll be the one to determine if it is relevant. So, why don't you tell me about that night."

"I don't really want to talk about it." Wayne looked down at the floor.

"As soon as someone doesn't want to discuss something, I do." Hunter picked up the beer can, pointing it at Wayne. "Now, you can sit in your comfy chair, have another beer, and provide to me the details for which I am looking. Or," he said, setting the can back on the bench, "we can continue our conversation downtown in a rather drab interrogation room."

Wayne pondered the equally unappealing options, then acquiesced. "What do you want to know?" he finally said.

"Start anywhere." He tossed the beer can to Wayne, who caught it and sat it on the table.

"My neighbor, Elroy, he was home between tours."

"Elroy Beggs?"

"Yeah. How'd you know that?"

"I'm a police detective. Go on."

"Anyways, Elroy, he was over twenty-one, so he bought us some beer and a bottle of bourbon. Cheap stuff, but, hey, what did we know? We were kids." He opened the beer slowly, watching the can top for foam. Seeing none, he took a drink.

"We was just riding around in Jeff's mom's car. Elroy was telling us army stories about being in Iraq, bragging about shooting the enemy, that sort of stuff. We were eating it up, although looking back, I think a lot of it was made up." He sipped some more beer from the can. "Next thing I know, I'm in the hospital, my arm's in a cast, my eye's swollen shut and my head hurt like a motherfucker."

"You don't remember the crash?"

"Not a bit." He took another drink. "And I didn't even know Jenny Harper died until I got back to school a week later. Mom said Mrs. Miller came by the house, told her everything was taken care of, not to worry."

"You weren't curious?"

He shook his head. "No. I know when to keep my mouth shut." After taking another mouthful of beer, he asked, "You think this River City Ripper is connected to that accident?"

Hunter stood up from the bench, straightening his suit jacket and tie. "I am looking into any and all possibilities."

"Am I in danger, Detective?"

"I can't determine if you are in any danger. I suggest you be cautious if there is a connection between the murders of Jeff Miller and Darryl Thomas that would impact you." He pulled a card from his jacket pocket. "If you think of anything that may help the investigation, please contact me."

Hunter handed his card to Wayne and walked to the front door, opening it. "Keep your doors locked."

Wayne regarded the card, flipped it on the end table, and finished his beer.

CHAPTER THIRTY

P hil had spent the first hours the Friday morning of his new position listening, taking notes, sorting how the new partnership would work—and getting caught up on the biggest case of the year. He was familiar with much of the case, having been one of the uniformed officers at both of the crime scenes. Hunter had been filling in the details while he sat in front of the detective's desk. He was prepared to be part of the team.

"So, based on your conversation with Wayne Peterson yesterday, do you think we need to confirm his alibi?" he asked.

"We should, even though I don't think he did it. Same for Tracy Thomas. Her new boyfriend was quite eager to disqualify her as a suspect. And they were out of town anyway." Hunter paused to look at the computer monitor. "Trevor Reed doesn't seem the type, like I said."

"He's got motive," Phil stated. "What if he only came to you after Jeff Miller's murder to make sure you were looking for someone else?"

"Diverting suspicion?" Hunter asked. "I don't know. He seemed pretty genuine."

"I can look into it," Phil offered.

"Okay. You do that. Meanwhile, we need to decide when to question Billy Ray Harper again."

"At the station, or do you want to go the halfway house?"

"Station. I don't want Amos Weller interfering. And our interrogation rooms can be much more intimidating." Hunter stood up and walked to the window. "Billy Ray's not a nice guy, and he really doesn't care for me. At all."

"Why?"

"My testimony at his trial is what put him in Eddyville." He pulled the cigarette pack from the pocket of his suit jacket. "Skeeter Thomas's house on Lisbon Drive is 2.6 miles from the halfway house on Manor Court. Billy Ray doesn't have a car, but he could walk the distance in less than an hour. It is very unlikely he would be seen walking through the side streets at night.

"Do you have any other good suspects?"

"Not yet." He pulled a cigarette from the pack as Irwin Betts walked into the office, wearing his usual grey, hooded sweatshirt, a file in his hand. Hunter put the cigarette back into the pack and slipped it into his pocket.

"Tell me you have good news, Irwin," Hunter said, returning to his desk chair.

Irwin grinned as he took the unoccupied seat next to Phil. "The security system at Fat Tony's is relatively low resolution, not designed to capture detailed information like a license plate image. Or facial images, for that matter."

"But you did get the license plate," Hunter stated flatly.

"Of course." Irwin smiled again. "When I blew up the still, it was pretty fuzzy. Put it through a few filters, and I got a decent image." He handed Hunter the file, from which he removed a grainy black-and-white photograph. "It's a bit blurry, but you can make out the plate numbers fairly well.

Looks like 248 RPA3, but the 8and the R could be Bs. It's the standard Kentucky license plate."

"Nice work, Irwin. Thanks."

"A digital copy's in your email." He turned in his chair to face Phil. "You want a copy too?" he asked.

"No. I'm good."

"Oh, you better have Fat Tony save that surveillance footage," Irwin added. "Most of those systems automatically erase files after a few days."

Hunter nodded as he handed the photograph to Phil. "Can you run down the owner through DMV?"

"Will do," Phil answered. "What about the girl? Did you get an image of her?"

"Not her face. The cameras are mounted in the eaves on both sides of the front doors. She had her back to them the whole time."

"Vinnie, the bartender, confirmed that the driver of the Volkswagen was the same girl who was with Skeeter Thomas inside the bar when he watched the video with Tony and me," Hunter said. "Even though he couldn't see her face in the playback."

"You need anything else, Hunter?" Irwin asked.

"Not today. What about you, Phil?"

"No."

Irwin stood up. "Phil, I'll have your computer and telephone set up in Hunter's old office on Monday."

"Sounds good."

After Irwin left, Hunter returned to the window, cigarette in hand. "Let's divide and conquer. I want to talk with Jeff Miller's widow, see if she can link the murders of Skeeter Thomas and her husband. Call me once you've found the owner of that Volkswagen. We can meet to question her together."

"You think she's involved?" Phil asked.

"I think it's unlikely. She's probably the last person to see Skeeter Thomas alive. She may know something without even knowing she knows it."

"And Billy Ray Harper?"

"Give us something to do this afternoon," Hunter said with a wink. He cracked the casement window open, and lit a cigarette with a wooden match, taking a drag. "I'll ask Mike Wagner to bring him to the station."

Phil slipped the file with the photograph of the license plate into the black faux-leather portfolio holding his notes, closed it and raised up from the chair. "I'm off to the DMV."

Chapter Thirty-One

The O'Neils lived east of Owensboro in a grand house on the Ohio River. There was a large two-level deck projecting from the back, with a zig-zag staircase down to the river, where their classic wooden cabin cruiser was docked. Hunter parked his grey Cadillac on the cobblestone circle drive behind Ann's Range Rover, straightened his black pindot tie, and stepped to the columned portico, pushing the doorbell. A faint ring could be heard through the bronze and frosted-glass double doors. The left-side door opened, revealing Ann O'Neil wearing a beige A-line skirt and crew-neck navy-blue sweater, her light brown hair hanging loosely, barely touching her shoulders.

"Detective Hunter," she said quickly. "I assume you are here to tell me you've apprehended the man responsible for the murder of my brother-in-law."

"I'd like to speak with Mrs. Miller, if she's available," he responded.

Ann scowled, then said, "I'll see if she's free," and closed the door.

After a few moments, Eve Miller appeared in well-worn faded jeans and an oversized dark-red sweatshirt. She was without makeup, her eyes red, her hair pulled back in a ponytail. Ann stood close behind her, a visual echo of look-alike siblings. She gazed up at Hunter without speaking.

"Mrs. Miller," he started, "I'd like to ask you a few questions about Darryl Thomas."

She nodded.

"You're no doubt aware that Mr. Thomas was murdered. I understand that Mr. Thomas and your husband were friends."

Eve eye-checked her sister before replying. "Skeeter. Jeff always called him Skeeter. They were buddies in high school."

"You think the murders are connected," Ann surmised.

"When was the last time you saw Mr. Thomas?" he asked.

"The funeral home. He came by the funeral home, the evening before Jeff's funeral." Eve started to tear up. Ann produced a tissue and handed it to her.

"Did he attend the funeral?"

"I don't know. If he did, he didn't make himself known to me." She turned to Ann. "Do you remember?"

Ann shook her head.

"And before the seeing him at the funeral home, do you remember the last time you saw Mr. Thomas?"

"Several years." Eve wiped her eyes with the tissue. "We didn't exactly run in the same social circles."

"What does this have to do with Jeff's murder?" Ann asked.

"I have reason to believe the murders of Jeff Miller and Darryl Thomas were done by the same man," Hunter stated. "As they knew each other and were friends, it is likely that the killer knew both of them. You say you haven't been in touch with Mr. Thomas for several years. Is it possible your husband was in contact with him without your knowledge?"

"Skeeter occasionally would arrange financing for some of Jeff's customers, but that was all business. It's not like he was over at the house for barbeques or anything. I never saw him."

Hunter twisted the wedding band on his left ring finger. "They were friends in high school. Did they have a falling out?"

"What are you getting at, Detective?" Ann questioned. "How is this going to help you solve Jeff's murder?"

Eve glared at her sister. "No, they didn't have a falling out, as you call it. I didn't care for most of Jeff's high school friends. I always thought they were a bad influence. Before we were married, he was always running around with Skeeter and another guy, Wayne Peterson. They were always getting into trouble. I told Jeff that had to end if he wanted to be with me."

"There's a suspect for you, that Peterson guy," Ann suggested. "Rather uncivilized."

"I've spoken to Mr. Peterson. He came to the funeral home also, it that correct, Mrs. Miller?"

"Yes. And before you ask, it was the first time I'd seen him in years."

"Would there be a reason for your husband to have remained in contact with Mr. Peterson over the years?"

"Not that I'm aware."

"You said that the three of them, Thomas, Peterson, and your husband, they were always getting into trouble. What sort of trouble?"

"I heard stories, mostly." Eve shook her head. "They could be real bullies, at least in high school. And I know Jeff's mom had to pick him up from the police station a few times."

"That's not unusual, Eve," Ann interjected. She looked up to Hunter. "How many teenagers have you apprehended for being out after curfew or underage drinking?"

"You're correct. It's not unusual." Hunter stepped back from the sisters. "Thank you for your time, Mrs. Miller, Mrs. O'Neil. If you think of anything that might help in our investigation, please contact me."

Eve went back into the house, leaving Ann on the portico. She closed the door behind her. "Look, Detective Hunter. My sister's been through a lot. I don't appreciate you putting her through an interrogation about Jeff's past or his old high school pals or anything else. She's been crying nonstop for a week, she was getting better, and, well, this is just going to dig it all back up. Next time you ring this doorbell, I expect it will be to tell me you've arrested the bastard."

Hunter silently watched her disappear into the house. As he walked to his car, he whispered, "Every time I interface with that woman, I need a cigarette."

CHAPTER THIRTY-TWO

Andrea Rhoades examined the contents of the refrigerator a second time, closed the door, then opened the left door to do the same in the freezer compartment. Four ice-cream containers, all different flavors, a gelid mass of frozen peas, and several frozen dinners.

"Who eats frozen peas?" she said softly as she closed the freezer, returning to the refrigerator side to retrieve a bag of spring-mix salad, a tomato and a cucumber. After rinsing the tomato in the sink, she pulled a cutting board from the cabinet and divided the tomato into eighths. She peeled the cucumber over the open trashcan, bisected and deseeded the halves with a spoon, then chopped it into small semicircles. She tossed the lettuce, tomatoes and cucumbers in a salad bowl with large wooden tongs and placed it in the refrigerator to keep cool. She checked the clock; Katie should be awake by now. A light meal would be ready for later. Just add some ranch dressing.

She was visiting her sister. With their parents both gone, it seemed a logical place to relax for a few weeks. Katie was older by seven years, had her own three-bedroom house, and had never married. Andrea sensed that Katie was avoiding men, avoiding the dating life, maybe just avoiding life in general, preferring to work the second shift at Daviess County

General Hospital. She had told Andrea that the second shift was easier on the respiratory therapists and the pay was better. Her sister always seemed to be exhausted when she returned home around midnight. Andrea was dubious that the evenings were not as hectic as the days.

Katie emerged from the hallway in a pink terrycloth robe and sat at the round glass-top kitchen table.

"Do I smell coffee?" she asked.

"Ready for a cup?" Andrea reached to the black metal mug tree by the drip coffee pot and pulled a red one with a VW logo. She poured the coffee, added cream and a spoonful of sugar, and stirred, before handing it to her sister at the table.

Katie cradled the mug in both hands, letting it cool before drinking. "I could get used to this," she said. "It's nice having you around. Making coffee, cooking dinner."

"Speaking of which, sis, we need groceries. Mind if I drop you at work and I'll go shopping?"

"I left out chauffeur," Katie said with a grin. "Of course. Can you pick up some more black licorice?"

"Did you already eat all the licorice?"

Katie frowned. "Maybe." She started on her coffee.

"Anything else you want from the store?"

"Chips. You know, the ones with salt and pepper?"

Andrea shook her head. "Is that what you eat? Licorice, chips?"

"And chocolate-chip cookies and diet soda. It's a well-rounded diet." They both laughed.

"Cracked-pepper and sea-salt chips, yeah, I know the ones you like." Andrea got up from the table. "I made a salad for later, when you're hungry." She plucked a mug from the tree, filled it, then returned to the table. "There was another article in the *Gazette* about the River City Ripper today. Mostly a rehash of yesterday's front-pager." She sipped from her coffee mug.

"It's all everyone at the hospital can talk about." Katie stared into her coffee. "Let's go out for lunch. Let me finish my coffee and I'll hop in the shower."

"Good idea." Andrea thought about the salad she had made. Rather dull. "You want to try that sushi place by the mall?"

Katie drained her coffee. "Sounds good to me." As she was getting up from the table, the doorbell rang. "I'll get it."

"In your robe?"

"Sure, why not?" She turned to walk to the front of the house.

∞

Phil was parked on Landsdowne Road, within sight of the silver Volkswagen Beetle parked in the driveway. He had driven past, confirming the license plate, 248 RPA3. It was registered to Katie Rhoades, and it was parked at the correct address. Hunter pulled to the curb behind him. Phil got out of his car and joined Hunter, slipping into the passenger seat.

"That's the Beetle from the surveillance video," he said as he pointed down the street. "It's owned by a Katie Rhoades."

"Katie?" he asked. "Not Katherine? *Katie* is a diminutive."

"It's Katie on her driver's license." He handed Hunter a file.

He opened the file, pulling out an enlargement of her driver's license. "Hmmm. She's blonde."

"Huh?"

"She's blonde. Vinnie said the girl who was with Skeeter Thomas was a brunette. She had dark hair on the surveillance video."

"Women do change their hair color, Hunter," Phil observed.

"Usually to become blonde. Not the other way around." Hunter closed the file and handed it back to Phil. "Good work. Let's go meet Miss Rhoades."

∞

When the front door opened, they were met by Katie in her pink robe and matching pink fuzzy slippers. Hunter held up his badge to introduce themselves as he stared at her tousled blonde hair.

"Miss Katie Rhoades?" Hunter asked.

"Yes, I'm Katie Rhoades." She gazed intently at Hunter. "What's this about?"

"You are the owner of the silver Volkswagen Beetle, license plate 248 RPA3?" He pointed to the car in her driveway.

"Yes, that's the Baby Bug," she answered, raising her left eyebrow.

"Your car was seen leaving the parking lot of Fat Tony's Pizzeria Saturday night. Were you at Fat Tony's Saturday?"

Katie scrutinized the detectives. "I worked second shift on Saturday. Andie had the Baby Bug. Hang on a sec." Leaving the door open, she walked into the house. A faint and unintelligible conversation could be heard from the kitchen. Moments later, Katie returned with Andrea in tow.

"Yes?" Andrea asked.

Hunter considered her. Dark hair, pulled back into a pony tail, as Vinnie had described. She was wearing a loose-fitting long sleeve T-shirt with a Reds logo and black yoga pants.

"I'm Detective Hunter with the Owensboro Police Department. I understand you were driving Miss Rhoades's Volkswagen Saturday night."

"Why? Is there a problem, detective?"

"Please, just answer the question."

"Yes. I had the car Saturday." She looked up at Hunter, her face uncertain.

"And you are?"

"Andrea Rhoades. Katie's my sister."

Hunter glanced at Phil. "We're investigating the murder of Darryl Thomas. You were seen with Mr. Thomas on Saturday. Do you know Mr. Thomas?"

"He told me his name was Skeeter. And no, I don't know him, or didn't know him. I met him at Fat Tony's." She moved closer to her sister, slightly hiding behind the right shoulder of her taller sister.

"You didn't tell me about this," Katie said to Andrea, who shook her head.

"How did you come to meet Mr. Thomas?" Hunter asked.

"Well, I went to the bar to watch the Reds play the Cardinals. I'm a big Reds fan. I arrived after the game had started and the place was packed. This Skeeter was sitting by himself, and there was an empty chair. I asked if I could sit there to watch the game, and he said yes."

"And after the game?"

She hesitated, then looked at Katie. "Is Andie a suspect?" Katie questioned.

"What happened after the game?" Hunter probed bluntly. "When you left with Mr. Thomas."

"He invited me to his house. I followed him, but when we got there, I realized how late it was getting so I didn't stay."

"Did you go into the house?"

"Yes, but only briefly. I had to pick up Katie after her shift ended."

"She was waiting for me in the parking lot when I got off," Katie confirmed.

"Where do you work?" Phil asked.

She turned to face Phil. "At Daviess County General. I'm an RT, err, respiratory therapist."

"And what time did your shift end?"

"Eleven. But it's always around eleven thirty or so before I ever get out of there, sometimes even later."

Phil took a quick look at Hunter. "And what time did you leave the hospital last Saturday?"

She glanced at Andrea. "Closer to midnight, I think."

"Yes, it was almost midnight," Andrea said. "I had to wait for you."

Hunter scanned Andrea and Katie. "Okay. You would have left Mr. Thomas sometime soon after eleven, maybe eleven fifteen, eleven twenty, correct?" he asked.

Andrea nodded. "That sounds about right."

"What was he doing when you left him?"

"He was flipping through the sports channels to find the game recap."

"We have reason to believe that Mr. Thomas was murdered sometime Saturday night. How was he when you left the house?"

"Very much alive." She fidgeted. "He seemed like a nice guy. He was dismayed about his wife leaving him."

"And he was alone when you left for the hospital?"

"Yes."

"You said he was killed Saturday night, but it wasn't in the papers until yesterday," Katie stated. "I thought he'd been killed Wednesday or something."

"His body was found Wednesday," Phil explained.

"One other question. Do you know Jeff Miller?" Hunter looked at Andrea.

"The other man killed by the River City Ripper?" Katie asked. "I don't."

Andrea shook her head. "No, I didn't know him."

Hunter turned to Phil. "You have any questions?"

"Yes. Do you two live together?" he asked.

"No," Andrea answered. "I'm, uh, between jobs, so I'm visiting my sister for a few weeks."

Producing a card from his grey suit jacket, Hunter handed it to Andrea. "You may the last person to see Mr. Thomas alive. If you think of anything that may aid in our investigation, please contact me."

As the detectives returned to their cars, Hunter started the conversation. "If Andrea was out of the house by eleven thirty, Skeeter Thomas would then be alone. Once again, our killer knew when his victim would be isolated. Billy Ray Harper is usually done on Saturdays before midnight. He's looking guiltier with every passing hour."

Phil stopped at his car. "I agree."

Hunter leaned against the door of Phil's car. "I wonder why she didn't tell her sister that she'd met Skeeter Thomas. If you were aware that you had been with someone who was then found dead, would you not tell your own sister?"

"Maybe the time frame? The murder didn't make the news until yesterday."

"Maybe. Sisters always talk, and no doubt about the men they meet. My wife is on the phone with her sister almost daily. Seems odd that Katie didn't know about Andrea's Saturday night adventure."

"Can't answer that," Phil shrugged. "You said that Vinnie described her as not good-looking."

"Vinnie said, and I quote, 'Her face was like a five, six maybe.'" Hunter surveyed the neighborhood, then focused on the Beetle. "She seems attractive enough, although Katie is the prettier sister."

"I thought Andrea was kinda cute." Phil paused. "Did you see her man hands?"

"Were you checking her out?" Hunter asked as he regarded Phil.

"No." Phil's eyes shifted to the right. "Maybe."

Hunter smiled. "See you back at the station. Time to grill Billy Ray."

CHAPTER THIRTY-THREE

B illy Ray Harper was sitting alone in the same dull room he had occupied a week previously. The bottle of water offered to him was on the table, unopened. He checked his reflection in the two-way mirror, as if speculating about who might be watching him. He was wearing his tan custodial uniform, the sleeves rolled down, the front placket buttoned to the collar.

Phil joined Hunter, who was intently observing Billy Ray, waiting for the right moment to enter and engage Billy Ray. Hunter liked to keep a suspect waiting, let their minds fear the unknown horror of a police interrogation.

"Guess he's not thirsty," Phil said.

"Suppose not," he responded. "Showtime." He left the observation room, passing into the interrogation room, taking the chair opposite Billy Ray.

"What do you want this time, Hunter?" Billy Ray uttered through clenched teeth.

"I'm interested in the murder of Darryl Thomas, known by a nickname, Skeeter. He was murdered sometime Saturday night or Sunday. You know anything about that, Billy Ray?"

"I know he's dead." Then he added, "And I'm not exactly unhappy about it."

Hunter pointed to Billy Ray's right arm. "You mind rolling up your sleeves?"

"What?"

"Roll up your shirtsleeves."

Billy Ray slowly turned his left sleeve up, then his right, revealing both forearms. Along the inside of both were a series of parallel lines, scabbed over, surrounded by faint redness.

"Interesting thing about his murder, Billy Ray. Seems that Mr. Thomas tried to fight off his attacker." He aimed at the wounds with his right index finger. "Care to explain those injuries?"

"Happened at work," he said curtly.

Hunter leaned back in his chair. "Not from when you attacked and killed Mr. Thomas?"

Billy Ray stared at Hunter without responding.

"How did you come to have these wounds on your forearms, Billy Ray?"

"Repairing a floor buffer."

"Why don't you save us a lot of time and trouble and confess to the murders of Jeff Miller and Darryl Skeeter Thomas?" He smoothed his tie against the white shirt. "Or are you going to continue to be a burden on the taxpayers?"

Billy Ray reached for the water bottle, taking a long drink. "Ain't confessin' to a crime I didn't commit."

Hunter put his elbows on the table, his nose resting on his clasped hands. Then he raised his head slightly and said, "You must be aware that you have a motive for killing both of these men. You want to change my mind about that, then why don't you tell me something that will help me."

He considered the detective. "You said that Skeeter Thomas fought off his attacker, right?"

"Yes." He dropped his arms to the table.

"How do you know that?"

Hunter debated the response. If he revealed too many details, he might jeopardize the case. Alternatively, divulging the tissue evidence may aid in eliciting a confession. "Mr. Thomas scratched his assailant. There was tissue under his fingernails."

"And you can get DNA from that," he surmised.

"Correct." Hunter studied his face. He was blank, emotionless. "You want to give us a DNA sample?"

"If it will get you off my fucking back, yeah." He opened his mouth wide, exposing his yellowed teeth.

Hunter turned and crooked his finger at Phil through the two-way mirror.

∞

Amos Weller and Keith Embry were sitting in Hunter's office when he returned from questioning Billy Ray Harper. Hunter closed the door as he entered, walking to a coatrack in the corner.

"I didn't anticipate seeing both of you today," he said as he pulled off his grey suit jacket, placing it on a wooden hanger, and hooking the hanger on the rack. He then adjusted the holster on his left shoulder, resecuring the Glock handgun.

"Why are you harassing Billy Ray, Bob?" Amos asked.

"I'm not harassing him, Amos. He was brought in for questioning." He sat in the desk chair, facing them.

"In the murder of Darryl Thomas? He didn't do it." Amos shook his head. "He didn't leave the house Saturday night."

"What about Sunday? Or Sunday night?" Hunter questioned. "The time of death cannot be confidently confirmed. He could have committed the murder Sunday as easily as Saturday."

Amos grimaced. "Can't be certain about Sunday."

"He has motive, undoubtedly has opportunity, and the knowledge. One can only hypothesize what he learned in Eddyville." He leaned back in the chair. "And he has marks on his forearms where Skeeter Thomas tried to fight him off. He claims the wounds are from repairing some equipment."

"What motive?" Embry asked. "What reason does Billy Ray Harper have to kill this Skeeter Thomas?"

"Darryl Skeeter Thomas was in the car driven by Jeff Miller that killed his younger sister, Jenny Lynn Harper," Amos answered, turning to Embry. "Happened before your time, Keith."

"Didn't know he had a sister," Embry stated.

"Oh yes, there was one," Hunter replied.

"Bob, you still haven't got enough to hold him," Embry said. "If you're not going to charge him, let him go."

"He's working tonight," Amos added. "Billy Ray is not going to miss his shift with Craig because of your theories. I'm taking him home, now." Amos stood up.

"He's still in the interrogation room. Phil was getting an oral swab for DNA." Hunter said. "Go ahead. Not much else for me to do, and you're right, Keith, I haven't enough to hold him. Yet."

"DNA?" Amos asked.

"Tissue under the fingernails of our victim. Looking for a match. I get a match, Billy Ray gets a one-way bus ticket back to Eddyville."

"I'm going with you," Embry said as he joined Amos leaving in the office.

Hunter opened the casement window and lit a cigarette. Billy Ray was more than eager to offer a DNA sample. *Maybe he is innocent. There is a link between Jeff Miller and Skeeter Thomas I haven't exposed*, he thought. Wayne Peterson knew both of the victims, knew them well. It is likely that he would have known that Skeeter had dextrocardia. But he doesn't have a motive. Trevor Reed may not even know who else was in Jill Miller's Mercedes when the accident occurred. He doesn't have a motive either. Miller and Thomas were friends in high school, as was Wayne Peterson. Maybe the connection is old. Someone who knew Miller and Thomas. And that someone knew Skeeter Thomas had his heart on the wrong side.

"I'm missing something," he said softly. He finished the cigarette, crushing the end into the ash tray. *If the killer didn't know about the dextrocardia, he would have needed to recognize that at the time of the murder. Dr. Turner didn't think that was likely. I need another opinion.*

He reached into his hanging suit jacket and pulled out his phone. He called Louis Mercier, who answered on the third ring.

"Hey, bubba. Catch you at a good time?" Hunter asked.

"Yes. I'm done for the day. Just sitting in the OR lounge listening to the surgeons whine about next week's schedule," Mercier replied. "What's up?"

"I want to bounce something off you. Want to meet me for a beer, say, in about an hour?" he asked.

"Sure. Where?"

"O'Sullivan's Pub. It's on Second Street, opened a few years ago. You can't miss it."

"See you there." He ended the call. As Hunter slipped the phone back into his jacket, Phil entered the office.

"They're gone. I walked the oral swab over to ECU already." He sat down. "Amos looked pretty pissed."

"He thinks I'm going after the wrong man." Hunter said as he returned to his desk chair.

"Oh, by the way, Trevor Reed called me back. Says he knew Mr. Thomas was in the car with Jeff Miller. And that he was in the ER Saturday night." He pulled a notepad from his pocket. "His wife had false labor. Thought the baby was coming early."

"So, Trevor is probably not our killer," Hunter concluded.

"What if he is?" Phil questioned. "His alibi doesn't entirely clear him."

"Doesn't make sense, Phil. He has a lot to lose—his marriage, a family with a second child on the way. And why now? Why would he seek vengeance now?" He shook his head. "He's cleaner than a nun's browser history."

"Hear me out, Hunter, okay? Trevor Reed harbors his anger until Billy Ray Harper is out on parole. Why? So he can murder Jeff Miller and Skeeter Thomas while deflecting attention. He even comes into the station to speak with you, giving you the target in the case you were lacking. Harper. And he even provides Harper's motive. He's had a decade to sort out the details, years to plan the perfect murders. We've got blinders on, focusing on Harper. All the while, Reed is knocking off his former classmates in plain sight."

Hunter leaned back in his chair. "Good points. Let's say that you're right, that Trevor Reed is the River City Ripper. We know Thomas was murdered sometime after Andrea Rhodes left his house Saturday. That leaves the Saturday night and Sunday. He was dead by Monday morning.

The Saturday–Sunday time frame fits with the condition of his corpse and his absence from the bank starting Monday. Could Reed get to Skeeter Thomas's house without detection? Without his wife's knowledge?"

"I don't see why not," he answered.

"I'm not convinced." Hunter tapped the desktop with his fingers. "Of course, it should be pursued."

Phil looked at his watch, then stood up from the chair. "I'll question him. Reed should be home soon."

"Harper, Reed. We're a bit short on suspects."

"Maybe it's someone we haven't discovered yet," Phil offered.

"We know the murders are connected, definitely done by the same man. The assailant also knew when both Jeff Miller and Skeeter Thomas would be alone. He must know both of them. Leaving the knife in the chest, sending a message." Hunter shook his head. "What's the message, and to whom is it being sent? If the DNA exonerates Billy Ray Harper, and Trevor Reed's not our man, we're a long way from solving this case."

CHAPTER THIRTY-FOUR

Phil parked on the street in front of the Reed's house, a white-brick two story with an attached two-car garage. A child's plastic tricycle, with an oversize front wheel, was parked on the front walk. The concrete driveway was empty.

The door was answered by a very pregnant, very barefoot Robin Reed. Phil could hear the faint jingle of a children's television program from some distant room. Before he could finish a sentence, she asked, "Is Trevor a suspect?"

"Mrs. Reed, I'm just following up on some questions involving the recent murders in Owensboro. Is Mr. Reed at home?"

"No, he's not home from work yet." She moved forward into the door frame. Phil slid back slightly on the small concrete porch. "Do you want to come back later?"

"I can, but in the meantime, do you mind if I ask you a few questions now?" he asked.

Robin pursed her lips, then said, "Okay."

"I understand that you were in the emergency room Saturday. Is that correct?"

"Yes. We thought R Two was coming." She patted her pregnant abdomen. "What's this have to do with Trevor?"

"We're just trying to establish a timeline." Phil pulled out his notepad. "What time were you released from the ER?"

"Sometime after nine, I suppose. We were home in time for Trevor to watch the ten o'clock news."

He wrote a note on the pad. "Did you watch the news with Trevor?"

She shook her head. "No. I was wiped out. I put our daughter to bed, then crawled into bed myself."

"Any idea at what time your husband joined you in the bedroom?"

She peered closely at Phil. "Are you sure my husband is not a suspect?"

He looked up from the notepad. "Like I said, we're establishing a timeline."

"Well, I have to get up to pee about every hour, it seems. I'm not sure when Trevor came to bed."

"Okay," Phil said. He checked his notes. "And Sunday. Were you at home Sunday?"

"Seems to me you're fishing for information." She crossed her arms over her protuberant abdomen.

"Can you answer the question, Mrs. Reed?" he asked.

"Trevor was at his brother's house most of Sunday. They're renovating the kitchen, and Trevor was helping him. He was gone most of the day, but home for dinner. Is that all you need, Detective?"

"You've been very helpful. Thanks." He closed his pad. "Just one more thing. Did you know Jeff Miller or Darryl Thomas? Darryl was known by a nickname, Skeeter."

"No. I know of them, and I know about the accident Trevor was in when he was in high school. But I never met either of them."

"Thank you, Mrs. Reed. Have a good evening."

Robin closed the door firmly without a word.

Back in his car, Phil called Hunter as he pulled away from the curb. As Hunter answered, he simply declared, "I spoke with Trevor's wife, Robin Reed. His alibi's pretty weak."

CHAPTER THIRTY-FIVE

O'Sullivan's Pub was slowly filling with Owensboro's downtown workers, who were starting the weekend early. The high-back stools at the long wooden bar were all occupied, and several people were standing nearby, most engaged in lively conversations. Louis Mercier chose an empty table by the window, as far from the bar gathering as the pub's space allowed. He ordered, pulled out a paperback, and waited for Hunter.

"Reading in a pub?" Hunter said as he took the chair opposite Mercier. "You've spent too much time at the university."

Mercier put the book away. "Didn't know how long you'd be." He studied Hunter's dark-grey suit. "Your sartorial tastes have definitely changed to the ascetic. You always wear a suit?"

"Mostly, yes. Detectives wear suits. At least, they should." He looked over Mercier's navy blazer, blue oxford-cloth shirt and chino trousers. "If you had on a navy-and-white striped tie, you'd still be wearing our high school uniform."

"Well, I spend most of my life in OR scrubs." He waved to the waitress, who hurried to the table.

"A pint for my buddy," he ordered.

"Same thing?" she asked.

"Yes, please," he answered before Hunter could respond.

After the waitress left, Hunter sighed. "I want to talk about these murders."

"You looking for a confession?" Mercier smiled.

"Well, bubba, if you would just confess, it would be good for my career, and save me a lot of trouble."

Mercier put his forearms on the table, palms up. "You caught me. I confess. I'm the River City Ripper."

"Don't tempt me. I'm short on suspects."

The frosted mug of beer arrived. Hunter inspected the reddish-brown liquid, sipped, then asked, "What am I drinking?"

"Irish red ale," explained Mercier. "This is an Irish pub."

"It's pretty good." He took another drink, then set the mug down on the table. "I assume you've read the papers about these murders."

"Correct."

"I need to provide some details that are not public–only known to some of the officers and Brenda. And the killer, of course. You'll need to keep quiet."

"Not a problem," Mercier replied.

"To start, both murders were committed with a knife used by Navy SEALs."

"I have one of those, Bob. A Ka-Bar. I could still be the River City Ripper."

"Be serious, will you?" Hunter scowled.

"Okay, so you're looking for a Navy SEAL, or a retired one, or another ex-military type. Right?"

"No. The particular tactical knife that was used is available at most hunting retailers. And here's one of the interesting bits. The knifes were left in the chests of both victims, sending a message."

Mercier twisted his mouth. "Hmmm. Sounds like you need a psychiatric opinion on that. Revenge killing? Some warped personal vendetta?"

"That's one of my theories. Jeff Miller and Darryl Thomas were friends in high school, but had drifted apart, from what I can determine. I'm convinced the killer knew both of them, and likely knew them well. What I need to talk with you about is the second murder, the murder of Darryl Thomas. Oh, and everyone apparently called him Skeeter."

"Skeeter? You would hope to outgrow a childhood nickname like that," Mercier observed.

"No kidding. Here's where you come in. Skeeter Thomas had dextrocardia."

"Just dextrocardia, or were there other anomalies?" He pulled the mug to his lips.

"He had situs inversus totalis."

"Wow. That's pretty rare. I've only seen it three, maybe four times."

"Exactly what Jean Turner said. She'd only seen one case in medical school."

"Remember, I was at a university medical center. We saw all the rarities."

Hunter nodded. "True. She also said that he would have known it, and his doctors, probably his family, close friends, that sort of thing."

"Makes sense. If you had situs inversus, you'd want people to know."

"Why?" Hunter picked up the mug.

"Think about this. You know how people with certain diseases and allergies wear medical-alert bracelets? So that in an emergency, a physician or other healthcare provider knows in advance? Say you had dextrocardia, and were in a car accident. You're taken to the ER and if the ER doc doesn't know, he'll freak out and do something stupid, like they usually do."

Hunter laughed. "Like they usually do?"

"Most ER docs are, well, you know what they call the person who graduates last from the worst medical school in the country?"

Hunter smirked. "This is a posteriori knowledge?"

"More like a priori, Bob." Mercier lifted his mug for a long swig.

"Back to Skeeter Thomas. Tell me more about situs inversus."

"You said he had situs inversus totalis? All the organs reversed?"

"Yes. Why?" Hunter asked.

"Well, there can be incomplete forms of situs inversus. Some, but not all of the organs are reversed, and some may be incompletely formed, or malformed. Those patients can have multiple medical problems related to their congenital anomalies, but each one is different, as the malformations tend to be very case specific. Meaning, it depends on which organs are formed correctly, just in mirror image, and which are misshapen."

"His was total. Heart was on the right, liver on the left, complete mirror image, according to Jean."

Mercier sipped more of his beer. "In that case, you would not expect him to have any medical issues."

"Jean said that. Why?"

"The organs function normally. They're just reversed." He paused for a moment to collect his thoughts. "Think about it this way—ten percent of the population is left-handed. Now, lefties do everything righties do, except they do it backward. Lefties bat from the wrong side of the plate. Left-handed quarterbacks put a counter-clockwise spiral on the football, righties a clockwise spin."

Hunter made a passing motion with his right arm. "Okay."

"That's why when we played football in high school, I always preferred the plays in which I would line up on the right side of the line. I could then run a pattern that would cross the field from right to left, from your perspective as the quarterback. The clockwise spiral of the ball—"

"It would spin right into your chest," Hunter interrupted. "Yeah. If I was left-handed, you want to run from left to right."

"Yep. Although I never played with a southpaw quarterback."

The waitress returned to the table, her hands filled with laminated menus. "Appetizers are half-off during happy hour."

"I'll take a look," Mercier said. "Thanks."

"Happy hour ends at six." She handed each of them a menu and continued to the other tables.

Mercier started to look over the menu. Hunter set it down without looking.

"Another thing bugging me, Louis—there were three shallow wounds on the left chest which Jean called hesitation marks. Made me wonder if the killer started to stab Skeeter Thomas in the left chest, where the heart should be, then switched to the right chest."

"See those in suicides. They're self-inflicted superficial wounds, made before the final cut that causes death. This guy didn't commit suicide, Bob. You may be right in that the killer hesitated, then realized he needed to stab the right chest to get his heart."

"Which brings up the next question—if you were about to stab someone in the chest, how would you know if they had dextrocardia?"

"Unless you knew it beforehand, you wouldn't look." Mercier replied. "You talking about a condition that is seen in less than a hundredth of a percent of the population. I'll bet most people don't even know it exists."

"Humor me. How would you determine if the intended victim had a right-sided heart? Jean said something about feeling for the pulse of the heart on the chest."

"PMI. Point of maximal impulse. Found by palpating the precordium." Mercier shook his head. "Bob, that exam technique requires a certain level of medical knowledge and has to be taught. I can't even do it reliably. I seriously doubt a nonclinician could read about it or find some video on the internet and successfully palpate PMI to ascertain the presence of dextrocardia. And certainly not in the midst of an endorphin-enhanced act of murder."

Hunter stared at his half-full beer. "So, the killer had to know."

"Would be my opinion. Had to know Skeeter had dextrocardia."

"Thanks." Hunter lifted the mug, draining the remaining beer. "By the way, Brenda really liked Carmen."

Mercier smiled. "She's a nice girl. I'm seeing her again tomorrow."

"Not tonight?"

"She's working." Mercier finished his beer. "And you, what do you think about Carmen?"

"I think she's too tall for you, bubba."

"And I think I'll have another pint." He picked up the menu. "You want to try the Reuben Rolls?"

CHAPTER THIRTY-SIX

The office conversion in Lewisport was still behind schedule. Wayne spent Saturday making overtime, laying floor tiles in what was to become the patients' restroom. By midafternoon, the crew was done for the day. He drove Earl home and met Arlene at his townhouse. Arlene had offered to accompany him to the Fulkerson Funeral Home for Skeeter's visitation, so Wayne accepted. He pulled two cans of beer from the refrigerator, handed one to her, then headed upstairs gulping the other one.

His back was sore; the shower helped as he aimed the hot stream at his lower spine. He walked downstairs to the kitchen with a towel wrapped around his waist, his hair still wet. Arlene was seated at the kitchen island, a slim cigarette in her hand, the ash glowing with a faint spiral of smoke arising from it.

"I know this sounds silly, but what should I wear to the funeral home?" he asked her.

She gazed up at him. "You look pretty good like that," she smiled. "Put that on later, willya?"

He chuckled. "If you play your cards right."

"It's not silly. You're going to pay your respects to an old friend, Wayne. Don't you have some nice slacks? A shirt with a collar that doesn't have some construction company's name on it?"

"Okay. I can do that." He peered at the island. "What are you doing?"

"Looking at your high school yearbook." She picked up the album to show him. "You've got several nice pictures in here. I found one with you and Skeeter. Oh, and I love that prom picture with the burgundy tuxedo." She smirked. "Not."

"I proposed to Karla in that tux," he said as he returned to the second floor.

"We see how well that turned out," she responded as she continued to flip pages in the yearbook.

∞

Dorothy Thomas was a short, chubby woman, with short silver-grey hair and round cheeks. She stood at the foot of her son's casket in her best maroon dress. Her husband, Rodney, his navy suit hanging on his tall, thin frame, was next to her. Behind was their eldest son, Rodney Junior, known as Rod, who was even taller than his father. Noticeably absent was Tracy Thomas. Being the matriarch of the Thomas family, Dorothy had taken charge when they met with the funeral director on Friday. She decided on the arrangements, picked out the casket and set the visitation and funeral times when Tracy had failed to show up for their appointment with Todd Fulkerson, funeral director and direct descendant of the founder, Zacharias Fulkerson.

Rod had spent the morning pulling old photographs from shoeboxes in his parents' hall closet to create a collage of Skeeter's life on a twenty-four-by-thirty-six-inch poster board.

He had even found a yellowed third-place ribbon from some long-ago science fair. It was positioned near the head of the open casket, alongside a standing wreath of red-and-yellow flowers, the Owensboro South High School colors.

Bank colleagues, friends from high school, and some of Dorothy and Rodney's neighbors had dropped by and said a few nice words while avoiding the details of the murder. No one seemed to be aware of the missing wife, Tracy, or at least they hadn't asked about her. The room was lightly filled when Arlene and Wayne arrived.

They made their way through to the Thomas family and the casket. Wayne walked directly to Dorothy Thomas. She spoke before he could utter a word.

"Well, Wayne Peterson. It sure has been a long time since I've seen you." She pulled him in with a motherly hug. His eyes teared; his throat was dry.

"I'm so sorry about Skeeter," he finally mumbled as she released him.

"I'm sure going to miss him."

Wayne stepped back to Arlene's side, then introduced her to Mr. and Mrs. Thomas.

Rodney Thomas offered his hand. "Thanks for coming," he said.

"I'm so sorry for you," she uttered softly. She then looked up to Rod. "You must be Skeeter's big brother. Wayne told me all about you. How you were the star of the basketball team, took the Bulldogs to state when him and Skeeter were freshmen."

Rod smiled. "I would have thought by now everyone had forgotten about that."

"Arlene, you have to see the pictures Rodney Junior put together." She pointed at the collage. "There's some of Wayne, and some with Wayne and Jeff Miller. They were big pals back in high school."

She took Arlene's hand and walked along the front of the casket to the collage. Wayne followed, his right hand gently sliding along the smooth, dark wood of the casket's concave ogee. He stopped at the head to take one last look at Skeeter Thomas. His blond hair was neatly combed back, revealing his pale, gaunt face. On his chest, his long, thin fingers were intertwined, clasping his steel-rimmed glasses.

After pointing out a few pictures, Dorothy peered at Wayne. "I know you and Skeeter drifted apart over the years. I really appreciate you coming." She glanced at Arlene. "You and Arlene should drop by for dinner sometime. I'd love to see you."

"You still put a hard-boiled egg in your meatloaf?" Wayne asked.

She smiled. "Sure do."

Arlene and Wayne sat down on the end of a row of folding chairs in the middle of the room. She reached across his thigh to hold his hand. He dabbed at his eyes with a tissue she had handed him.

"We wait a while, then you walk up to Mrs. Thomas, give her a big hug," she said. "Then, we go have dinner, take me back to your place, and take me home." She squeezed his hand. "If you know what I mean."

Wayne looked down without responding. When he looked up, Rod was standing next to Arlene's chair.

"Wayne, mind if we talk for a minute?" he asked.

Arlene stood up quickly. "I gotta go to the bathroom. I'll leave you boys alone."

Rod took her vacated seat. "What do you think about this River City Ripper? Any idea why both Jeff and Skeeter been killed?"

"No idea." Wayne shook his head. "Some detective came by my house the other day. I got the sense they don't have a clue. Asked me if I'd killed them."

"Mom said that you and Skeeter didn't really hang out anymore. When was the last time you saw him?"

"Here. I saw him at Jeff Miller's viewing." He scratched his chin. "Before that, I'm not sure. Been a long time." He stared at the casket. "I can't believe Skeeter's gone. Wish we'd stayed in touch."

"People change, they move on," Rod said. "We're not the same individuals we were in high school."

"Yeah, well, too late now." He wiped tears with a tissue.

"Thanks for coming, Wayne. I know Mom and Dad really appreciate it." He awkwardly leaned forward, up and out of the chair, then clasped Wayne's shoulder. "Take care of yourself." Rod walked to the back of the room to speak with another cluster of visitors.

Arlene returned, grasped Wayne's hand, and said, "Time to go hug Mrs. Thomas."

∞

Wayne reached for the lamp on the bedside table, turning it on. Arlene was sitting on the edge of the bed, her back to him.

"What're you doing?" he asked.

"Putting on my clothes," she replied.

"Why?" He rolled to face her, propping his head on his right hand.

"I'm going home. I can't stay the night."

"Why do you always leave?"

"I'm more comfortable at home." She tipped back on the bed to kiss him. "Don't take it personally."

Completed redressed, she made for the bedroom door. "Let's do this again next week, only without the funeral home."

Wayne listened to her heels click down the stairs, then on the hardwood floor of the hallway. The door opened, followed by a clunk as it closed and then locked.

He turned off the lamp and lay on his back in the darkness of his bedroom, the only light a faint red glow from the digital alarm clock on the bedside table. He thought about seeing Skeeter Thomas in a casket, and Jeff Miller in a casket. He wouldn't miss them, not really; their paths had diverted long ago. Maybe if he had a second chance, they would have remained close. No second chance, not with Jeff or Skeeter.

The doorbell rang. Wayne sprung from the bed. "Arlene changed her mind," he said excitedly.

Still in his boxer shorts, he took the stairs two steps at a time, and threw open the door.

"You're not Arlene," he said to the stranger on the front step.

CHAPTER THIRTY-SEVEN

Mere blocks from the modest downtown of Whitesville, the procession turned from Walnut Street into the main entrance of Whitesville Memorial Gardens. Fulkerson Funeral Home's black hearse and matching six-door limousine was followed by a string of purple-and-white funeral-flag bearing cars. Hunter had taken the back entrance on Main Street and parked the family minivan nearby. He walked through the grass to the edge of a tree line from where he could discretely watch the graveside ceremony.

He finished his cigarette and waited for the procession to halt. He pulled out his deer-hunting 10x42 binoculars and scanned the series of vehicles. One of the funeral directors opened the tail door of the hearse as several men poured out of cars, meeting up to pull the casket. Once out and on a carrier, the men towed Skeeter Thomas toward a small canopy tent by an open grave. Dorothy and Rodney Thomas were escorted from the six-door limousine, along with a tall young man who resembled Skeeter; Hunter assumed he was the older brother. Sergio Perez emerged from the next car, walked around the front to the passenger side, and opened the door for Tracy Thomas. He suddenly peeked over the roof in Hunter's direction, scanning the tree line.

"Should have worn camo," Hunter whispered as he moved behind a tree trunk. After Tracy and Sergio were turned toward the tent, he resumed his surveillance. He wasn't really sure for what he was looking. He just had a hunch, really, that the killer would show up at the funeral. Like how an arsonist will often remain to watch the building burn. Although he was convinced of Billy Ray Harper's guilt, he had been a detective long enough to know that such conclusions could turn out to be incorrect. He felt that the case for Trevor Reed's guilt was less substantial, despite the convictions of his new associate, Phil. A third suspect just might be here.

He viewed each of the mourners as they walked from the cars, but was not always able to see faces. The gravel path through the cemetery on which the procession was parked was between the trees and the gravesite. They were moving away from Hunter.

The line of chairs for the Thomas family was opposite Skeeter's casket, with a small lectern at the head, to Hunter's left. He watched as the family was seated. Then the minister spoke briefly; Hunter was too distant to hear anything. The minister finished, moved to Tracy, then to Dorothy and Rodney Thomas. Some grievers lined up to speak to the family, others started to leave. Hunter trained his binoculars on them, better able to see their faces on their return trip. A few faces seemed familiar—bank employees he had seen in the conference room Thursday morning, including the young woman in the yellow dress, now clothed in black and wearing oversized, oval black sunglasses. They all seemed to have equally blank looks. Some exchanged a few words; others went straight to their waiting autos.

A slight curve in the cemetery road to the Main Street exit allowed Hunter one last view of the mourners as the refilled cars left Skeeter's final resting place. As Sergio drove out of the cemetery, he once again examined the trees where Hunter was standing. His curiosity must have been satisfied, as he continued to the exit without slowing.

Nothing seemed out of place among the funeral-goers, nothing new learned, Hunter thought. If the River City Ripper had been amidst the mourning family and friends, he had not revealed himself.

CHAPTER THIRTY-EIGHT

When he relocated from Louisville to Owensboro, Alan Maddox had wanted two things: a quieter life and space. His former neighborhood in the old part of Louisville was filled with majestic shade trees, restored Victorian mansions and quaint restaurants within walking distance. And it was space deficient. Like many older areas, each house sat close to the next one, and the yards were tiny. Cars lined the leafy streets, as garage space was lacking. Maddox had found his space and his place—five acres southwest of town. He built a modest three-bedroom ranch with an oversized garage to accommodate his collection of woodworking equipment.

Maddox had always been a runner, three miles most days, until he was sidelined by his recent operation. He still had the runner's look—tall and thin with a mop of greying hair. He was on the wooden deck, sitting in the umbrella's shade at a teak outdoor dining table, wearing plaid shorts and a golf shirt, and reading a fishing magazine when Hunter arrived.

"Thanks for letting me drop by," Hunter said.

"You're welcome anytime, Bob." Maddox pointed to an empty chair. "How are you managing as the new chief detective?"

"Borderline." He sat down, removing his sunglasses. "How's the new hip?"

Maddox aimed his index finger at the cane leaning against the chair's arm. "Not ready to give this up yet. I think my marathon days are over. And I'm damn glad I didn't build a two-story house. Stairs are wicked."

His wife appeared through the sliding glass patio door, carrying an opened beer bottle. "Hello, Bob. So nice to see you."

"Thanks, June," Hunter replied. "How're you enjoying Alan's retirement?"

She laughed as she handed the beer to her husband. "It'll be better when the doctor lets him drive again. You thirsty? Ready for a cold one?"

Hunter looked at his watch. "Sure, sounds good."

"Stay seated. I'll be right back." She returned to the house.

Maddox took a sip and then set his beer bottle on the table. "I wasn't ignoring your calls, Bob. We were at my sister's cabin on Lake Barkley. She doesn't have a land line, and there's no cell phone reception. I didn't know you'd called until yesterday when we drove home. I must have had a million voicemails."

"How was the fishing?"

"The fish population of Lake Barkley was not endangered in any way," he said with a chuckle. "You didn't come here to talk about my angling adventures. This River City Ripper case bugging you?"

"I think I've got a serial killer on my hands. I know it's only two murders, but the pattern is suggestive. I'd like to stop him before there's more."

"Okay. Walk me through the cases."

June reappeared with a beer for Hunter and an ash tray, which she sat on the table. He thanked her, swallowed some of the cold liquid, then leaned back in the chair to sketch the details to Maddox. Maddox remained silent while Hunter provided the summary.

"So, let's look at the consistencies," Maddox said. "Both men were likely murdered on Saturday nights, late. Both were home alone. Why would the killer pick Saturday nights?"

"Less likely to be seen. Both Miller and Thomas lived in quiet neighborhoods. The choice of weapon, a knife, is silent compared to the blast of a handgun. No reason for any of the neighbors to be alerted."

Maddox nodded. "I agree with you. The murderer had to know them well enough to know that both Miller and Thomas would be alone on those Saturdays. In Thomas's case, he lived alone, so that's not particularly useful. Miller, on the other hand, was married. Your killer knew his wife was going to be out of town."

"That's what I've concluded. In addition, the killer had to know about Skeeter Thomas having dextrocardia, from what I can determine." Hunter downed some of the beer. "He would not have been able to determine that at the time of the murder."

"Add in the fact that these men knew each other, high school buddies, but had not been in close social contact for years, and I think you've got to go back to high school. Leaving the murder weapon in their chest, sending a message—that's a serial-killer characteristic."

Hunter pulled a pack of cigarettes from his pocket and lit one, taking a long drag. "Holding a grudge for some recondite reason for years."

"Fits with the pattern. Had plenty of time to plan."

"Hence the dearth of clues," Hunter added.

"Bob, there's more than you think. When there's crime, there's clues. Just keep looking." He paused to take a drink of beer. "I was in a running club in Louisville with an FBI agent, Kurt Nelson. Ran the marathon with him last year in Lexington. He's had some experience with serial killers. I'll get his number for you. Give him a call tomorrow, run it past Kurt. They may be interested."

"Even though it's two murders, and not three?"

"FBI considers two or more, so what you're seeing fits their definition."

"Got it." Hunter drew on the cigarette, then exhaled slowly. "That leads me to another subject. How familiar are you with a car accident involving Jeff Miller and Skeeter Thomas? Miller was a teenager, drunk driver, and a young girl died when she was ejected from the other car. Jenny Lynn Harper was her name."

Maddox sighed and reached for his beer, which he finished.

"Jenny Harper's big brother is Billy Ray Harper." Hunter studied Maddox's blank face. "He was released on parole from Eddyville last month."

Maddox ran his fingers through his salt-and-pepper hair. "Shit."

"So, you do know about it."

"I know all about it, Bob. How did you find out?"

"Chief Hartmann filled me in. He has secret files locked in his desk and has kept track of all the persons involved." Hunter puffed at the cigarette. "I'd always thought of him as more of a kakistocrat who got in the way than a proper policeman."

"Before Hartmann became a brown-nosing ass kisser, he was a good detective, Bob."

"Tell me what happened that night." Hunter crushed the cigarette in the ashtray, replacing it with the beer bottle.

"I knew this would haunt us someday," he grumbled.

"Exactly what Hartmann said."

"The crash was on Calhoun Road. Neighbor heard the crash, ran out to take a look, saw a body on the hood of the car, so he runs back into the house to call 911. One of the uniforms recognized the Mercedes, knew it belonged to Jill Miller. He called the chief."

"Wade Elkins was chief back then, right?" Hunter asked.

"Yes. So, Elkins drives over, calls Hartmann and me on his way, vehicular homicide. And it's Jill Miller's kid. Only child, mind you." He looked at the empty beer bottle. "I need another beer."

Hunter stood up. "I'll get it." He slid the patio door open, called for June, then walked into the kitchen, returning with two bottles.

After taking a long drink, Maddox continued. "The cars were a mess, both obviously totaled. Jenny Harper was lying on the hood of a, uh, I think it was an older Oldsmobile coupe. She was barely alive when I got there, but as you are aware, she died later at the hospital. Miller and his buddies were sloshed. Trevor Reed, Jenny's date, he was sober. Elkins confirmed Jeff was Jill Miller's son, then walked out of ear's reach and made a call to Jill, I assume. Next thing I know, he's standing in the middle of the crime scene. They were all taken to the emergency room. The rear-seat occupants in Miller's car were injured. I can't recall the specific injuries."

Hunter filled in the information. "Trevor Reed, Jeff Miller, and Skeeter Thomas were uninjured. The others,

Wayne Peterson and Elroy Beggs, were in the rear seat of the Mercedes. They sustained injuries, probably because they were unbelted." He took a drink from the beer bottle. "Miller, Thomas, and Peterson went to Owensboro South High School together, as did Trevor Reed and Jenny Harper. Beggs was Peterson's neighbor."

"Yeah, that sounds right. Anyway, Elkins pulls the memory chips out of the ECU rats' cameras and crushed them on the asphalt under the heel of his cowboy boot. Then he informs everyone that this accident is to be kept quiet and if anyone reveals what actually happened, not only will they be fired, he will make it his life mission to blackball them from every police force in North America."

Hunter shook his head. "Explains why I don't remember it."

"That's exactly what the Fulkerson family wanted. Jill Miller got her way. And the great-grandson of three-time former mayor Bruce Fulkerson got away with murder."

"They circumvented the entire judicial system."

"Sure did." Maddox stared at the bottle of beer. "You're convinced Billy Ray Harper did this?"

"Yes. He has motive, has opportunity, and certainly has the knowledge. I don't think it's a coincidence that he's out on parole and the next thing that happens is the driver of the car who took his sister's life is murdered. The next murder is an occupant of the same car." Hunter twisted the bottle in his right hand, then took a long drink.

"I can't argue with that, Bob, I can only say that it seems a bit too obvious."

"Like Harper is being framed?"

"No, more like you're digging in the wrong place. Step back, keep looking. I think there's more to this high school connection than you're seeing." He downed some more beer. "I wouldn't be in a rush to arrest Harper. Not just yet. Wait for the DNA. It matches, you're good to go."

Maddox leaned back in his chair. "And call Kurt Nelson."

CHAPTER THIRTY-NINE

The sun was beginning to reach the horizon, casting a warm glow over Owensboro, when Earl Cravens pulled his F-250 into Wayne Peterson's driveway. The townhouse was dark, like the other townhouses on Goetz Drive. Wayne was not on the front step waiting, as usual. Earl turned off the diesel engine and climbed down out of the lifted truck.

"Better not be hung over again, Wayne," he hissed.

Earl listed to the faint chimes after ringing the doorbell. No movement inside, no lights being turned on. He pulled out his cellphone to illuminate the keypad of the front-entry lock and punched in the four-digit code. Swinging open the door, he reached inside for the wall switches.

"Wayne, get your ass outta bed," he bellowed into the townhouse as he found the wall switch, flipping it up.

As the front room came to light, Earl shuddered. Wayne was laying in the middle of the floor in a pool of blood. The black handle of a knife was poking out of his left side. He knew Wayne was dead.

Earl remained standing the doorway, frozen, trying to grasp what he was seeing. He remembered that on the police shows on television there was always this issue about disturbing the crime scene, whatever that meant. He didn't move into the room. Leaving the lights on, he closed the door and stepped back to his truck before calling 911.

∞

Brenda Hunter was not quite awake when the bedside telephone rang. She answered with a groggy, "Hello."

The caller introduced himself as an Owensboro policeman, apologized for waking her, and asked for Detective Hunter. She walked into the bathroom to find her husband still in the shower.

"Bob, they need you on the phone," she said over the racket of the streaming water.

"What?" He cracked open the frosted-glass shower door, peering through the gap.

"The phone. You're wanted on the phone."

He turned off the water, moved out of the shower, and pulled a towel around his waist. Sitting on the bed, he picked up the corded handset.

"Hunter," he said into the mouthpiece. After a few moments, he said, "I know the address. I'll be there," and replaced the handset on the receiver.

"What's up, Bob?"

"Murder number three." He rubbed his right hand against his still-wet forehead. "I need to stop this villain before he claims victim number four."

"You sure it's the same guy?" Brenda moved to sit next to Bob.

"Yes. It's the River City Ripper. His trademark knife was left in the chest. He's struck thrice now."

"Thrice?"

"*Thrice*. Three times is thrice, although it's not commonly used."

"What's four times?" Brenda asked.

"I don't think there is a numeral adverb for 'four times' in English. Good question for Dad. Hopefully, I won't need to know."

"Get dressed, honey. You're getting the sheets wet." She kissed him on the cheek. "I'll go start coffee."

CHAPTER FORTY

There were two patrol cars in front of Wayne Peterson's townhouse, with the ECU van backed into the driveway behind and blocking a lifted Ford F-250 pickup truck. Otherwise, the street seemed to still be asleep. A few windows were glowing in the row of townhouses, cars still in driveways, no curious neighbors nosing about.

"Last one to the party," Hunter said as he parked his Cadillac behind Dr. Turner's car. He started to the entry as Mike Wagner exited the front door, joining him on the short concrete walkway.

"It's the same guy, Hunter. Looks just like the other crimes."

"You're here early," Hunter observed.

"Relieved the night shift," Mike answered. "How's Phil working out? Tough to lose him as a partner. We've worked together for four years."

Hunter studied Mike. "You blew the exam on purpose, didn't you?"

"I like being in uniform."

"Like your father."

"Yes, like my father," Mike reiterated. "I'll fill you in."

"Let me guess. The neighbors saw nothing," Hunter declared. "Wayne Peterson was last seen sometime Saturday afternoon or evening."

"Close. He was seen leaving around six with a woman. Not sure when he returned."

"Arlene. The woman would be Arlene."

Mike shook his head. "And you know this how?"

"Trade secrets," Hunter answered with a wink. "Who found the body?"

"Coworker, Earl Cravens. He's on the back patio waiting for you. Says he and Peterson have been working a rehab construction job in Lewisport and been ride-sharing. It was his turn to drive today. He arrived, no lights were on, so he goes into the house and finds the body on the floor. He called 911, knew Peterson was dead. Says he didn't touch anything except the light switch."

"Does he usually go into the house?" Hunter asked.

"No. Says that Wayne has overslept on occasion. Earl would wake him up."

"And he thought that today Wayne has just overslept again?"

"Yes."

"Thanks, Mike." He walked to the front door and into the room where he had questioned Wayne Peterson a few days before. Dr. Turner was standing over the body, writing notes on a yellow pad, her reading glasses far down on her thin nose. She nodded to acknowledge his presence. One of the ECU techs was by the stairs, reviewing photographs on the camera's small screen.

Wayne was wearing only a pair of boxer shorts, his lifeless body lying at an angle to the room, feet closer to the door. The familiar knife was in his left chest, an irregular pattern of blood around the body reaching the recliner Wayne had occupied on Hunter's last visit to this room. He noticed small specks of pink, green, and yellow in the blood. He kneeled closer on the left side of the body, holding his burgundy pindot tie against his white shirt.

"You have pictures of this already?" he asked the tech.

"Yes."

He slipped a pen from the inside pocket of his grey chalk-stripe suit jacket to pull a small, round piece of pink paper from the sticky mass. He could just make out a series of letters and numbers.

"Confetti," he said softly.

"What, Bob? Did you ask me something?" Jean asked.

He looked up to Jean and spoke loud enough for her to hear. "Confetti. This is confetti from a taser gun." He stood up, moved to the right side of the body where the blood pool did not extend very far and kneeled a second time to get a closer look at the bare chest. Wayne's chest was bare, with only a sparse amount of hair; Hunter was able to see what he expected to find.

"Jean, see these two red marks on his chest?" He pointed with the same bloodied pen. "Those wounds are from the electrode projectiles of a taser gun. These little pieces of confetti spew from the cartridge when a taser is fired." He stood up. "That's how he subdues his victims. Tase them, then he's got a brief window when they are defenseless to bisect their heart."

"I wondered about that. They look like the little pieces of paper you get when you use a three-hole punch. Didn't occur to me that they're taser confetti. And I missed the marks on his chest."

"You didn't know to look, Jean."

"I will next time," she predicted. "Plan an autopsy as soon as the body's in the morgue, but I don't anticipate finding anything you don't already know."

"Estimated time of death?" Hunter asked.

"I'm guessing twenty-four to thirty-six hours." She looked at her pad. "The body's at room temp, and it's still in rigor mortis."

"Fits with the timeline." He turned to the ECU tech who was still checking his camera. "See the confetti from the taser gun?"

"Yes." He moved toward Wayne's lifeless body, gazing down.

"We'll need to bag it. They're contaminated by the blood, but you should be able to lift the serial numbers."

"Will do, Hunter," he responded.

One of the uniformed officers walked into the room. "Detective, Mr. Cravens is ready for you. The patio's through there," he said as he pointed the way to Hunter.

Hunter moved into the kitchen but stopped at the island. There was an ashtray with two different types of cigarettes, one the slim ones favored by many women, the filter remnants ringed with bright-red lipstick.

"Arlene," he whispered. "She was here. I need to find her." Then he spoke to the uniformed officer. "Have ECU bag these cigarettes. One will be from the victim, the slim ones, his girlfriend."

"Yes, sir," the officer answered and walked back into the front room for the ECU tech.

On the patio, Earl Cravens sat with another uniformed officer at the cast-iron patio set, two empty beer cans on the table, surrounded by cigarettes ashes. The officer stood up when Hunter arrived. Hunter introduced himself and let Earl talk through how he found the body and called the police.

"Have you known Mr. Peterson long?" Hunter asked.

"Coupla years. We've been working on some of the same jobs for a while."

"And outside of work?"

Earl shook his head. "No. We've just worked together. He's a hard worker. I like working with Wayne. And when we do jobs like this one in Lewisport, we take turns driving to save gas money."

"That's your F-250 in the driveway?"

"Yes. Wayne drove Friday and Saturday. Today it was my turn. That's why I found him this morning."

"About that," Hunter paused. "Was the door locked when you arrived?"

"Yes. And the lights were off."

"How did you get into the house?"

"Oh, I know the code for his keypad. He gave it to me a long time ago."

Hunter turned to the uniform. "Find Mr. Peterson's cell phone." Then he returned his attention to Earl. "Did Wayne have a date on Saturday with Arlene?"

A look of surprise came across Earl's face. "Yes, he was supposed to see her."

"Do you happen to know Arlene's last name?"

"No. I know she's a paralegal in some office downtown. Don't know her full name."

Phil walked through the open patio door with a mobile telephone in a labeled clear evidence bag. "You wanted Mr. Peterson's phone?"

Hunter took the bag. "Has this been fingerprinted yet?"

"Yes."

"I love the smell of fingerprint dust in the morning," Hunter said as he opened the bag to retrieve the telephone. It was on and still well-charged. He peered at Earl. "What is his door entry code?"

"Sixty-nine, sixty-nine," he answered.

Hunter regarded Earl. "Seriously?"

Earl nodded his head, softly adding "Yes."

He keyed in the number sequence. The phone's screen switched to a dark-red home screen full of icons. He scrolled through the recent numbers to find Arlene. There was no last name, just "Arlene" in the calls, along with a single voicemail from Arlene on Sunday, which had not been played. *If Wayne had been alive on Sunday, I would expect him to answer a call from Arlene*, Hunter thought. The murder occurred Saturday night, or early Sunday morning.

"Mr. Cravens, you've been very helpful. I don't think we need to detain you any longer. We have your contact information?"

Earl rose from the chair. "I gave it to one of the officers."

"I can understand that this morning has been quite a shock to you." He pointed to Phil. "My colleague will escort you from the townhouse."

Phil signaled the patio door with his open right hand. "After you Mr. Cravens. We'll have the van moved so you can get your truck out."

After they walked into the house, Turner emerged through the doorway. "I'm finished, Bob. Any questions?"

"No. This is the third episode of the same show. A River City Ripper hat trick. I know the plot now." He fished a pack of cigarettes from his pocket, pulling one out. "Hang on, yes. I do have a question. Do you think that you just missed the taser wounds on the other victims, or is it possible that they just weren't there?"

Turner shook her head. "Don't know. Miller had a pretty hairy chest, so it would have been easy to miss. Thomas—well, I just didn't see them, nor did I think to look. I've never seen a taser wound before. If I had found them, I'm not sure I would have known that's what they were." She paused. "I suppose you might see them on the autopsy photos."

"I'll drop by later. We can review the photographs together." He struck a match as Phil reappeared on the patio. He flicked his wrist to extinguish it without lighting his cigarette. "Jean, have you met Owensboro's newest detective?"

Turner glanced at Phil, looked back to Hunter, then returned her gaze to Phil.

Hunter thought he saw a smile start to develop across her face.

"No," she said softly.

Hunter introduced them. After a brief handshake, Turner announced that she would be in the pathology lab and would see them later.

"How is it that you've never met the medical examiner?" Hunter asked once she was out of earshot.

"Uniforms are invisible to her," he stated flatly.

Hunter sighed. "Back to work. Peterson was with a woman named Arlene Saturday night. Track her down. Her number's in the phone." He handed Wayne's cell phone to Phil. "Think you can remember the passcode?"

"I can remember." Phil grinned.

"I almost forgot. Peterson had an ex-wife. We'll need to find her. Her first name is Karla."

"I'll see what I can turn up," Phil offered.

"We need to bring Billy Ray Harper in again. Assuming he was knocking off the former teenagers responsible for the death of this sister, Wayne Peterson was the last one on the list."

"You still think he's the River City Ripper?"

"Yes. And no. He's got motive, but I'm not sure that even Harper is stupid enough to commit a third murder when he knows I've got him in my crosshairs." He struck another wooden match against the box. "Unless he really wants to return to Eddyville."

Hunter lit his cigarette. "I had a beer with Alan Maddox yesterday. Gave me the name of an FBI agent in Louisville who is knowledgeable about serial killers. I'll give him a call after I update the chief."

"What about Trevor Reed?" Phil asked.

"Yes. We'll need to question Trevor Reed also."

He took a long drag, slowly exhaling the smoke into the still morning air.

CHAPTER FORTY-ONE

Arlene was Arlene Young, a paralegal in the law offices of Baker and Baker, a father-son firm located just off Frederica on Third Street. Accustomed to speaking with police officers, she didn't ask Phil any questions on the telephone, readily agreeing to meet him in the office.

Phil waited in the reception area until Arlene opened the privacy-glass door to join him. She was of average height, her straight red hair was cut in a bob, and she was wearing too much bright-red lipstick. His eyes were immediately drawn to her oversized chest, which tented the front of her Kelly-green scoop-neck dress. Once he gained his composure, he produced his badge, introducing himself.

"Is there someplace we can speak privately?" he asked.

Arlene turned to the receptionist. "Nadine, is anyone in the conference room?"

She checked the computer screen. "There's a deposition at nine."

"Okay." She looked at Phil. "No one else is in yet. How about the paralegal cube farm?"

"That's fine." They walked down a short hallway to a moderately sized room with four cubicles, two each on opposite walls, and a rectangular table in the middle. Books and files were stacked on the table, and a collection of overflowing cardboard file boxes sat against the far wall under the window.

"You'd better sit down, Arlene," Phil said.

She pulled a chair from a nearby cubicle. He noticed a slim purse pack of cigarettes next to an oversized brown leather satchel purse on the deck surface—the same brand that was found in Wayne's kitchen.

"Wayne Peterson was found dead this morning."

She closed her eyes, tears started to form. "Stabbed? Was he stabbed like his friends?"

"Yes."

She reached for a tissue box on the adjoining cube, taking one to her eyes. "I just can't believe this. He can't be dead."

"I need to ask you a few questions about Mr. Peterson."

She exhaled slowly, then said, "Go ahead."

"When did you leave Mr. Peterson's townhouse after your date Saturday?"

She seemed surprised at the question. "Uh, I guess around 1 a.m. or so."

"Didn't stay the night?"

"No. I don't sleep well in other people's beds." She reached for another tissue. "He's really gone?"

"Yes, he is. When you left the townhouse, how was he? Anything unusual?"

Arlene twisted in the chair. "Didn't want me to leave. But, no, nothing odd. He stayed in bed when I left. I let myself out."

"And he would have been alone at that point?"

She nodded. "Yes. When I left, he was by hisself."

"Where did you go on Saturday?"

"We went to the funeral home for the visitation of his old friend Skeeter. Met Skeeter's parents, that sort of thing. Had some barbeque, then went back to his place." She paused. "He kept talking about how him and Jeff and Skeeter had been big buds in high school. I think he kinda regretted losing touch."

"Had you met Skeeter Thomas before?"

"No. I don't think him and Skeeter talked for a long time." She grabbed the cigarette pack. "I need a smoke. Do you mind if we continue this out back?"

Phil followed her farther down the same hall to a windowless back door, which opened onto a steel-grate landing and the alley. She pulled a slim cigarette from the pack and lit it with a disposable plastic lighter.

"This is that River City Ripper, isn't it?" she asked after taking a long drag.

"We believe so."

"They all knew each other, you know. I've seen the high school yearbook. Wayne had it out, looking at it. The three of them, they was buddies. Like I said, he was talking about Jeff and Skeeter Saturday night. This River City Ripper—he knows them, or knew them," she concluded. "The murders are connected, right? This isn't some random serial killing."

"You might make a good detective, Arlene. How long have you known Wayne?"

"About five or six months."

"How did you meet?"

"Here. We met here. We had some renovation done on the second floor to add more offices."

"How about family? We can't seem to locate any relatives," Phil said.

Arlene blew a smoke ring before answering. "Wayne didn't talk much about his family. His mother died several years ago, he didn't have no brothers or sisters."

"I understand he was previously married."

"Yeah, Karla. They met in high school. Sounds like it didn't last long." She took a drag from the cigarette. "She's still in town, I think. Remarried and popped out a kid or two."

"You wouldn't happen to know her married name, would you?"

"No."

"One more question. Do you have any idea who might want to see Wayne Peterson dead?"

She finished the cigarette, crushed it against the building brick, and dropped the butt through the steel grate. "No." She could contain her emotions no longer. The tears erupted as she sobbed, pulling Phil against her.

Chapter Forty-Two

Chief Hartmann closed his eyes and clenched his teeth when Hunter told him that Wayne Peterson had been murdered. After an unusually long pause, he tightly gripped the mahogany-stained wooden arms of his chestnut leather chair and opened his eyes.

"I don't know if I should be frustrated or furious. Frustrated that we were unable to prevent this River City Ripper from committing a third murder, or furious that these three young men would still be alive if Elkins had handled that damned accident the right way."

Hunter shifted in the chair. "Still convinced it's the residual effect of Jenny Harper's death?"

"Yes. Even more so now." He rubbed his temples, avoiding his comb-over. "Billy Ray Harper is our man."

"I'll be interrogating him this afternoon."

"Good. Get a quick confession, we'll have a press conference in the morning, and soon it's back to normal around here. And the mayor will be off my ass."

"I'm not so confident, Chief. Harper was a little too quick to submit to a DNA swab. He knows that I have DNA from the second murder, Skeeter Thomas. It's possible I've been too focused on the wrong person. Trevor Reed remains a suspect."

Hartmann shook his head. "And it's possible Harper did it. It all fits, Hunter. He's out on parole and suddenly the people he holds responsible for his sister's death turn up dead. All you need is a confession."

"Yes, Chief." Hunter stood up, buttoning his suit jacket. "I'll leave you to get back to work."

∞

The police station was already abuzz with the latest River City Ripper murder when Hunter arrived on the third floor. There were several officers in the breakroom, all speculating on the identity of the serial killer. Hunter made his way to the coffee, filled his mug and mostly deflected questions. Once in his office, he closed the door and slowly wandered to the window. He sipped coffee as he gazed at the few cars on Crittenden Street below. Miller, Thomas, Peterson. Will there be a fourth killing? He sighed, then sat at his desk and dialed the number for FBI Special Agent Kurt Nelson.

Nelson answered on the second ring. Hunter identified himself, to which Nelson responded, "I've been expecting your call."

"Is that good or bad?" Hunter asked.

He chuckled. "Don't worry. Maddox called me yesterday. After he finished whining about his hip and lying about all the fish he caught, he filled me in on the case of the River City Ripper."

"Then I've additional information for you. We found the third victim this morning."

There was a pause on the line. "The same MO?"

"Yes, he used the same method. The murder occurred sometime late Saturday night to Sunday, the victim was stabbed in the chest, and the knife was left in place. Same brand and type of knife was used. I also have determined that the third victim was subdued with a taser gun. I suspect that is how the others were subdued as well, as there was no sign of a struggle with Jeff Miller."

"But there was evidence that the second victim tried to fight off his attacker, right?"

"Correct. Skeeter Thomas. There was tissue under his fingernails, suggesting that he scratched his killer. DNA is pending."

"Any other sign of a struggle with him?"

"No. I have a theory that may explain why."

"I'm listening."

"Skeeter Thomas, the second victim, had a rare cardiac condition called dextrocardia. His heart was on the right side, not the left side, the normal position."

Nelson interrupted Hunter. "Dexter what?"

"Dextrocardia. Latin for right-sided heart."

"Never heard of it."

"It's quite rare. I confirmed with a local physician. I think the assailant hesitated before slicing into Skeeter's chest, either because he suddenly recalled that his heart was on the wrong side, or because he had made that determination before the act. The latter, however, seems unlikely."

"Hmmm," Nelson purred into the telephone. "So, your River City Ripper probably knew about the heart condition."

"That's my conclusion."

"Any connection between the third and the two prior victims?" Nelson asked.

"Yes. They were friends in high school, the three victims, albeit their relationships became more distant over time. They were also involved in a car accident that resulted in the death of another high school student. There does not seem to be a direct current relationship between the three. Except that Jeff Miller and Skeeter Thomas did have a business relationship."

"Maddox mentioned the accident. Told me that he thought it was handled poorly at the time."

"I agree, the entire affair was mishandled." Hunter shifted in his chair. "The older brother of the deceased girl was released on parole about a month before these killings began. He's a prime suspect."

"Maddox said that also. Harper, right?"

"Yes. Billy Ray Harper."

Nelson made a clicking sound with his tongue. "Okay, so you've got a serial killer on your hands. Fits the general description. Let's take this Harper character out of the equation for right now and sort through the details."

"Okay," Hunter agreed. "I'll readily admit, I'm an abecedarian when it comes to serial killers."

"Not exactly the sort of expertise one sets out to gain," Nelson declared. "Victims of serial killers often have something in common. For example, Jack the Ripper's victims were all destitute women, Jeffrey Dahmer's were handsome younger men. In this case, the common thread is high school. Knowing what the victims have in common does not necessarily help you identify either the next victim or the identity of the serial killer."

"So, we work with that. The high school connection," Hunter concluded.

"Then, let's discuss motives. There is usually some sort of psychological gratification in serial killing. We've identified four categories of motives, but, frankly, there is overlap. There are visionaries, who are usually psychotic and believe that they are on a mission from some other entity. Second, the hedonistic, who experience pleasure in killing. Then there is the power or control type, which is self-explanatory. Finally, the mission-oriented. My guess is that is the type that you're dealing with. A mission-oriented serial killer."

"How is that different from a visionary killer?" he asked.

"Well, there is overlap. The mission serial killer is not psychotic, not hearing voices telling them to kill people. It's more personal."

"Like taking out the people responsible for the death of a family member."

"Yes. If Harper is your man, then that's how the FBI would categorize him. But it could be other things. Many serial killers had rough childhoods, were abused, may have been bullied. They became socially isolated as a result of being rejected by their peers."

"This is very useful, Kurt," Hunter said. "What do you make of the killer leaving the murder weapon at the crime scene?"

Nelson cleared his throat. "Definitely leaving a message. And making it very personal. Subconsciously, most serial killers want to be caught. It may be his way of helping you apprehend him."

"An interesting perspective. I hadn't thought of it that way."

There was a long pause, then Nelson spoke. "Bob, I know the reputation the FBI has when it comes to cases like this. The feds storm into town to exert their authority and seize control of the investigation. The local LEOs think we just get in the way, calling us the Federal Bureau of Incompetence behind closed doors. Trust me, I'm glad to help you. I can be in Owensboro this afternoon, look over things with you, and have an experienced team there sometime tomorrow."

Hunter took a deep breath and slowly exhaled. "I'm interrogating Harper again this afternoon. Give me a day or so, then I'll take you up on your offer."

"It's a deal, Bob. You've got my number. Don't hesitate to call."

"Thanks." Hunter placed the handset back in the cradle and walked to his side window again. He pulled a cigarette from the pack in the pocket of suit and lit it with a wooden match before opening the casement window.

"Most serial killers want to caught," he said aloud to no one. "Not this one, bubba. He's a clever one." He blew smoke softly at the window.

∞

"It's the same thing," Dr. Turner said as she pulled the green sheet from Wayne Peterson's corpse, standing on the right side. "More like the Miller murder, though, except evidence of recent coitus. No hesitation marks like the Thomas murder. Just a clean slice through the fourth intercostal space, bisecting his right and left ventricles. Pretty much instant death."

"Didn't expect it to be different," Hunter responded as he leaned over the open torso, inspecting the long gash in the left chest.

"There's evidence of old healed fractures of his left forearm and the left zygomatic arch. He also has hardware in his right ankle, a plate and three screws, which likely was to repair an ankle fracture. His lungs showed some moderate emphysema," she pointed to his right hand, "and there's mild clubbing of his fingers. I'm guessing he was a heavy smoker."

"The arm and facial fractures are from a car accident when he was a teenager. Not sure about the ankle, but I don't think it germane to the case."

Turner pulled off her exam gloves, tossing them into the bin, then reached up to turn off the overhead lamp. "Not much else to add then, Bob."

"So, three weeks, three murders. All done in the same efficient and effective manner, leaving us with a paucity of clues as to the killer's identity."

"Seems that way." She started to walk to her desk. "I've got the autopsy photos pulled up for you." He joined her, standing behind her desk chair, looking at the oversize computer monitor.

"First, Jeff Miller." She pointed to the slash in his left chest. "There's a lot of blood matted into his chest hair. If there's a taser wound, there's not a way you'd be able to see it."

Hunter nodded. "Agreed."

She clicked through a few more shots—different angles of the chest wound. "Yeah, I don't see anything, and, honestly, Bob, I doubt I could have found any small wounds even if I knew where to look." Turner closed Miller's file, and opened the folder with the pictures of Skeeter Thomas. After scrolling through a series of small icons, she opened a direct photograph of Skeeter's chest.

"His sparse chest hair is light blond, lighter than his scalp hair. Lot of blood splatter over his torso." Turner pointed to the gash in his right chest. "Maybe some of these spots are taser wounds." She enlarged the area.

Hunter shook his head. "No way to determine if they are." He stepped back from the screen. "It makes sense that he, the killer, this River City Ripper, that he would first tase the victims to incapacitate them. I'm convinced that's the technique."

She closed the photo viewer and stood up from her chair, pushing her reading glasses into her curly black hair. "Where's Phil? I thought he'd want to see all this."

"He's talking to Wayne Peterson's girlfriend. They were together Saturday night."

"You think she could have killed him? After sex? Like a black widow spider?"

"No, she's not a suspect." He twisted his wedding band. "Where are we on the DNA?"

"I'll check. It should be available by now, or soon. Call you when I have the results."

Hunter started for the door. "I'll be in the office."

CHAPTER FORTY-THREE

The county clerk's office was located on the third floor of the courthouse, a short walk from Arlene and the Baker and Baker law office. Phil flashed his badge to the young clerk behind the window and was escorted to see the manager, Crystal Mattingly, a hefty, overly made up bleach-blonde in a too-tight black dress with acrylic nails and enough gold costume jewelry for three women. The small office had a casement window, opened, under which a dusty camel trench coat was draped on top of stacks of files. Her desk was cluttered with more files, loose papers, and several five by seven notepads in pastel colors.

She held the telephone handset between her right cheek and scrunched shoulder, mumbling, "Uh-huh," repeatedly while taking notes. Phil sat down after she pointed to the empty chair in front of her desk.

"Okay, listen, someone just stepped into my office. I'll get on this right away," she said into the phone, ending the call.

He told Crystal that a third murder had taken place, then simply stated, "Mr. Peterson, the victim, does not seem to have any family except an ex-wife. I understand that she has remarried and still lives in town."

"And you want to find her through the divorce and marriage records," she concluded in her raspy voice.

"Yes."

"Hang on." She slipped on a pair of squarish black-framed glasses and tapped at the keyboard. "Okay, what is her name?"

"The first marriage would have been Karla and Wayne Peterson. I don't have her maiden name."

After a few minutes, Crystal looked up over the readers. "Karla Ann Compton. Married Wayne Monroe Peterson."

"That was quick," Phil said.

Crystal winked at him. "I assume you don't know if she returned to her maiden name or kept Peterson."

"That's correct."

"I'll try both." A few more clicks, then she said, "A marriage license was issued for Karla Ann Compton and Steven John Gaines."

"So, Karla Gaines."

"Would seem so." She leaned back in her chair, looked at Phil's left hand, then smiled while looking directly at him, revealing a sliver of red lipstick on her nicotine-stained teeth. "Anything else I can do for you, Detective?"

"No, thanks. You've been very helpful." He stood to leave.

"When you catch this River City Ripper, can I tell my friends that I helped apprehend him?"

"Couldn't have done it without you."

Crystal chuckled as he left her office.

∞

Phil obtained a copy of Karla Gaines driver's license from the Department of Motor Vehicles, located a single flight of stairs up from the county clerk. Address in hand, he drove to her home on Lake Forest Drive, a two-story red-brick house with black shutters and a professionally kept lawn. He parked on the street and moved along the concrete walk to the double front doors, painted in the same satin sheen black.

Karla matched her driver's license picture—dark-brown eyes and curly blonde hair that flowed past her shoulders. She was wearing a white, long-sleeve cable sweater and tan capri pants in the same shade as her espadrilles. Phil held up his badge as she opened the door.

"Something bad has happened to Wayne, hasn't it?" she said before he could introduce himself.

He nodded. "Yes, Mrs. Gaines. Mr. Peterson was found dead this morning."

She lowered then shook her head. "I was afraid something like this would happen. Jeff, then Skeeter. Now Wayne." She looked back to Phil. "It's this River City Ripper, right?"

"We have reason to believe the same person has committed these murders."

"So, it's real. There really is a serial killer haunting Owensboro. How was Wayne killed? Was he stabbed like the others?"

"Yes. All of the victims were stabbed in the chest." Phil hesitated. "I understand that you and Mr. Peterson divorced years ago. Even so, I'd like to ask you a few questions, if I may."

"Yes, of course. Where are my manners?" She fully opened the door. "Please come in. May I offer you something to drink? There's fresh sweet tea in the kitchen."

"Tea sounds good." He followed Karla through the high-ceilinged foyer, her soft shoes silent as she slid across the terracotta Mexican tile floor. The entry opened into a spotless kitchen with bright-white cabinets contrasted by hardwood floors. A glass pitcher of tea rested on the dark-grey granite-topped kitchen island. She filled two glasses with ice, reached for the pitcher to pour the sweet tea, then carried both to a rectangular wooden table in front of the large bay window overlooking an in-ground pool.

"Please have a seat." She motioned to an empty chair as she placed the sweet tea on the table, then sat down on the long side facing the window. "How can I help you?"

"When was the last time you spoke to Wayne Peterson?" He tried the tea.

"Oh, it's been several years." She took a sip of tea. "John and I are, well, we are part of a different social stratum. Our lives don't intersect."

"Your iced tea is very good, Mrs. Gaines."

"Please, call me Karla. And thank you."

"John? I thought your husband's name was Steven."

"Steven's his dad. John uses his middle name. You've probably seen his billboards."

"John Gaines, the realtor?"

She smiled at Phil. "That's him." With her smile, Phil noticed her left eyelid narrow, giving her face a mild and attractive asymmetry.

"How long were you married to Wayne Peterson?"

"Not long, and too long at the same time. Almost three years." She took another small sip of tea, gently replacing the glass on the table. "If I don't seem grief-stricken, please understand, that chapter of my life ended long ago. Two-thirds of teen marriages fail. We were too young to get married."

"It was an amicable divorce?"

"I thought we'd remain friends. I moved back in with my parents and started college. That's when I met John." She beamed. "Something about the allure of an older woman, the divorcée, I suppose. Little did he know we'd fall in love." She peering into her tea, a hint of sadness in her expression. "I'd always hoped that Wayne would meet someone, remarry—hoped that he would find some happiness. His life, well, it wasn't exactly the best life. Raised by a single mom, a childhood devoid of a positive male influence, the perpetual financial insecurity." She wiped a tear from her eye.

"Do you know if there are any of Wayne's family members we should notify?"

Karla shook her head. "His mother passed away four or five years ago. I attended her funeral." She looked out at the pool. "I don't recall any other family. At least, I never met anyone."

"We know that Jeff Miller, Skeeter Thomas, and Wayne were friends in high school, but drifted apart since then. Assuming that the murders are connected, that connection may go back to their school days. Can you think of anyone who would want to kill any of them?"

"That's difficult to say, Detective. They were bullies in high school, and Wayne was the leader of the pack. I didn't see it then, or maybe I just didn't want to see it."

Phil leaned forward on the table. "Do you recall a car accident involving Jeff, Skeeter, and Wayne?"

Karla took a deep breath, exhaling slowly. "Jenny Lynn Harper."

"Yes."

"How do you know? Jeff Miller's mother made it vanish, as if it never happened."

"I'm a detective, Karla. The accident didn't completely disappear."

"And you believe there's a connection to Jenny's death." It was a statement, not a question.

"It's being considered." He took a long drink of the sweet tea.

"They did a lot of bad things back then. Her death was probably the worst of it. I knew Jenny. She was a year behind us. Lovely girl. Had a bright future that was taken from her."

"How about Jeff Miller or Skeeter Thomas? Any contact with either of them?"

"We would occasionally see Eve and Jeff Miller at country club dinners, although they were never very friendly. They're not members. Eve's sister is a member, as are Jeff's parents. They would bring them along as guests. Skeeter? I haven't any idea. It's been years." She glanced at the wafer-thin rectangular two-tone gold and silver watch on her right wrist.

"Do you need to get going?" Phil asked.

"Our son is at preschool. I'll need to collect him before too long. We're okay on time."

"I don't have any more questions right now." He laid his card on the table. "If you think of anything that may help the investigation, please give me a call. And thank you for the tea. It's quite good."

"Hopefully you'll be successful in bringing this killer to justice. Feel free to contact me if I may be of any assistance in your investigation."

Karla walked Phil to the front door. "You have a lovely home, Mrs. Gaines."

"Thank you. It happens when you marry a realtor, I suppose." That smile again. "Have a good afternoon."

CHAPTER FORTY-FOUR

Hunter stood at his office window, smoking, running through the details. The killer used knives that can be easily obtained, leaving each one in the victim's chest. He subdued them with a taser gun. He wore latex gloves, leaving a few powder traces and no fingerprints. Hid in the night. Knew his victims would be alone. Knew when to complete the stealthy strike. No eyewitnesses.

He recreated the events in his mind. Jeff Miller, stunned by a taser, giving the killer only a brief moment to pull up his shirt and slash his left chest. Skeeter Thomas, also stunned, but the killer dawdled, as if suddenly remembering that Skeeter had dextrocardia, leaving the hesitation marks on his left chest. The delay gave Skeeter time to partially recover from being stunned; however he was unable to fight off his killer. Wayne Peterson must have been asleep, clad in his boxer shorts. Tased, stabbed. River City Ripper kills not once, not twice, but thrice.

He took one last drag and crushed the cigarette in his ashtray. He knew the murders were meticulously planned, not random killings. Revenge killings, leaving the knife, leaving a message. Revenge for what? Was it as simple as avenging the unfortunate death of a teenager who was sister to one, girlfriend to another?

228

His thoughts were interrupted when Amos Weller limped into his office.

"Billy Ray's in an interrogation room, Hunter." He sat in one of the chairs in front of the desk. "Waiting for you," he added.

Hunter turned from the window, remaining on his feet. "Still think he's innocent?"

"Billy Ray's not dumb enough to murder Wayne Peterson right in front of you. Yeah, could he have slipped out of the house during the night? Sure. Three times? Sure." Amos shook his head. "I told you that I doubted he would go after Miller when you showed up at my halfway house three weeks ago. And two more murders, well, just doesn't make sense to me."

"What if Billy Ray wants to return to Eddyville? He learned how to adapt to the difficulties of being in the state prison and has found outside life too demanding?"

"That certainly occurs," Amos agreed. "I'm not buying it, Bob. Not in this case. He's cleaning up his act."

"Afternoon, Amos," Phil said as he walked into the office, taking the remaining empty chair.

Amos gave Phil a thumbs up with his right hand. "I understand congratulations are in order, Detective."

"Thanks." He looked up to Hunter. "I can fill you in later. Talked to Arlene—she left Wayne Peterson's townhouse around one in the morning. She did help me locate his ex-wife, Karla. She's still in town. Didn't have much to add. Wayne didn't seem to have any family other than his mother, and she's passed away."

"Good work." Hunter remained standing by the window. "Billy Ray's here. Ready?"

"Yes. Oh, and Trevor Reed will be stopping by on his way home from work."

Amos turned to Phil. "Trevor Reed? He was the driver of the car—"

Hunter interrupted him. "The car Jenny Harper was in, yes. He's also a suspect."

"I think Reed's guilty," Phil pronounced.

"He's got this theory that Reed waited until Billy Ray was out on parole to commence his killing spree." Hunter shook his head. "In doing so, diverting our attention to Harper and away from him."

"Or, they could be in it together, Bob. Phil might be on to something here." Amos waved his index finger in the air. "The two men collaborating to avenge Jenny Harper's death? Vigilante justice when the system failed them?"

"Both Harper and Reed have motive," Phil added. "Harper has acknowledged that he doesn't hold Trevor Reed responsible for his sister's death."

Hunter glared at Phil. "Harper's paroled, they meet for coffee to reminisce about old times and hatch a plan to take out Miller, Thomas, and Peterson?" he asked sarcastically.

Amos nodded in agreement. "Works for me, Bob." He turned to Phil. "What about this? They're working with a third man? The logistics man. Has the medical knowledge, knows when the victims will be alone and vulnerable to a three-man blitz?"

"Yeah," Phil exclaimed. "I like it."

"The two of you read too much detective fiction," Hunter pronounced. "I'm going downstairs."

∞

"This gonna take long, Hunter?" Billy Ray Harper asked calmly.

"As long as it takes, Harper." He spread three pictures on the table on front of Billy Ray. He pointed to the first one on the left. "Jeff Miller, driver." Then the middle picture. "Darryl Skeeter Thomas, front-seat passenger."

"I get it, Hunter."

"Wayne Peterson, back-seat passenger," as he pointed to the last picture.

Billy Ray stared at him.

"You didn't have to murder Elroy Beggs, did you? Someone did that for you." Hunter leaned forward, his elbows on the table. "All three stabbed in the heart. Well-planned murders, almost perfect, really. You've had plenty of time to sort all the details, Billy Ray. Plan every last detail." He took a deep breath and leaned back in the chair.

"Every person who was in the car that killed your little sister is now dead. So, why don't you confess, Harper, and I can be home in time for dinner."

"Like I said, Hunter. I ain't confessin' to no crime I didn't commit."

"Tell you what, Billy Ray. I will personally drive you back to Eddyville in my Cadillac after you're convicted. We'll even stop in Hopkinsville at that little restaurant that makes those famous burgers. My treat."

The door to the room suddenly opened. Chief Hartmann glared at Hunter, then Harper.

"This interrogation is over," he said in a firm voice. "Detective Hunter, in the hall." He held the door open.

Hunter carefully rose from the chair, eyes fixed on Billy Ray. He buttoned his suit jacket and walked through the doorway. He stood facing the chief, gazing down, spotting areas of bare scalp the combover failed to cover.

Hartmann waited until the door closed. They were alone.

"You've got the wrong man," he said as he slammed a file folder into Hunter's chest. "DNA doesn't match."

Hunter took the folder, opening it as Chief Hartmann stormed down the hallway to his office.

CHAPTER FORTY-FIVE

Trevor Reed was sitting on the same brown couch he had occupied two weeks ago in the reception area next to Hunter's office, opposite Phil. He was wearing a short-sleeve tennis shirt embroidered with a company logo. Hunter looked at Trevor's forearms as he arrived at the open doorway. No wounds.

"Since we last spoke, Trevor, there have been two more murders." Hunter blocked the doorway with his large frame, the DNA file folder still in his hands. "Darryl Thomas, known as Skeeter, and Wayne Peterson, the other occupants of the car Jeff Miller was driving."

"And you think I did it?" Trevor asked. "Why am I a suspect? I came to you freely with the information about Jeff Miller and the car accident that killed Jenny Harper." He looked at Phil. "I even told him that Jenny's brother contacted me. And now, I'm being accused of murder?"

"Can you account for your whereabouts Saturday night?" Hunter asked.

"When Saturday?"

"After midnight," Phil said.

"Asleep. At home."

"And Sunday?" Hunter questioned.

"Sunday? I was helping my brother doing some renovations on his house."

"All day?" Phil asked.

"Most of the day." Trevor gazed up at Hunter, then to Phil. "I was home for dinner. Check with my wife, or did you already talk to Robin? Oh, yeah, that's right. You already did that."

Hunter put his right hand into his suit jacket pocket and fiddled with the pack of cigarettes.

"Would you mind standing up, Mr. Reed, and removing your shirt?"

"What?" Trevor looked bewildered. "Here?"

"Yes. Your shirt. Remove it." Hunter repeated.

Trevor shook his head, then stood up and pulled the tennis shirt over his head.

"Turn around." Hunter stated flatly.

He held his arms out and turned in a circle. No marks, no scratches, no wounds. A tattoo on his left shoulder of a bird with grey wings and an orange breast.

"You're free to go, Mr. Reed." Hunter walked to his office, closed the door, then pulled shut the venetian blinds covering the window between the two rooms.

Trevor slipped his shirt on, leaving the tails untucked. "What was that all about?"

Phil rose from the arm chair. "Skeeter Thomas injured his assailant. Hunter was looking for wounds."

"I'm pretty sure this is police harassment." He stared at Phil. "My wife is due any day now, so, tell you what, Detective, I'm going to let it go." He moved to the doorway, then pointed his finger at Phil. "But the next time I get pulled over for speeding, you're my Get Out of Jail Free card."

"I'll escort you out." Phil followed Trevor down the hallway to the elevator.

∞

When Phil returned to Hunter's office, he was sitting at his desk, forehead propped up by his right hand, tapping the fingers of his left hand on the closed file with the DNA results.

"I've walked Trevor out of the building." Phil took a seat. "Kinda hard on him, don't you think?"

"Frustrated," Hunter said. "Harper's not a DNA match." He pushed the file across the desk as he sat back.

Phil opened the tan folder and scanned the report. He closed the file and replaced it on Hunter's desk.

"I've missed something, Phil. Something important." He twisted his wedding band. "You uncover anything useful from Arlene or Wayne's ex?"

"Arlene, not so much. The slim cigarette butts found at Wayne's are the brand she smokes. She's also generous with lipstick, so I'm pretty sure they were hers."

"What I suspected."

"But, like I said earlier, she did help me find his ex-wife. She's Karla Gaines, married to the realtor, John Gaines. Talked to her before coming back to the station."

"Karla Gaines is Wayne's ex?"

"You know her?" Phil asked.

"I know both of them. I didn't know about her previous marriage. Difficult for me to see Karla with Wayne. He was a bit rough around the edges." Hunter paused, leaning back in his desk chair. "John took over his dad's real-estate business.

He's been quite the success, turning his father's little two-room real-estate office into a booming enterprise."

"I'll say. Their house belongs in a magazine." He nodded slowly as he smiled. "Anyway, here's the interesting thing. Karla said that in high school, Wayne and his pals Jeff and Skeeter, they were the bullies. She also knew all about Jenny Harper's death. Seemed surprised that I knew. And she knew that Jeff's mother, quote, 'took care of things,' so to speak."

"That's concordant with what Eve Miller told me. She said that the three of them were always getting into trouble. She also described them as bullies." Hunter walked to the window and looked down on the street. "We have three high school bullies who didn't remain in close contact after graduation. The connection must be from high school. Otherwise, there doesn't seem to be a link." He picked the football off the stand on the file cabinets, palming it in his right hand.

"Seems that way," Phil agreed.

"When I spoke with Nelson, the FBI agent, he said that serial killers were often bullied as adolescents."

"The River City Ripper is taking out his high school bullies?

"Quite efficaciously, Phil." Hunter shook his head. "We've gone from two suspects, to no suspects, to an entire high school full of suspects." He spiraled the football in the air, catching it with his left hand. "Let's take the evening off. Look at things tomorrow after a good night's sleep."

CHAPTER FORTY-SIX

A good night's sleep was not to be had. In the office before eight, Hunter was already on his second cup of coffee. He'd been over the reports, then started to review the crime scene photographs. He was clicking through when Phil walked into his office.

"Morning, Hunter," he said as he took a chair.

"You know, you can call me Bob." Hunter glanced away from the computer screen to look at Phil.

"Does anyone call you Bob?"

Hunter scratched his chin. "My wife does." He shrugged it off. "I'm reviewing the crime scenes. Not seeing anything new."

"Like you, I've been to all the crime scenes. There's something that's bugging me."

"Go on," Hunter encouraged.

Phil shifted in his chair. "See, you found some confetti in the blood around Peterson's body. But a taser blows more confetti than what was found in the blood. There were just a few pieces, right?"

"Hold that thought." Hunter searched for the pictures of Wayne Peterson's body in the crime photos. Finding the right set, he positioned the computer monitor so that Phil also could view it. "Here we are. This is taken from the foot of the body. Blood pool on the left." He zoomed in, pointing at a few spots on the screen. "There's the confetti."

"So, why isn't there more confetti? Or confetti all over the floor? There are dozens of pieces in each cartridge."

"Because the killer cleaned them up," Hunter concluded. "Assuming he tased Miller and Thomas, we should have found confetti."

"But we didn't," Phil acknowledged, "because he cleaned it up."

"Good catch." Hunter turned the monitor back to face him. "We need to walk through the crime scenes again."

"Afraid you'll be doing that solo, boss. The rangemaster called me a few minutes ago. I'm to report this morning for regular firearms training and recertification."

"Boss?"

"You'd prefer Hunter?"

"Okay. Boss." Hunter acquiesced. "When you've completed your range time, follow up with ECU about the confetti serial numbers. Assuming they can resurrect the numbers, we may be able to track down our River City Ripper through the taser gun purchase." Hunter smirked. "Of course, *may* is the critical word in that statement."

"Will do."

As Phil walked out of the office, Hunter picked up the telephone handset. He had two calls to make.

∞

Ann O'Neil and Eve Miller were sitting at an umbrellaed patio table drinking coffee, watching a barge roll by on the Ohio River, discussing Eve's future. Eve was still in her bedclothes and robe, her sister already dressed, makeup on, letting her hair air-dry in the morning sun.

"I don't think I can live in that house," Eve told her sister. "Every time I close my eyes, I see Jeff lying on the kitchen floor in a pool of his own blood."

"You can stay with us as long as you'd like, Eve," Ann responded. "There's plenty of room."

Eve followed the barge's wake in the brown-green water. "I'm late," she said softly.

"For what? We don't have any plans today."

"That's not what I mean," she responded.

Her eyes wide open, Ann looked at her younger sister. "Oh my God—you're pregnant!"

"Yes, I think so." Eve turned her gaze from the water to Ann. "What am I going to do? A pregnant widow. I can't stay here forever. It's not just about me anymore."

"One step at a time, Eve. We can put your house up for sale, say, in a few months, when the story is old news. You can remain here. Then, we'll find a new place, a place of your own to start a new life." Ann suggested. "A place without Jeff memories. For you and the baby."

"Maybe." She peered into the coffee cup. "I'll think about it."

A telephone rang in the kitchen. Ann peered through the open French doors. "I'd better answer that," she said, then walked into the house. She returned after a moment, handing the cordless handset to her sister. "It's that detective."

Eve took the handset from her sister. "Hello." She listened for a moment, then pulled the phone away from her ear. "Detective Hunter would like to look inside my house. Part of the investigation. I can't bear to even think about it. Would you let him in?"

Ann rolled her eyes, checked her watch, then sighed. "Only because I love you, Eve. Twenty minutes."

"My sister can meet you there in about twenty minutes. Will that work?" Eve nodded as she listened to the answer. "Okay."

"I wonder how looking through your house again is going to help him find the man who killed your husband," Ann said.

"He didn't say." Eve twirled the cup around on the saucer. "You think they'll ever find him?"

"Well, if they don't, we'll hire a private investigator. One way or another, the man who murdered Jeff will be found."

∞

Miller's house on Christie Place no longer had the appearance of a crime scene. Just another house in a quiet neighborhood. Hunter parked on the street in front of the house and waited for Ann O'Neil. When she arrived, she pulled her Range Rover into the driveway. Hunter met her on the concrete walkway.

She viewed his sedan. "I didn't know that the Owensboro Police Department paid so well. The detectives drive Cadillacs?"

Hunter slowly exhaled. "That particular Cadillac is property seized during the drug bust of a rapacious stockbroker who was managing both his client's portfolios and a thriving methamphetamine business."

"My husband's a stockbroker," she declared firmly.

"I know."

Ann glared at Hunter. "I don't like you very much, detective."

"I'm aware of that fact." Hunter smiled. "Now that we've engaged in the obligatory small talk, will you let me into Mrs. Miller's house?"

Ann scowled, then walked to the porch, unlocked and opened the door. Hunter followed her into the front room.

"I've had the place professionally cleaned already. Not sure what you'll find."

"Do you happen to know where your sister keeps her vacuum cleaner?" he asked.

"I don't." She glanced around the room, then looked down the hall toward the bedrooms. "Try that closet in the hallway."

Hunter walked down the hallway. The closet was filled with cleaning supplies, a broom, and an upright vacuum. He dragged the vacuum to the front room.

"I may need a witness," he said as he kneeled down. He pulled the cover off the front of the vacuum. The compartment was empty. The vacuum bag was missing.

Ann was surprised. "Why is there no bag? The cleaners I hired have their own equipment. They wouldn't have used Eve's vacuum."

He replaced the panel before standing. "I didn't expect to find one."

"Why?"

"I think Jeff Miller was tased—stunned with a taser gun—before he was brutally murdered. When a taser gun is fired, there is a cartridge that spews confetti. There was no confetti when your sister found her husband, nor when we arrived at the house, because the killer vacuumed the floors." He looked directly at Ann. "He took the bag so we wouldn't find it."

∞

"Thank you for meeting me on such short notice, Mrs. Thomas," Hunter said. Dorothy Thomas had willingly agreed to meet him at her son's house. She was waiting for him on the front porch, keys in hand. "I hope I haven't kept you long."

"Just arrived, Detective Hunter." She handed him the set of keys. "Skeeter kept an extra set at the house. After Tracy left him, he changed the locks. Good thing you called me instead of her." She held her head down. "I still can't believe he's gone."

"Would you like to come inside with me?" he asked.

"No. I'll stay out here."

"Shouldn't be too long, Mrs. Thomas." He unlocked the front door. The putrid odor of his last visit had diminished, yet remained faintly present. He made his way to the hallway, looking for the logical hall closet with a vacuum cleaner. He found it. A bagless upright with a clear bin. He could easily see that the bin was empty. He placed the vacuum back in the closet.

The blood on the kitchen floor had hardened. He stepped around it as much as he was able while he rummaged through the kitchen. Hunter located the waste can in a cabinet pull-out next to the sink. The receptacle was empty. Under the sink, he found an opened box of white drawstring kitchen waste bags the correct size for the bin.

"He took the confetti in the victim's own trash bag," he murmured. "This guy's good."

Back on the porch, he returned the housekeys to Dorothy. "Thanks again, Mrs. Thomas."

"Did you find what you needed?"

"Yes." Hunter straightened his tie. "Would you like to call a service to have your son's house professionally cleaned?

I can provide a recommendation. At this point in our investigation, we will not need to examine it any further."

"Yes, I would appreciate that. Rodney wasn't sure if we should yet, and, well, you know Tracy won't do anything."

"I'll write their number on the back of my card." He pulled a pen from his inside pocket.

CHAPTER FORTY-SEVEN

Third stop, Wayne Peterson's townhouse. As he pulled his Cadillac into the driveway, a man walking a yellow dog stopped on the sidewalk and waited for Hunter to exit the car.

"Are you investigating Wayne's murder?" the man asked. A short man with a bushy black moustache, he was wearing an untucked plaid shirt and ragged jeans.

Hunter nodded. "Yes. I'm Detective Hunter. And you are?"

"Dave Bellamy. I'm his neighbor, live back down that way," indicating with his thumb over his right shoulder.

"Well, Mr. Bellamy, how can I help you?"

"My wife told me that the police been around yesterday morning, asking about the goings-on at Wayne's on Saturday. I was sleeping, so didn't talk to no one. Lisa didn't wake me up."

"Sleeping?"

"Yeah. I'm the evening manager at Roper's Electronics. We stay open until nine on Saturdays and Sundays."

Hunter leaned against his car and unbuttoned his suit jacket. "Okay. You saw something?"

"Well, I don't know if it's important or not."

"Tell me. It may be relevant."

244

"Okay." He looked down at his dog. "Sit, Sparky." The dog obeyed, sitting near his feet.

"Well-behaved," Hunter commented.

"Sometimes. Working on it. He's still a puppy."

"Golden retriever?"

"Yes. Sparky's about six months old now."

"Nice-looking dog, Mr. Bellamy."

"Thanks. Anyways, Saturday night I was walking Sparky before I went to bed."

"What time was that?"

"Oh, well after midnight. I got home around ten from the store, then watched a movie after I had some supper. Lisa, my wife, she went to bed before then. Anyways, when the movie ended, I took Sparky here down to the park by the tennis courts to do his business." He pointed to the end of the row of townhouses. "When we were walking, I saw this woman leave Wayne's place. I seen her leave Wayne's before. She's kinda chunky, if you know what I mean."

"Could you otherwise describe what she looked like?" Hunter probed.

"No, not really. It was dark."

"But a larger woman, then" Hunter said.

"Well, large in a particular place, if you know what I mean. Anyways, that's not the interesting part." Dave checked his dog, then returned his attention to Hunter.

"Go on," he encouraged.

"So, after Sparky gets done doing his business, we're heading back home, and I see another woman knocking at Wayne's door. And I think, wow, this Wayne's some kinda stud, you know. One leaves, then another one's ready to go."

"That is interesting, as you said." Hunter surveyed the front door, seeing the lantern-style outside light fixture. "Did you get a good look at her?"

"No. Her back was to me, and, well, I was kinda laughing about it all, and didn't give it too much thought."

"Was the porch lamp turned on?"

"Yeah. That's how I knew it was a girl. She had a pony tail. I could see that."

"Did she go into Wayne's house?"

"Don't know for sure. Me and Sparky, well, we just went on home. I didn't know about Wayne getting killed until Lisa told me." The dog whined. "Did that help you?"

"Yes, very much, Mr. Bellamy." Hunter straightened up from the sedan. "Looks like you better get Sparky to the park."

Dave laughed. "Got that right, Detective." He tugged the leash. "C'mon, Sparky." They resumed their walk toward the park and the tennis courts.

Hunter punched the code in the front-entry keypad that Earl Cravens had provided the previous day. The lock clicked open. The front room of Wayne's townhouse was still a mess. Dried blood on the hardwood floors, the furniture in disarray after the investigation, the fading stench of death. Finding hall closets the most likely place for a vacuum, he looked there first, a right-trapezoidal door under the staircase. Wayne had a canister vacuum. He removed the lid. The bag was missing, as he expected.

"I wonder how he missed some," he whispered. "Or why? Maybe serial killers really do want to be apprehended."

He continued further into the townhouse, into the kitchen. A stainless-steel step trash can was positioned next to the island. Hunter pressed the pedal, opening the lid. The bag was missing, the bin empty, clean. The lid silently closed.

The ashtray Hunter had noted yesterday had been emptied, the cigarettes bagged as evidence. As Phil had confirmed Arlene smoked the same brand, that information no longer seemed to be important. Next to the ashtray was Wayne's Owensboro South High School yearbook. Hunter turned the book so that he could read it, then opened it.

In the middle of the front endpaper, in large printed letters of black ink, was the motto "One for all and all for one." Below, the signatures of Jeff and Skeeter. Skeeter's name was written in cursive with a backward slant. The remaining signers had the usual juvenile quips, like "2 good 2 be 4 gotten" written as a vertical addition problem and "I'm the first one to sign your crack" along the crease. Hunter flipped through a few pages, stopping to look at Jeff Miller's senior picture, then Wayne Peterson. His eyes were drawn to the photo immediately below Wayne's, Andrew Rhoades.

Hunter sat down on one of the two counter stools. "He looks like he could be the brother of Andrea and Katie Rhoades, or maybe a cousin," he said aloud. "Definite family resemblance." He spun the book to view the spine. Katie Rhoades is too old for this yearbook, he concluded. He searched through the yearbook for Andrea Rhoades. There were several other Owensboro South Bulldogs with the family name Rhoades, but not one was named Andrea.

He was closing the yearbook, pushing it to the center of the counter, when the cellphone in his pocket vibrated. He checked the screen. Dad. He answered with the speaker button.

"Hey Dad, what's up?"

"Your mother made ceviche this morning. Want to drop by for lunch?"

"Fresh shrimp?" he asked, the hunger pangs starting.

"Is there any other way?" the elder Hunter asked with a laugh.

"Sounds great, Dad. I could use a break from this case."

"See you around noon, Bobby." He pressed the end button.

"Bobby," he moaned. "I could be inaugurated as our next president and my father would still call me Bobby."

He visually inspected the kitchen once more, then proceeded out of Wayne Peterson's townhouse, locking the front door as he departed.

CHAPTER FORTY-EIGHT

On the occasion of becoming a tenured professor at Verona College, Thomas Hunter, PhD had given a gift to himself. He had had the wooden deck of their bungalow expanded and a screened-in room added, complete with an outdoor ceiling fan for those humid summer days. Dr. Hunter was sitting at the rectangular teak dining table with his iced tea, the *Gazette* folded to the crossword puzzle in his hands. He looked like a smaller, older version of his son, with the same clear-blue eyes—except for the horseshoe of short grey hair ringing his bald head.

Hunter pulled his medium-grey Glenurquhart-check suit jacket off, draped it across one of the empty chairs and joined his father, taking the wicker chair on the long side of the table. "How's today's puzzle, Dad?" he asked.

"Not too much of a challenge." Dr. Hunter laid the newspaper on the table, placing his yellow pencil on top. "How's this River City Ripper case going? I read about the third murder this morning."

"Turns out I was chasing the wrong guy," he answered. "Have some new developments, so, we're getting there."

"That was pretty vague, Bobby."

"Maybe after I've had some lunch. I've managed to only move from the shadow to the penumbra in solving these murders." He smoothed his black grenadine-silk tie into his white shirt and adjusted his shoulder holster. "Speaking of lunch, why are you home? Shouldn't you be in the office or some lecture hall?"

"Finals week. I'm taking a break from grading final exams."

"That reminds me, I've got a question for you."

"Make it a tough one, son. I'm feeling particularly smart today." He winked at Hunter.

"In the sequence, once, twice, thrice, is there a word for 'four times'? I don't know of one."

Dr. Hunter laughed. "Is this the sort of debate one encounters at the police station?"

"No, this is not a police matter. Brenda asked me."

"Well, in Latin the sequence of adverbial numbers continues. One, two, and three have special treatment in Latin of course, with masculine, feminine, and neuter forms. Similarly, the adverbial numbers for these are irregular, *semel*, *bis* and *ter* for once, twice, and three times or thrice. Four times is also irregular, *quater*. After that, the series continues by adding a suffix to the root of the number, hence *quinuiens* for five times, *sexiens* for six times, and so on." He paused to drink some tea. "As Vulgar Latin evolved into the Romance languages, the sequence was lost. However, the special treatment of the number one persists."

Hunter shook his head. "Dad, English is a West Germanic language, not a descendant of Vulgar Latin."

"You were always such an impetuous student." He frowned at Hunter. "You've forgotten that Latin influenced English as a result of the Norman conquest of 1066. That's why the English vocabulary leans more to Romance than Germanic. In fact, the very word you've chosen, descendant, entered English from Latin by way of French."

"That's all very interesting, Dad," Hunter said. "Can we return to my question?"

"Of course, son." Dr. Hunter picked up the glass of iced tea and took a sip. "At a conference several years ago, one of the professors talked about the use of *quadrice* for four times and *quintice* for five times. He thought the adverbial numbers should be continued in a manner similar to Latin, using *ice* as the suffix and the Latin root word for the number."

"So, *decice* would be ten times, using *dec* as in decade or decathlon?"

"Exactly. I pointed out that while his idea had merit, the words were modern inventions that would find scant audience and be of little use."

"The bottom line is that there is no number adverb for 'four times' in English," Hunter said. *Which is what I wanted to know in the first place*, he thought.

"Correct, son. No English word." Dr. Hunter said with a chuckle. "Although you could start to popularize quadrice as you seem to be so fond of thrice. You'll have an uphill battle. Bobby. Thrice has really fallen into disuse."

"I'll leave the English department to you, Dad."

Betty Hunter emerged from the kitchen door which opened into the screened-in room. "Bobby, when did you arrive?"

"A brief etymological lecture ago, Mom."

"Can you help me put lunch on the table?" Hunter got up from his chair and walked into the kitchen.

∞

After lunch, Hunter helped his mother clear the dishes, just like when he was younger. The dishwasher full, he returned to the table with two refreshed glasses of iced tea.

"Tell me about this River City Ripper, Bobby," his father said, taking a glass from him.

Hunter retook his seat. "The murders are connected, not random killings. The three of them, Miller, Thomas, and Peterson, were close friends in high school. Although they remained in Owensboro, they lost touch over the ensuing years."

"Not unusual, son. Although it's easier to remain in contact with today's technology."

"True. Since their present lives were not interconnected, the theory is that the link goes back to high school days. I was at Wayne Peterson's townhouse when you called. His high school yearbook was on the kitchen island."

"Reminiscing about his high school days, perhaps?" Dr. Hunter offered.

"I think so. Two of his old pals are murdered. Pulls out the old yearbook, takes a trip down memory lane. Funny thing, written on the front endpaper was 'One for all and all for one,' signed by Jeff Miller and Skeeter Thomas."

"The Three Musketeers motto," Dr. Hunter observed. "Wonder how many class albums have the same?"

"Many, unquestionably. The comma was missing, of course," Hunter grinned at his father.

"You need to find d'Artagnan. What if the jilted fourth Musketeer is your serial killer?" Dr. Hunter offered.

"Dad, they attended public schools which apparently lacked a grammar class. I doubt they've ever read anything written by Alexandre Dumas." He shook his head. "And I seriously doubt that they knew there were four Musketeers."

"It would have added a certain literary flare to the story." He sipped some of his tea. "Find anything else interesting in that yearbook?"

"Yes, actually, as you asked." Hunter leaned forward, folding his forearms on the table. "In the senior class pictures, I noticed a classmate named Andrew Rhoades. He bears a striking resemblance to two sisters we interviewed last week with the same family name, Rhoades."

"Like their brother?"

"Exactly. One of the sisters even has a similar name. Andrea."

Dr. Hunter sat back, looking up at the ceiling fan. "It's not uncommon for families to give their children feminine and masculine versions of the same name, like Patricia and Patrick. Especially if they're fraternal twins. I have also seen cousins named that way, notably when their mothers are sisters and the cousins are close in age. Once had a Lauren and a Lawrence in Eighteenth-Century British Literature who were cousins. Double cousins, as I recall."

"Good notion. Except, I looked through the yearbook, and didn't find an Andrea Rhoades." Hunter countered. "If they're fraternal twins, they should be in the same class."

"Not necessarily, Bobby. Boys are much more likely to be held back in school than girls."

"She would have graduated the prior year," he concluded.

"Correct."

"I need the prior year's album." Hunter stated.

"If they're twins. If they're cousins, then all bets are off." He looked directly at his son. "Why don't you just ask this Andrea?"

"If they are twins, then she went to Owensboro South. She lied to me." He opened his left hand and fiddled with his wedding band.

"How so?"

"Andrea Rhoades was with Skeeter Thomas the Saturday night we believe he was murdered. They met while watching the Reds game at Fat Tony's. She said that she didn't know Thomas before she met him that night. She was likely the last person to see him alive. When we questioned her, she also denied knowing Jeff Miller."

"If her defense, she may not have known either of them. Owensboro South's a big school, Bobby. Public schools are like that, lots of students, a mass of nameless faces. It would not be expected that the students all know each other."

Hunter twisted his lip. "Maybe. I know an easy way to resolve this issue." He reached for his suit jacket, pulling out his cellphone to call Phil.

"Are you done at the range?" he asked once Phil answered.

"Just finished. I'm about to head back to the office. What's up?"

"Go to Owensboro South High School. When I was at Wayne Peterson's townhouse, I noticed that there was an Andrew Rhoades in his graduating class. He looks a lot like Andrea and Katie Rhoades. We need to determine if Andrea Rhodes attended OSHS. Katie's too old for that era. Andrea may have graduated the year before Miller and the others. If she did, I think she lied to us about knowing Skeeter Thomas."

"You got it, boss."

"I'll meet you back at the office later."

Hunter stood up and snatched his suit jacket. "Thanks for the idea, Dad. I'd better get back to the office. Have fun grading those finals."

Dr. Hunter smirked at his son. "Sure thing, Inspector Thrice."

CHAPTER FORTY-NINE

After flashing his badge to the security guard at the entrance of Owensboro South High School, Phil was directed to the principal's office on the second floor. Phil eyed a teen in his gym uniform seated on one of the red-and-yellow plastic chairs holding an ice pack over his right face as he opened the glass door to the office.

"Having a bad morning?" he asked the high schooler.

"I hate volleyball," he responded, checking Phil with his uninjured left eye. "Waiting for the school nurse."

He addressed the receptionist, who was standing behind a chest-high counter painted in an oversized gingham of the schools red-and-yellow colors, and held up his badge. She looked up from the spiral notebook she was holding and removed her reading glasses.

"Can I help you?" she inquired after she scrutinized his credentials.

"I'm with the Owensboro Police Department. I'm interested in finding out if a person attended Owensboro South. It would have been about fourteen years ago or so."

"Don't you need a subpoena or a warrant for something like that?" she questioned.

"Hmm. I don't think so," Phil answered. "Can I speak with the principal? Is he available?"

"She," she snarled at him. "The principal is in her office. Let me check." She disappeared through an open door at the back of the reception area. On her return, she was accompanied by a tall, slim woman with long, dark, feathered hair wearing a fitted navy dress with matching flyaway jacket.

"I'm Principal Jones. How can I help you, Detective?" she asked.

"I'm investigating the recent murders which I'm sure you've read about in the *Gazette*. All of them were students of this high school," he stated flatly.

She studied Phil, then said "Please come back to my office where we can speak privately." She looked over at the student with the ice pack.

"Volleyball?" she asked.

"Yes. I hate that game."

She shook her head, then led Phil to her office. "I have no idea why the gym teachers feel it necessary to punish the students with volleyball. Keeps the school nurse busy every spring," she said softly to Phil so that the student wouldn't hear her.

Principal Jones's office was as neat as her appearance. Black metal bookshelves and matching four-drawer filing cabinets lining the far wall, a series of curtainless windows overlooking the baseball diamond were behind a minimalist desk on which sat a green-shade bankers' lamp, a matte-grey multi-line corded telephone and little else, with plush light-crème carpet underneath. She motioned to the two black leather chairs.

"Please have a seat," she said as she closed the door then sat in her own black leather desk chair.

"Your office is gorgeous. The principal's office didn't look like this when I was a teenager," Phil commented.

She smiled at him. "Spend a lot of time there? The principal's office?"

"Enough," he said.

"A gift from my husband for my sixtieth birthday. It's not school property," she explained.

"Nicely done," he responded. "As I said, I'm investigating these recent murders."

"I wondered when, not if, when the police would be around. You were correct, all of the victims are, or were, that is, graduates of this high school."

"That explains why you didn't seem surprised by my presence."

"No, not at all. So, before you ask, yes, I remember Jeff Miller, Darryl Thomas—oh, he had that awful nickname, Skeeter, and of course the most recent victim, Wayne Peterson. I was the vice-principal back then."

"Why do you remember them?" Phil asked as he produced his notepad. "A lot of kids pass through these halls."

"They were trouble. I remember the senior class Halloween party. The three of them dressed up like they were auditioning for the next Godfather sequel. I recall thinking how appropriate that was since they had so often been the bullies." She adjusted the position of the lamp on the desk. "I always expected that Wayne Peterson would pursue a life of crime and end up behind bars. He was the real leader of that clique. Like most bullies, he inspired the same in others."

"What about the others, Mrs. Jones?"

"Oh, call me Judy." She pushed back from her desk, crossing her slender ankles. "Well, Miller, he was only bad when he was around Wayne Peterson. Never could figure that one out, being from a good family as he was. Thomas was living in the shadow of his older brother, who had been the star of the basketball team and an excellent student. A tough act to follow."

"That's all very helpful, Judy." Phil flipped his notepad. "There's another person who may be involved in these murders. My colleague noticed an Andrew Rhoades was in the same graduating class. We were—"

Judy cut him off. "I remember Andy."

"You do?" Phil sat upright.

"Oh yes. Most students are just a bunch of faceless teenagers who show up, do just enough to get by, don't participate in any of the extracurriculars—no clubs, no sports teams. They pass through without footprints, without memories. Andy, he wasn't that student. He was quite bright, ran track, but wasn't a great athlete because of his small stature. I liked him, although I don't think he had a lot of friends in school. You remember how challenging those teen years can be, right?"

"I do," Phil admitted.

"Speaking of Wayne and his posse, to let you know what bullies they were, they locked Andy in his own locker one time. I had to get the janitor to cut the lock off. Andy was sobbing so much, we couldn't understand him when he was attempting to give us his locker combination. Poor kid."

"That sounds terrible."

"It was." Judy sighed.

"Let me redirect you. When my colleague noticed his picture, Andrew, in the OSHS yearbook, he was struck with the resemblance to one of our witnesses, Andrea Rhoades. We thought perhaps they were siblings, or otherwise related."

"I don't recall a sister."

"Do you have a database of students that you can query?" he asked.

Judy chuckled. "You're joking, right? This is an under-funded public school. We have stacks of paper records." She pointed to the file cabinets to his right. "Lots of records. There's more in the storage room."

Phil scratched his forehead. "I can't look through all of that without a subpoena."

Judy rotated in her chair, arose and walked to the book-shelves. "I want to help you, detective. I have an idea. All the yearbooks since I've been at the school are right here." She pointed at a series of matching volumes on the bottom shelf. "Mind searching the good old-fashioned manual way? I'll start with the years before that trio graduated, you can have the later ones."

"Works for me." He stood up to help her remove the books.

After flipping through several years, Phil commented, "There seems to be a Rhoades in most classes."

"It's a common enough name in Owensboro," Judy answered. "I think I found her. Andrea, right?"

"Yes." Phil put down the yearbook he was holding and moved closer.

She laid the opened book on her desk, positioned so that both of them could see Andrea. "Two years before their graduation. Here's her senior picture."

The senior class pictures were printed in color, the underclassmen in black and white. Judy pointed to a female on the top row of the page with a mop of curly red hair and freckles.

Phil was disappointed. "Not her, unfortunately."

"Keep looking," Judy encouraged.

After looking through the remaining years, Phil closed the last book and added it to the stack on the adjoining chair.

"She must have gone to another school," Phil surmised. "Maybe they're not siblings."

Judy picked up the stack of books from her desk and walked to the bookshelves. "Or their parents separated them, putting the sister in a different school than her brother for some family reason. We've had some students with siblings at Owensboro North, even St. Andrews. At any rate, Andrea Rhoades wasn't an Owensboro South Bulldog."

Phil collected his yearbook stack to replace on the shelves. "Guess not. Thank you for your time, Judy."

CHAPTER FIFTY

The calling line identification screen read "ECU." Hunter tapped the speakerphone button to answer.

"It's Barry. I've got some good news, Hunter," said the voice on the other end.

"I could use some good news," Hunter responded.

"We were able to obtain the serial numbers on the confetti. That cartridge was in a lot shipped from the manufacturer to a distributor in Georgia. Waiting on a callback from the warehouse manager at the distributor to find the retailer."

"That's progress."

"Call you when I've got an update."

Hunter clicked the speakerphone button to end the call. He leaned back in his chair, tapping his fingers on the desktop. *Yes*, he thought, *making progress.*

He arose, walked to the file cabinets and pushed open one of the casement windows. He pulled the pack of Marlboros from his pocket and lit one. *What about the third man theory Phil and Amos advanced? Was I too quick to dismiss it?* Hunter thought.

He took a puff from the cigarette. Plausible, he decided. Billy Ray and Trevor collaborate, engage a third assailant. Billy Ray would have sufficient contacts in the criminal world to recruit an accomplice. An accomplice who possessed the necessary medical knowledge to know exactly where to place a knife to bisect the heart and the type of knife necessary to do the job. They use the taser to incapacitate the victim, drag him into the kitchen for the execution, away from the discharged taser confetti. One of them holds him down, the third man slices his chest. Either Billy Ray or Trevor is cleaning the confetti with a vacuum, which also removes the marks made in the carpet from the body being dragged into the kitchen. Leave the knife as no prints were left on it, and the type is common enough to be untraceable. In and out, five minutes. Silent.

"Brilliant," Hunter uttered aloud. He checked his cigarette, tapped the ash, then took another drag, slowly exhaling the smoke at the casement window. "Absolutely brilliant."

Billy Ray allowed the DNA swab without protest, almost demanded it, because he knew he wasn't the one Skeeter Thomas had scratched. It was the third man. Trevor knew Skeeter in high school. He likely knew Skeeter had dextrocardia. Perhaps he remembered it as the third man was about to stab Skeeter. The hesitation, that's why Skeeter was able to mount a resistance, although a futile one. I can envision the scene, Hunter imagined. Third man is straddling Skeeter's torso, knife in hand. Trevor has his arms pinned to the tan linoleum floor. As third man is about to stab him, Trevor halts his action, remembering, then directs third man to the right chest. A brief discussion takes place before third man agrees and proceeds. Time for Skeeter to partially recover.

Wayne Peterson's body wasn't dragged into the kitchen. His townhouse has hardwood floors, no carpet, just a few rugs upstairs. He considered the rooms. The townhouse kitchen was small, crowded with that island in the center. There was more space in the front room, however it made the cleanup more difficult. With three men around Wayne's body, the area would have been cramped. Whoever was vacuuming at Wayne's could have easily missed some of the confetti, which he did.

"So, who's the third man?" Hunter asked himself. "And, how do I find him?"

No fingerprints at the crime scenes, no witnesses. These acts were accomplished by organized criminals. The process was well thought out. They've minimized their mistakes. The only real clue is the DNA.

Hunter finished his cigarette. "I have the third man's DNA."

He returned to his desk. The FBI's database should be queried. If the third man has a criminal record, he would be in the Combined DNA Index System, or CODIS, the United States' national DNA database. He called ECU, and Barry answered.

"Did you check the DNA from the Skeeter Thomas murder against the CODIS database?" Hunter asked.

"No. We got the information back too late yesterday. We haven't gotten to it yet today."

"But you will," Hunter stated. "Today."

"Yes, Hunter. I'll do it as soon as I'm off the phone."

Phil entered his office as he hung up the telephone handset and took a seat in front of the desk.

"I've given some thought to the theory you and Amos concocted about Billy Ray and Trevor working together with a third man," Hunter said.

Phil sat up in his chair. "Really?"

"Yes. Billy Ray would be able to recruit someone who has the medical knowledge, Trevor probably knew about Skeeter Thomas's dextrocardia, and having three men would allow one of them to be cleaning up the confetti while the others are committing murder." Hunter exhaled slowly. "The vacuums at all three crime scenes had been used, and the bags removed. They vacuumed the confetti, and took the bags which contained the evidence. The taser confetti."

"It makes even more sense to me now."

"Billy Ray has wounds on his arms. I assumed that was from Thomas fighting him. What if the third man is the one who was injured by Skeeter Thomas in his unsuccessful effort to ward off the attacker?"

"Would explain why Billy Ray didn't push back on having a DNA swab done," Phil deduced.

"I agree. The DNA is from the third man." Hunter pointed at the desk telephone. "ECU will query CODIS today. It's plausible that this third assailant has a criminal record."

"And you dismissed the theory, boss." Phil smiled.

"True," Hunter agreed. "Oh, Barry called. They did get the serial numbers off of the confetti. Tracking it down now."

"I hadn't called them yet."

"And now you don't have to do so," Hunter said. "How was your trip to the high school?"

"The principal was the vice-principal when they attended Owensboro South. She said that Peterson was the leader of the group, Miller and Thomas tagalongs. They were the school bullies. Told me that she was surprised Peterson didn't end up in prison."

"The fact that they were bullies is a recurring theme. What about Andrea Rhodes?

265

"When I told her that you saw the high school yearbook picture of Andrew Rhodes and how he resembled one of our witnesses, she quickly stated that she remembered Andy. She even told me a story about how Peterson's gang trapped him in a locker, and the janitor had to cut the lock off to get him out."

"They must have been horrible teenagers," Hunter declared.

"No doubt about that," Phil agreed.

Hunter scrutinized Phil. "Hang on a sec. What did the principal say about Andrew Rhodes?"

"She said she remembered him."

"No. What exactly did she say?" Hunter peered directly into Phil's eyes.

Phil paused, closed his eyes briefly. He spoke slowly. "Principal Jones … not surprised by my questions … I said, 'Another person may be involved.'" He opened his eyes. "She said, 'I remember Andy.' That's her exact words."

Hunter leaned back in his chair, reached for the wedding band on his left hand and twisted it back and forth several times. Then he aimed his right index finger at Phil. "When we questioned Katie and Andrea Rhodes, Katie called her sister Andie. Andy is a diminutive for both Andrea and Andrew, albeit spelt differently."

"Yes. I had a female classmate who went by Andie."

Hunter softly whistled. "Man hands. You thought she had manly hands."

"Yes, I did," Phil agreed.

He twisted the desk chair, a smile developing on his face, his eyes opening widely. "I don't think Andrea and Andrew are siblings or cousins, Phil." Hunter shook his head. "It's been right in front of me. Andrea is Andrew. Or was Andrew."

"You mean he became a she? Had a sex change?"

"Yes." Hunter smiled. "All this time I've been focused on how the River City Ripper murders were linked to Jenny Harper's death. What if this has nothing to do with Jenny Harper, Phil? Consider the alternative. A neighbor saw a woman at Miller's house the night he was murdered. Andrea was with Skeeter Thomas the night he was murdered. And when I was at Peterson's townhouse this morning, a guy walking his dog told me he saw a woman who matches Arlene's description leave Peterson's, then another woman with a ponytail appeared at the door. The mystery woman in the blue polka-dot dress at Millers, Thomas's last date, and Peterson's late-night guest are the same person. Andrea Rhodes."

"I don't know, boss. Your theory is based on what? The fact I thought Andrea had man hands. Seems far-fetched. Andrea looks like just another woman to me."

"Is it? How many teenagers have been on the receiving end of a bully and would like an opportunity to retaliate?"

"Many, I suppose."

"We know Andrew Rhoades was bullied. Now, Andrea Rhoades has found the perfect method to amerce those adolescent bullies, Jeff Miller, Skeeter Thomas, and Wayne Peterson. She has a new face, a new look, she's a new person. No one knows Andrea. They might remember Andrew, but Andrea slips under the radar."

Phil shook his head. "I'm not convinced."

"What about the chance meeting at Fat Tony's?" Hunter leaned forward in his chair. "Chance? Unlikely it was mere kismet that she shared a table with Skeeter. Very clever.

Andrea has harbored a grudge for over a decade. She's had plenty of time to plan this killing spree."

"Sounds pretty weak, boss," Phil said.

"Does it?" Hunter asked. "Andrea gored Skeeter Thomas, but because of the hesitation, she is wounded as Skeeter desperately tried to save his own life. She may, or may not, know that some of her skin is trapped under Skeeter's fingernails. If she knows that we have her skin as evidence, and if Andrea knows anything about DNA analysis, she knows that we have male DNA and therefore wouldn't be looking at her as a suspect."

Phil sighed. "And this is all because I thought she had man hands?"

"I know a way to solve this." Hunter picked up the telephone.

CHAPTER FIFTY-ONE

The operating-room supervisor, Sara, checked through the window before opening the door to the OR where Louis Mercier was working. Things seemed to be under control. She entered.

She walked to the head of the OR table where Mercier was seated with the anesthesia equipment. Head down, he was hand-writing notes in the anesthesia record and didn't notice her presence until she tapped him on the shoulder.

"Dr. Mercier," she said, "there's a Detective Hunter of the Owensboro Police Department who wants to speak with you."

A surgeon peered over the ether screen at Mercier. "Hey, Louis, that old cannabis charge finally catch up to you?" he joked.

"That was no mine," Mercier answered with a Spanish accent and a chuckle. "You mind if I take this?"

"As long as you return to finish this case. They can arrest you after I'm done," the surgeon stated flatly.

He stood up and faced Sara. "I'm looking at train tracks. Would you keep an eye on the monitors?"

She smiled at him. "Of course, Dr. Mercier." She pointed at the wall phone. "He's on line three. It's blinking."

Mercier slipped past her, grasped the handset from the wall telephone as he pushed the line button to connect. He moved out of the OR into the hallway next to the scrub sinks, letting the door softly close.

"Mercier," he announced as he tugged his OR mask from his nose and mouth.

"Louis, it's Bob. I've got a medical question for you," Hunter said.

"Sure. What's up?"

"When you were talking about plastic surgery with Brenda the other day, you mentioned that a surgeon can't change someone's hands. Correct?"

"Yes, that's correct."

"So, if a person had a sex change operation—"

Mercier interrupted him. "It's called gender-reassignment surgery or gender-confirmation surgery, not sex change."

"Uh, okay," Hunter responded. "Go on."

He continued. "The procedures are performed as a component of the treatment for gender dysphoria in transgender people. Gender dysphoria is the term used when the sex and the gender assigned at birth do not match the person's gender identity."

"Gotcha. If a person had gender reassignment surgery, their hands wouldn't change, right?"

"The general appearance, no. That can't be altered."

There was a pause, then Hunter said "If a man was changed to a woman, he would have man hands, then."

"Bob, he would be a she, and yes, if it was male-to-female gender reassignment. She could paint her nails, have regular manicures, but her hands would still have a masculine appearance."

"Man hands."

Mercier shook his head. "Yes, man hands."

There was a pause, then Hunter said, "One more thing. I know the answer, but I'll ask anyway, just to confirm."

"Hang on a sec." Mercier looked through the OR door window to view Sara and the monitors. Seeing nothing of concern, he answered. "Go ahead."

"DNA. With the gender reassignment, the DNA doesn't change, right?" Hunter asked.

"Correct. In medical terms, that would be the genotype, the genetic identity, which isn't altered by a change in the phenotype. The phenotype, the physical characteristics, is what is altered with the gender reassignment operations."

"Thanks, bubba," Hunter ended the call.

Mercier pulled the handset from his ear, and stared at the it in his left hand. "I wonder what that was all about," he whispered softly to no one.

CHAPTER FIFTY-TWO

Andrea handed a chilled glass of chardonnay to her sister, then joined Katie on the concrete patio's sage-green cushioned sofa. The sun was starting to set, its rays streaking though the wispy clouds, the sky changing to a mixture of yellow, red, blue, and purple. The warm, humid air had yet to become the night's chill.

"You went to high school with all those men who've been murdered. Did you know any of them?" Katie asked.

"Yes, I did. They were the bullies, especially that Wayne Peterson," Andrea answered. "He was the ringleader. I'm not sad that they're gone. They did some pretty awful things in high school."

"Why didn't you tell me? You met up with that Skeeter Thomas fellow, even went to his house." Katie sipped at her wine.

"I was curious if he would recognize me. He didn't know me, had no idea who I am. Or was." Andrea looked at her untouched wine. "It was a mistake to go to his house."

"And why didn't you tell the police about it? Why did you lie and tell them that you didn't know him?"

Andrea drank before answering. "I wanted to avoid the explanation."

"What explanation? That you used to be Andrew?" Katie shook her head.

"Don't call me that. Andrew is my deadname. I'm Andrea now."

"Did they bully you, Andie?" Katie looked at her sister. "Did they?"

"They bullied everyone." She took another drink. "Can we talk about something else?"

Katie sat quietly, looking at the setting sun from her patio. "Can I ask you about the operation?"

"Yes," Andrea replied quietly.

"Did it hurt?"

"A lot. But before you can even have the operations, you have to be on hormones for a few years, pass the psychiatric exams, and live as the opposite sex for several years, that sort thing." She sipped more wine. "You know, I probably would have benefited from seeing a psychiatrist or a psychologist when I was a teenager."

"Wouldn't we all?" Katie agreed. "Somehow I doubt Mom and Dad would think so. Take it like a man, he would have said."

"I'm not sure Mom or Dad would have understood how uncomfortable I felt in that male body." Andrea stared at her wine glass.

"And then the operation?"

"Actually, there are several procedures. It's done in stages. First, they do what's called the top surgery. I understand that's a bigger operation for the females transitioning to males. They have to have mastectomies. For me, the female hormones I'd been taking only gave me a small mound of breast tissue. That's why I decided to have breast implants."

Katie looked at Andrea and smiled. "You know I'm a little jealous," she said as pointed to her own chest.

Andrea laughed and then sipped a little chardonnay. "Then, the bottom surgery is done. It's called a vaginoplasty, making a vagina. That was the most painful."

"Sounds like it," Katie observed.

"The last part was some cosmetic surgery on my face, facial feminization."

"Oh, that's why you look so different." She hesitated. "I mean, you look like you, just, well, different."

"I look like the woman I've always felt I was meant to be." Andrea took a sip of wine. "Now, when I look in the mirror, I see Andrea. The girl I always knew was inside."

Katie put her arm around Andrea. "You're so brave to do all that, Andie. You seem much happier than ever."

She turned to face her sister. "I am happy."

"What's next? Do you want to stay here in Owensboro with me?" Katie smiled. "There's plenty of room."

"No, but I appreciate the offer." Andrea finished the wine, then sat the empty glass on the concrete. "I saved up quite a bit when I was in Atlanta. There's a small town on Lake Michigan I want to try out. On the Michigan side. It's called Saugatuck. It's a very accepting place. I can find a little apartment to rent, maybe work in one of the art galleries."

Katie drained her wine, then rose from the sofa, picking up Andrea's glass. "My turn to refill. If there's any left."

"I put another bottle in the frig," Andrea said.

As Katie slid the glass door open, the doorbell rang. She twisted to see Andrea. "Expecting anyone?"

"No. Are you?"

"Probably some kid selling popcorn," Katie joked. She walked through the kitchen, setting the empty wine glasses on the table, then hurried down the hallway to the front door. She was surprised to find Hunter filling her doorway, with Phil standing behind him, to his left.

"Miss Rhodes, is your sister Andrea at home?" Hunter asked.

"Yes. She's on the back patio."

"We'd like to speak to her. May we come in?"

Katie hesitated, then fully opened the door. "Follow me," she said. Hunter and Phil trailed Katie to the kitchen, then through the sliding glass door to the patio.

"Andie, the policemen are back," she announced as she emerged onto the patio.

Hunter followed. Immediately, he checked her hands, then noted the long-sleeve coral sweater she was wearing. Finally, he examined her face. And the look of terror she bore.

"Seems to be a bit warm for long sleeves, Miss Rhodes," Hunter observed. "Would you mind pushing your sleeves up?"

Andrea stared at him. "Why?"

"Just push them up."

Katie positioned herself between the detectives. "What's going on?"

"You'll see soon enough," Phil answered.

Hunter was becoming impatient. "Sleeves up." He shifted his six-foot-four bulk to directly face Andrea.

Andrea stood up, then slowly pushed up the left sleeve of her sweater. At the midforearm, Hunter could see the thin scabs of several healing wounds.

"That's enough," he said abruptly.

She pulled the sleeve back to her wrist, covering her watch.

"Andrea Rhodes, you are under arrest for the murders of Jeffery Miller, Darryl Thomas, and Wayne Peterson." He pulled a pair of handcuffs from the right pocket of his suit jacket and dangled them from his index finger.

"Phil, hook her up."

CHAPTER FIFTY-THREE

Three photographs were on the table in the interrogation room. Hunter tapped his right index finger on the middle one, the photograph of Wayne Peterson. He looked across the table at Andrea, his eyes meeting hers. They were alone in the room, Phil behind the one-way mirror.

"He was the leader of the pack, right Andrea? Wayne Peterson. His pals, Jeff Miller and Skeeter Thomas. The three high school bullies who tormented the students of Owensboro South High School. And tormented you." He paused. "You made a mistake when you killed Wayne." Hunter moved his hand from the photograph and leaned back in the chair.

Andrea sat silently, blankly staring at Hunter.

"The confetti that is discharged when firing a taser gun is imprinted with a serial number. You missed some confetti in the clean-up. We found your taser gun in Katie's house, Andrea. Your prints were on it. We also found several unused taser cartridges." He ran his left hand along his chin before letting his chin rest in his palm, elbow on the table. "The serial numbers match the confetti we found in the pool of blood around Peterson's dead body."

Andrea remained mute.

Hunter picked up the photograph of Skeeter Thomas. "The other mistake, Andrea. You hesitated before stabbing Skeeter Thomas. Just long enough for Thomas to partially recover from the stun, just long enough for Thomas to make a futile attempt to fight off his attacker, leaving those wounds on your forearms. You were his attacker." He leaned forward on the table. "That unsuccessful strike also left your skin under his nails."

Tears formed in Andrea's eyes. She wiped them away with the sleeve of her sweater.

"The DNA from that tissue is going to match the DNA sample you will be compelled to provide. It's over Andrea." Hunter ran his right hand over his tie, pressing it against his shirt. "Why don't you tell me who helped you? Was it your sister, Katie?"

"Katie had nothing to do with this," she said.

"How about Billy Ray Harper? Did he help you plan the attacks?" Hunter asked.

Andrea shook her head. "I don't know anyone named Billy Ray Harper."

"You don't? Jenny Lynn Harper's brother?"

"I remember Jenny, but I didn't know her that well. She was killed in a car accident." Andrea looked at Hunter. "I didn't know she had a brother."

"So, you killed Jeff Miller, Skeeter Thomas and Wayne Peterson all by yourself?"

"I'd like to speak to a lawyer now," Andrea said.

CHAPTER FIFTY-FOUR

Hunter turned onto Manor Court, then slowly pulled the grey Cadillac to the empty space in front of the halfway house. The street was quiet, that tranquil time after noon before the children return from school, the adults from work. The front porch was empty. He slipped from the car, straightened his tie and made his way to the steps before Amos opened the door.

"What are you doing here?" Amos questioned. "I heard you arrested someone last night for the murders."

"I did. Chief Hartmann has a press conference planned for this evening."

"Again, what are you doing here?"

"I'd like to see Billy Ray Harper." Hunter stepped onto the porch.

"What's it about, Bob?"

"Just get him for me." He leaned against the porch rail. "I'll wait outside."

"Damn right you'll wait outside." Amos looked Hunter in the eye, holding the gaze momentarily, then disappeared through the door. He returned, Billy Ray Harper close behind, wearing a white, full-length bib apron with water spots.

"I'm in the middle of washing dishes, Hunter," he scowled. "Whadda you want?"

"Sit down for a minute, Billy Ray." He took one of the lawn chairs on the porch. "Amos, you should stay."

"Oh, I'm staying, Hunter." He remained at the door, arms crossed on this chest, feet planted shoulder width apart, as if standing at attention in his old police uniform.

"Okay, I'm sittin'," Billy Ray said.

Hunter lit a cigarette, slowly exhaling before continuing. "You may or may not be aware that we've arrested the person responsible for the murders of Jeff Miller, Darryl Thomas, and Wayne Peterson."

"I could've read that in the paper. You the newsboy now?"

Hunter smiled. "Not hardly. And you're right, I didn't need to drive over here to tell you personally. I know that you had nothing to do with the three murders. And I also know that you've no remorse for their deaths."

"They got what wuz coming to 'em, yeah. Still don't bring my baby sister back." Billy Ray leaned rearward in the chair, pulling the front legs off the wooden porch.

"I've done some research into your time at Eddyville, Harper."

Amos relaxed his pose, moving his arms to his side and shifting his weight onto his good leg, off of the prosthesis on his left. Billy Ray was silent.

"You were very engaged in the rehabilitation program, specifically the culinary arts program. I am to understand you performed quite well. So well, in fact, that you were asked to cook in the prison kitchens." Hunter looked at Amos. "Were you aware of that?"

Amos shook his head. "News to me." He looked to Billy Ray. "Is that true?"

"Yes, it is," Billy Ray nodded. "What's your point, Hunter?"

"Craig told me you've been a stellar worker, getting the job done, no complaints. And Amos tells me that you're behaving." He stepped forward to crush the cigarette into the ashtray on the glass-top table next to Billy Ray.

"I've paid my debt to society. I aim to start a new life." Billy Ray looked to Amos, then back to Hunter.

"I would like to believe that everyone deserves the opportunity for the redemption of their past, whatever that past may have been." Hunter stood up from the rail. "Are you ready to redeem yourself?"

Billy Ray set the chair straight. "What are you talking about?"

"Are you familiar with Fat Tony's Pizzeria?"

He nodded. "I'll make you a pizza you can't refuse," he said softly.

"What you don't know is that Tony DeLuca is a friend of mine. When you're ready, he has a job waiting for you in his kitchen."

Billy Ray looked up at Amos, who was shaking his head in disbelief.

"Are you serious?" he asked.

"Yes. Second chances don't come around very often. This is your second chance, Billy Ray."

Billy Ray rose from the lawn chair. "I never, ever, in my entire life thought I would say this ..." He wiped his right hand on the apron and extended it to Hunter. "Thank you."

Hunter shook his hand while checking the bewildered face of Amos Weller, and winked.

ABOUT THE AUTHOR

Ian Kilgour is a widower. He lives in Montana with a rather goofy golden retriever and a grey cat who has seriously out-of-control whiskers.

Made in the USA
Columbia, SC
19 March 2020